THE TWIN BLADES

The Twin Blades

A LENOIR LEGACY STORY

Cristen Jennette

DragonNook Publishing LLC

A dream can become a reality.

Thank you to all my family and friends who have
encouraged me through this journey!

Prologue

After the arduous climb up the mountainside, Gailin wanted to pause at the cave's entrance. A small opening in the mountain's rocky facade, the entrance was backed by the vast valley which housed a myriad of plantations. Those blocks of color indicating abundant produce formed plantations his family now deemed a part of their land.

No one else stopped. Rather than appear weak and winded, Gailin followed the others. His curious blond-haired brother Xannan, who was older by mere moments and looked nearly the same as himself, tripped over a rock embedded in the caked mud which created the cave's floor.

"Smooth." Gailin nudged Xannan with a shoulder, earning a glare in response.

"Father said we'll see dragons." Xannan paused and raised himself to his toes, trying to look over those guiding them. Their parents, the Elder Elf Eonar, and two younger elves who appeared just as nervous as he—though they'd never admit it—all walked ahead.

Gailin chuckled and shook his head. "You're still half a foot shorter than Father." That earned another scowl. "And I doubt you wish to meet dragons while covered in mud, so maybe you should pay more attention to where you're walking."

"I am paying attention." Xannan settled back on his heels and crossed his arms.

"Quiet, boys," came their father's always slightly annoyed voice. A bold, brave man who'd founded a country. Years of fighting, arguing, and mediating had all led to this moment. Not only had their father, King Seth of Orda'an, provided for those who had less, he'd earned the support of both the dragons and the elves. A fine feat, all things considered.

While rubbing his arms to stave off the chill, Gailin slipped on the slick muddied cave floor and stubbed his toe on a jutting rock. A curse slipped from his lips before he could internalize it. His mother looked over her shoulder with one brow raised, and he mumbled a quick apology.

"Now who's distracted?" Xannan jabbed Gailin with his elbow.

Gailin rubbed his side, almost in tune with the slow drip of water from the cave's ceilings. It made the caverns smell like stale liquid.

Before Gailin could retaliate, their father said a simple, "Not now, boys."

With a huff, Gailin obliged, and Xannan snickered. His elder brother always seemed to get the first and last say, but at least they would all be there for this moment. Those ahead paused, and their father turned to them, brows furrowed and lips set in a manner which implied pain awaited if they did not obey.

"Do *exactly* as you are told." Their father exchanged a quick glance with the Elder Elf. "Stand where we tell you to stand, speak only when you are asked to speak, and please for the good of all, don't do anything stupid."

"If we do, it's Gailin's fault."

"You're the one with the crazy ideas, Xannan."

"Quiet," their father snapped at them. He shook his head and turned around, wrapping an arm around their mother's shoulders.

"Was that necessary?" Gailin asked Xannan. Mud squelched around his boots with each step. The sucking sound as he lifted each foot made him cringe. "My fault since when?"

"Quiet," their father said yet again and Gailin gritted his teeth.

When Xannan tapped against his arm, Gailin huffed and almost hit back but was distracted by the creatures he noticed in his periphery. Without the two awaiting dragons, Gailin supposed the cavern would appear incredibly expansive. With the two dragons' presence, the cavern appeared too small.

Gailin had heard stories of both. Stories from his mother and father, tales they'd passed from town to town as they built their own country.

One a deep black—Eilon. Deeper than the night sky, richer in color than anything Gailin had ever before laid eyes upon. His tail dragged behind him, a constant scrape against the caked mud that made Gailin forget about how his boots kept sinking into the cave floor. Beady silver eyes narrowed at them and made Gailin swallow before turning his attention to the other side of the cavern.

As white as a cloud, Magna boasted much softer features than Eilon's sharp ridges. Each had scales covered by feathers in a way that made Gailin think of Orda'anian birds mixing with the lizards of the Tenoan desert.

"What—"

Gailin pressed his lips together at their father's glare. Silence. Wait to speak. Do as they were told. Difficult for two curious fifteen-year-old boys to do. He wanted to ask if the dragons could speak, how hot their fire could burn, how long their flame could last, how old they were, and why they hid in this cave rather than stretch their wings in the wide-open sky. Instead, he bit his tongue as a reminder to not speak and kept Xannan in his periphery.

Eonar waved an arm, a silent indication of where Gailin and his family should stand. At first, Xannan followed, but when he strayed a step outside their indicated path, Gailin grasped the back of his brother's vest and tugged.

A series of looks which created a barely understood conversation between the brothers followed. During their silent attempts at communicating, Eonar spoke.

One of the younger elves, Eonar's son Arjun, laid a wrapped bundle between the two dragons. Reverently, he unraveled the cloth to reveal a shimmering crystalline sword. Exquisite craftsmanship, gorgeous enough even Gailin desired to inspect it closer. Without realizing it, Gailin held his arm out, halting Xannan's forward movement. While Gailin learned weapons use because of their father's persistence, Xannan learned because he enjoyed it. Perhaps a bit too much. Xannan muttered something Gailin hoped their mother would never hear and settled back onto his heels with arms folded.

"Here lies Praesidio." Eonar gestured at the sword and looked up at each dragon. "Forged by elves to be blessed by dragons so it may be wielded by man, this blade is meant to unify the races which remain on the continent of Ebios."

A huff from the black dragon made Gailin step backward. The white dragon lifted from her haunches as a glowing orange orb appeared at the base of her neck. The feathers adorning her wings ruffled as though wind had blown through them, but no wind was present. The blade no longer rested on the cave's ground. It had lifted and hovered between the two dragons. Another orb appeared at the base of Eilon's neck, pulsing in unison with Magna's.

Though Gailin wanted to take another step *away* from the enormous beasts who appeared to be cultivating their flame, Xannan stepped closer. Rolling his eyes, Gailin reached for his brother's arm to pull him back but held his breath. Heat filled the cave, pulsing outward from the streams of flame pouring from each dragon's jaw. Perspiration tickled at his skin until beads of sweat formed along his temple, his arms, his neck, his chest. He licked his lips, tasting salt from the forming droplets. Gailin couldn't look away, though a stray thought reminded him he should make sure Xannan didn't get too close.

He'd never seen fire so . . . pure, so vibrant, so rich in every fiber of its creation. No putrid smell of burning flesh filled the cave. Instead, all Gailin could scent was the heaviness of the air. The heat of their intertwining flames, a mingling of black and white, comforted him at first. As the dragons continued to spew their flame, Gailin's heart hammered in his chest. Faster and faster until something knocked him to his back. His head throbbed from the impact in time with his hammering chest, and his fingers dug into the mud as he tried to pull himself upright.

Whatever force had knocked him down did the same to his family and to the elves. None but the dragons remained standing. Gailin attempted to lift his head, grunting and straining, willing himself to sit up. Every finger pressed, further and further, until he knew it was useless. Gailin was stuck watching the two streams batter one another.

Beautiful and wrong. Awe-inspiring and torturous. Perfect and terrible.

Opposing emotions continued to well up inside Gailin. No matter how many times he shoved them back down, they reappeared, stronger than the last time. This wasn't supposed to happen. Whatever it was. The dragons were not blessing Praesidio. They were fighting.

Magna, an ancient monarch of her kind, fought Eilon, who was possibly the last of his own race of dragons. Flame upon flame met each other, colors different from those first breaths.

Gailin had to get to his family. He needed to help the others leave before the dragons' flame singed the far reaches of this cavern and burned them all alive. His mouth parched at the thought, and he struggled once more to find a grip. Already coated in mud, his fingers dug deeper, unable to find anything except more mud.

Another blast, similar to that which had knocked him to his back, made it so Gailin couldn't even change his facial expression to a scowl. The force of it reminded him of the times Xannan would pin him against the ground while sparring.

It was pointless to do anything but wait. His chest ached. His bones rattled. His thoughts raced. Glorious and tormenting. How could something appear so beautiful yet feel so terrible?

A subtle change, like the rush of air after being forced not to breathe for a time. Gailin gasped, pressing against the caked mud until it covered his wrists. As he sat up, he glanced around and brushed the chunks of dirt from his palms.

The earlier drip, drip, drip of water was no more. Eilon was gone, too. As was Manga. In her place... Gailin paused in his thoughts. She was there. But the powder-like white feathers drifted to the ground, and her scales deepened in color until they appeared as brown as his vest.

Beside him lay a clear crystalline sword. It beckoned for him to reach out, to grasp the hilt. And he did before he could decide not to. One at a time, he curled his fingers around the hilt and pressed his lips together. Necessary and tormenting were two emotions that did not make a good combination.

He stood, surveying the cave and found Xannan standing at his side with a crystalline blade of his own. Gailin flinched and rubbed his chest. An ache was forming. It wasn't from the lack of breath or whatever force had held them down. That ache was a reaction to seeing his brother with *that* sword. He studied the one in his own hand. Both weapons were necessary and tormenting.

"It's like it—" Gailin began.

"Molded to you," Xannan finished. He stared at the sword with a hungry eagerness.

Gailin grimaced and shook his head. "Called to me," he corrected and sighed.

As with everything in his life, these swords would further connect him to his brother. Despite being two different people, they were often considered connected. They looked alike—too much so sometimes. Their voices sounded almost the same. When one shared the womb, it seemed inevitable the other who occupied that same space would always be in your life.

Movement in his periphery caught his attention, and he rushed to his mother's side. "She's waking." He set the sword down, and his fears further eased when his father also sat up.

"What happened?" his father demanded as he homed in on Xannan holding the sword. "What is that? Where is Praesidio?"

Xannan approached, though he didn't look away from the weapon gripped in his hand. Across the cave, the younger two elves, Arjun and Celena, whispered to each other for a moment while Eonar remained seated. Magna lay nearby, brown streaking her once-pristine white scales.

"Be careful with those," Celena whispered, glancing between each weapon and back at Magna. Her red eyes churned a deeper shade. "Such power inside one. And if they touch. . ."

Celena shuddered and turned away, as though to hide whatever emotions might present themselves.

"What happens if they touch, Celena?" Arjun asked.

Celena closed her eyes, scrunched her lips together, and shook her head.

"What happens when they touch, Celena?" Arjun repeated, a tad more forcefully.

"Magna trapped Eilon's power in one of those weapons, and whoever is connected to them when they combine will be able to wield Eilon's power. But such a joining comes at a price for one wielder and for both. Once a connection is forged between the blades, and thus their wielders, it can only be undone through death.

Of one or both, I do not know. Nor does Magna," she blurted out before clasping her hands over her mouth and glowering at Arjun.

"Whoever is connected to them?" Seth pushed himself to standing and helped his wife up. "How could one be connected to a dragon-blessed weapon? That's preposterous."

All eyes looked to Celena, but she kept a hand clasped over her mouth, gaze darting between each person surrounding her and toward the tired dragon.

"Until now," Eonar murmured, stroking Magna's side and earning a deep, appreciative rumble in response.

Thoughts, frustrations, and warring emotions swirled deep in Gailin's gut. Wrong and right. Right and wrong. He picked up the sword. Delicate. Anxious. When Xannan lifted his new blade, Gailin shifted away. Bad idea to let the weapons touch.

"It feels . . . wrong," Gailin whispered, trying to recall exactly what Celena had said about these swords. "I can't tell you why, but it does."

"Until now, Father?" Arjun moved amid the others. "Meaning?"

Eonar's eyes bulged for a second before he responded. "The LeNoir twins have received the gift of the dragon's magic, though it is likely tethered to these weapons they now hold."

"There's more." Celena approached the tired matriarch of a dragon, hovering both hands above Magna's snout as she tilted her head. "I can hear. . ."

She shifted as though straining to hear, and her shoulders tensed. After a moment, Magna shuddered and lowered her head to rest atop her paws. When she turned to face them, Celena's light skin had paled, almost matching her shoulder-length white hair. It wasn't until Eonar urged her to explain that Celena said, "I can hear the dragon's thoughts. Magna's." She lifted her head, peering into the cave ceiling covered in stalactites. "And Eilon's. Not the images they share but what they wish to say."

A shudder racked Celena's body, and she closed her eyes. When she opened them, the red irises were the deepest shade Gailin had ever seen any elf's eyes become. "Eilon only agreed to come in hopes of capturing Magna's magic and using it to fix the species of droki he created." Celena glanced behind her at the dragon whose sad eyes faded to a dull white, and Celena's voice turned hoarse. "He considers the droki his children. They hunt magic because it is their missing piece. Magic is what the droki require to survive."

"Brainless fiends." Seth growled from behind Gailin, making him jolt at his father's voice. "Praesidio was meant to help us annihilate them. Can these blades do the same?"

After a brief exchange with Magna, Celena nodded. She inhaled to speak again, but Seth asked, "Did Magna know Eilon would attempt such?"

Tendrils of smoke escaped from Magna's maw, and Gailin stepped back, bumping into his brother who was too distracted studying the sword in his hand.

Celena laid a tentative hand on Magna's snout and bowed her head. "She had her suspicions. Praesidio should have been able to contain Eilon's magic."

An interminable pause lingered until Celena jerked her head up and her deep red eyes flickered between Gailin and his brother. He gulped and his insides churned with mingled suspicion, curiosity, and fear.

Eonar said, "The LeNoir twins' magic—"

"My sons have no magic of their own." Seth stepped forward, rounding his shoulders and peering down at Eonar. "You confirmed such before we came."

"I can only detect active abilities, Your Majesty." Eonar gripped the circular crystal hanging around his neck. "Theirs were dormant until today."

Seth's voice dropped lower, soft enough Gailin could no longer understand his father's words. What he did understand was the fear twisting his insides. When his mother rested a hand on his forearm, he flinched and dropped the sword. The kind Eonar approached Gailin and his brother, brows pinched together until they formed a singular line.

At his nod, their mother stepped back, and Eonar laid a hand on each of their shoulders. "I will bury the memory, but I refuse to take their magic. It is a part of them now, as are the weapons."

"Then we will give them new memories." Seth folded his arms and lowered his head. "Of which you must be a part to ensure this memory is never recalled. They cannot know they have their own magic; otherwise, their legitimacy to one day rule will be questioned."

Part One

"Sometimes things go wrong."

1

Five Years Later

"Ignore it," Xannan whispered, lips hovering above Anna's. He wanted to taste those lips again, their soft, sweet scent intoxicating him as he lowered his head to hers.

She leaned back, warm palm pressing against his chest above the divot in his brown leather vest. "That was the fourth knock, Xannan." A quick peck of a kiss and she murmured, "Answer it before Gailin knocks the door down."

"I wouldn't knock the door down," Gailin said through the closed door. "But Father might."

"Blazes." Xannan glanced around his room and grasped Anna's coat, laying it over her shoulders. A precaution, though she was fully dressed in the newest court design. A tight bodice accentuated her curves in the most distracting way, while the wide dark skirts showed off the delicate paleness of her skin. It was her display of that dress that had made him tug Anna into his chest for a lengthy kiss.

"That's a ridiculous *curse*." Anna tightened the coat around her and smiled at him, wiggling the first finger of her right hand, letting the torches alighting his room flicker across the simple silver band. "And there's no reason to hide me now that we're engaged."

"Blazes will catch on." Xannan pried her hand from the coat, holding it in his own as he lifted it and kissed the silver ring. "I'm shocked Father gave his blessing. The man is—"

"Outside your door and can hear you, Xannan."

Both Xannan and Anna shared a glance. She chuckled, he winced.

Gailin sighed loud enough to be heard through the door. "Please tell me you're decent."

As answer, Xannan opened the door to his room with an extravagant wave of his arm. "Decent and welcoming."

Their father, King Seth, pushed his way through, and Xannan frowned. The man was in full regalia. Not just simple clothing, but the king's most recent design to show off his station. Solid black coat and black pants, completed by the shimmering gold crown. If Xannan wasn't mistaken, this was another new crown, a shade of deeper gold than his father's hair, the blond locks which both he and his brother had inherited.

Seth watched without comment as Anna offered a slight curtsy and whispered honorifics. She paused next to Xannan, lifted to her toes, kissed him, and whispered, "See you soon."

Though he could feel his father's stare and his brother's annoyance, Xannan continued to lean against the door frame and watched Anna walk through the breezeway. Her black hair and dark cloak fluttered in the oceanic winds that made his room and this castle always smell like sand and salt. Xannan wanted to follow. Her company, even when planning every minute detail of a wedding ceremony, was becoming more enjoyable than any conversation with his brother and father. All he needed to do was listen to them, do as was requested, and then find Anna. Or she would find him.

Never one to mince words, his father said, "Pack your bags. Warmest clothes you have."

Xannan's groan earned a poignant stare from his father that made Xannan shiver at the memory. The northern lands were definitely too cold for his vest, though he'd tried to prove otherwise.

"Alkaanians have created a settlement in the far north, close to Falsumbra Forest."

Xannan looked back down the breezeway and sighed. "Can't Gailin go himself this time? I doubt Anna—"

"That's a risk she chose by saying yes to your proposal."

Xannan grimaced and lifted from the doorway, crossing his arms.

"Besides," his father continued, gaze flickering from one son to the other. "Why wouldn't I send the best?"

Xannan snorted. "Depends on which best you are referring to: mediating or fighting." He indicated his father's clothing. "Why the formality today?"

His father tugged at the black sleeves, brushed each arm with the back of his hand, and straightened the collar. "New design. Thoughts?"

As their father turned in a slow circle to show off the new outfit, Xannan shook his head. "Blazing foolish."

"Bad combination of words, that one," Gailin said absentmindedly, and Xannan silently agreed. "I quite like Father's new design. More elegant."

"Looks constricting." Xannan twisted his lips in thought. "Can you even lift your arms in it?"

"We need to distinguish more between our new country and our past." His father pulled on the edges of the coat. "But for now, pack. You leave at nightfall."

"Nightfall?" Xannan squinted at Gailin, who offered a subtle nod. "Edmund and Mikhael as battalion leaders again?"

"Always seems to work best," Gailin agreed.

Still fiddling with his sleeve-cuffs, their father said, "I look forward to your triumphant return, and mine own."

Xannan tried to ask Gailin what their father meant without speaking, but their silent communication didn't last long.

"Not battle, hopefully." His father picked up the sword which had earned the name Praeteritum and handed it to Xannan. "A meeting with Eonar."

"Again?" Xannan wrapped the sword belt around his waist and weaved between his brother and father to gather clothes, frowning at the few long-sleeved shirts he stuffed into the bag. "Nothing has changed in five years. We use the swords and that's that."

Gailin drummed his fingers against his own sword hilt. Futurae, they called it. "No, the swords gave us magical gifts, remember?"

"Ah, yes." Xannan cinched his bag together and patted his sword's hilt with mock reverence. "So useful. Relive my own past memories. At least yours is worth something."

Gailin drew his blond hair back from his forehead. "Let's not have this argument again, Xannan. Neither of us had any control over what magic we did or did not receive that day."

"So you say." Bag prepped, Xannan slung it over his shoulder. "I need to let Anna know. See you at the stables in an hour."

He followed the path Anna had taken, glancing over his shoulder and sighing as Gailin jogged to catch up with him. Not quite identical in appearance anymore, their facial expressions were always the first to give away who was whom. Pensive and melancholic, Gailin was the caretaker.

According to others, Xannan appeared annoyed more often than not. Unless he was with Anna, or training, or putting his skills to the test on the battlefield.

Tenuous peace had shattered once others knew of the magic he and Gailin now possessed. Some questioned how they had received the magic and debated if they were mentally capable of learning to rule, considering many humans with magic became corrupt. Others wanted to take it away, to possess the power for themselves.

Neither had asked for the abilities, but they had them. Now others wanted what neither Xannan nor Gailin quite understood themselves.

"You can stop scowling," Gailin said as he slowed to Xannan's pace. "You and I both know you enjoy battles more than you'll say."

Xannan grunted and glanced behind to make sure their father hadn't followed. Sometimes the man disapproved of the lengths Xannan would use to win these skirmishes. But better to leave none alive to bother them again, unless Gailin could persuade him otherwise. "And how do you feel about this impending confrontation?"

Several moments passed with naught but their footfalls and the swish of wind through billowing curtains.

"Tense," Gailin finally admitted. "Wary, but confident."

"Those are two words that do not go together, Gailin."

"Like Blazing and foolish?"

Xannan shrugged. "It was worth the attempt. And Father's new outfit *does* look foolish."

"Please don't make me force you to wear the proper attire on the journey."

"I'd prefer to keep feeling in my fingers this time." Xannan shoved his hands in his pockets, faintly acknowledging the bump of his sword hilt against his forearm and wondering how many more lives it would claim. "Father said it's a settlement? As in commoners?"

"That's where the wariness comes in. I think." Gailin shook his head, blond hair not much shorter than Xannan's own shifting from side to side. "I'm not so sure it's a settlement as Father was told."

Xannan paused, mulling over the implication. "Well, even if we were fed false information, we'll be prepared." He nudged Gailin with an elbow. "Confident, right?"

A muscle in Gailin's jaw twitched, but he nodded. "The two are warring with each other closer than I would prefer, but yes, confident."

"Otherwise Father wouldn't let us both go."

"He's always sent us both."

"True." Xannan glanced over the balcony railing where they had paused, smiling when Anna looked up. When she noticed his bag, her smile faltered. "But he always asks how you feel about it first."

"More often than you know," Gailin murmured.

With a chuckle and a soft sigh, Xannan jerked his head toward where Anna stood looking up from below. She'd removed the coat he'd placed around her shoulders. Black skirts matched her hair and the shimmering silver bodice almost made her skin appear lighter. Or perhaps that was the flickering torches that would never bathe Anna in the light she deserved.

Xannan didn't realize he was staring until his mother's solid white dress invaded his vision. The woman who'd survived birthing two sons at once despite many claiming one would die graced him with a brief, appreciative smile. She resumed her movement, waving her arms about as though she could magically decorate the spotless parlor that was any visitor's first view of Cantadad's castle. Grand staircases outlined either side, complete with the balcony where Xannan and Gailin now stood.

"Go. I'll prepare the battalions." Gailin leaned his side against the railing and held up a finger. "We leave at nightfall, Xannan. The moment that sun hits the horizon, we leave."

"There's plenty I can accomplish in that time." Xannan winked and gave Gailin a playful punch. After the first few stairs, he hollered back at his brother. "Don't forget to see Ella before we leave!"

2

As his brother descended the stairs, Gailin met his mother's observant gaze. Her tense smile meant his father had already shared what little he could sense. Often it bothered him they trusted those sensations almost without question. It was the only thing he felt good at doing anymore—taking care of others by sharing what emotions he felt in their presence or about their ideas. The mixture of wariness and confidence surged as one while he held his mother's gaze. In his periphery, Xannan and Anna were lost in their own embrace, complete with a lengthy kiss Gailin never would have committed to when their mother was within arm's reach.

Gailin allowed those emotions to fester. A myriad of unspoken words passed between him and his mother, much different from the silent communication which used to work so well between him and Xannan. She had tried to help them understand what abilities they had been gifted that day in the cave, but none of them would ever understand how every little piece of information created a new branch. An idea, however small, could grow into a forest. An overwhelming, overgrown, never-ending forest.

Gailin blinked and shoved away the often useless images that sometimes formed in his mind's eye. Where Xannan could relive that which he already experienced, Gailin could witness that which might come to fruition. What started with emotions that weren't his own turned into something more. Snippets, whirlwinds, vague statements—sharing them only ever led to chaos, so he claimed to stop seeing them. Based on how his parents continually questioned him and Eonar, he figured they didn't believe his lie about the images.

He stood a moment longer, turning to leave only after his mother's small nod. Several paces back down the breezeway was a second set of stairs which allowed a more direct path to the stables. Most of the stalls would, hopefully, be empty by now since he'd already sent word to Edmund to prepare the battalions.

Gailin paused at the entrance, allowing himself to smile at a welcoming sight that also caused him to mentally curse ever being trained in any capacity to fight. Head barely visible above the horse's back, Ella's arm moved in a slow and methodical movement, brushing the dappled gray stallion whose coat was reminiscent of the sword hanging about his waist.

The stallion pranced as Gailin approached. He wrinkled his nose at the mixture of hay and droppings caught in the breeze. Though Ella's arm continued its persistent motion, he heard her whispering to the horse falter.

While Gailin gathered the necessary materials to saddle the stallion, they shared a glance. Perceptive hazel eyes pierced through him, so he continued through the motions of preparing his mount, not knowing what to say. He'd always envied Xannan for that. The man spoke before he thought regardless of the potential repercussions. Granted, those repercussions usually came in the form of inciting enemy combatants' rage before it did their parents'.

"I recalled you suggested going for a ride this evening." She let the stallion nibble on a sugar cube in her palm. As the horse pressed his nose into her hand, she looked over at Gailin. "But your emanating worry indicates His Majesty has other plans for you, yes?"

Gailin tried to hide the wince. He'd known this would happen soon but hadn't anticipated how quickly they would be asked to leave. A quiet dinner with Ella in a nearby field would have been preferable to rallying two battalions.

"Father received news of a settlement near Falsumbra Forest and asked us to inspect." Gailin cinched the saddle and hooked his bag onto its side. "My guess is we'll be gone for at least a month. Edmund and Mikhael's battalions are coming, too."

"Longer, if the past is any indication." Ella folded her arms and frowned. "Two whole battalions for a settlement?"

He shrugged, checking the saddle one last time, led the stallion back to its stall, and gathered the supplies for Xannan's mount. "Father didn't disagree. Best to be overprepared."

Ella remained with arms folded, and now that a horse wasn't standing between them, he realized she wore a deep green dress he'd not seen before. It hugged close to her chest and hips in a way that was, admittedly, momentarily distracting. "Is Mother trying out new styles like Father has been?"

"Her Majesty and Anna designed it." Ella smoothed the velvety skirts and frowned at the gray hairs left behind while tucking a lock of blond hair behind her ear. "I'm uncertain how I feel about it, but Anna insisted I try it out. And she asked me to wear it while serving as her second for the ceremony."

"A second?" Gailin lifted the saddle onto Xannan's horse—another dappled gray stallion with kinship to Gailin's mount.

Ella held the saddle in place for him as he cinched the strap and explained, "One who stands in support of the union, aside from the priests and each betrothed's parents."

"Don't tell me it was Xannan's idea?"

"Definitely not." Ella chuckled and walked around Xannan's stallion, pausing to rub his nose and offer him a sugar cube. "Anna has many ideas for the ceremony." Slight streaks remained where she rubbed her hands against the dress-skirts. "Enough about those two."

Gailin had no reason to stiffen when she neared, but he did. Each day together, they shared this moment. It both calmed and infuriated him. Ella had no reason to carry the burden he had been given, but she knew him better than anyone now. At first, he'd tried to explain it to Xannan, but his brother harbored jealousy at the differences in their abilities.

She tugged his hand away from the saddle-strap, and he allowed the movement, chest clenching as she rested his open palm on her cheek. "Tell me."

When he tried to shift away, to tug his hand free, Ella's grip tightened. "If there were another way to ease it, I would," she whispered. "If you always hold it all inside—"

"Fear," he admitted, interrupting her with the one emotion he'd not mentioned to anyone else.

Though she flinched at the word, Ella didn't break her gaze. After a deep breath, he explained the concerns he'd shared with Xannan and his father, while adding those he'd thought to himself. As usual, Ella absorbed the information, allowing him to say what he needed to say, to share it with one who would not use his ability as a means to an end.

"Your jerky movements make more sense now." She lowered his hand from her cheek but did not let go, offering a reassuring squeeze as she lifted to her toes to kiss him. "Be careful, my love," she whispered, and his breath caught at the words.

Gailin leaned his forehead against hers. "As always."

She wrinkled her nose and rubbed it with her finger, a common habit she despised that Gailin found endearing. "And don't—"

"I know." He didn't want her to have to finish the statement. She knew how he kept most of what he felt contained. Emotions warred with one another so often inside that sometimes he found it difficult to determine what his own feelings even were.

Booted footsteps warned him of Edmund's arrival around the same time his friend said, "Might be easier to give the lady a proper goodbye when you aren't caring for a horse, Your Highness."

The solid black coat made Edmund's skin appear paler than most of the other soldiers, and he kept his hair so short Gailin had forgotten what shade it was. The second-son of the first duke their father had named, Edmund had initially been sent to the capital as a representative, but he requested to remain as a soldier. Edmund's father, who oversaw much of the land they were about to travel to inspect, had been hesitant to acquiesce to the idea, but Edmund disliked remaining in his brother's shadow, an element of life Gailin understood.

After a not-so-subtle wink, Edmund led the readied mounts outside the stable, leaving Gailin with nothing to occupy his hands.

Ella chuckled, holding both his hands as she lifted to her toes and kissed him again. "Remember that this ability does not define or control you, Gailin." She placed her hand on his chest, above his heart, and Gailin wished he knew what to say in response. Once more, she knew how to comfort him while he had nothing to offer in return. "One branch does not a tree make."

"How do you always know what to say, Ella?" He tapped her nose, grinning as she wrinkled it and rubbed with her finger again, earning him an uncharacteristic glare. "Will you stay in the castle this time?"

She nodded and continued rubbing her nose. "Apparently a second is supposed to help keep the bride-to-be company and assist with the preparations."

"Ah, I'm sure you can accomplish much without Xannan around to distract Anna every time they turn a corner."

At the doors, Edmund cleared his throat. "Apologies for the interruption, but His Majesty requested we leave by nightfall, yes?"

Gailin's jaw clenched as he nodded, and Edmund pointed at the sky with his dagger—a weapon he had no need to pull from its sheath when not in danger. The sun's descent neared the horizon, and a glance at the castle gates found the courtyard filled with soldiers ready to leave. After one final squeeze, and a firm request Edmund prevent Gailin from suppressing all of his emotions, Ella walked back to the castle. She glanced back several times, pausing at the doorway.

"So," Edmund leaned against the open stable door and idly tossed his dagger, chuckling when Gailin glared at him. "Who gets the honor of reminding Prince Xannan he's to join this journey?"

Gailin folded his arms. "He's a good judge of time."

"Ah yes, in battle, true." Edmund smirked and tossed his dagger again. "But he's been engaged for how many days now?"

Gailin's shoulders tensed, and his gaze trailed the dagger's movement as Edmund tossed, caught, and sheathed the weapon. "Six." Saying the number aloud made claws of jealousy resurface. Societal convention would require him to wait until *after* his brother's wedding to even ask for Ella's hand. While hoping Ella didn't grow too curious in his absence, Gailin's gaze roamed over their mounts and mentally checked off each item present. "Where's Mikhael?"

"Checking supplies." Edmund tilted into his line of sight and lifted a brow. "You're more distracted than usual."

"Later." Gailin walked around Edmund, unsure if his chest felt tighter or looser as Xannan exited the castle. Gailin called over his shoulder to Edmund, "And keep that dagger away until you need it. Unless you want a repeat of—"

"The boy shouldn't have tried to snatch it!" Edmund called back as he walked toward his gathered battalion.

"How many times will you remind Edmund of that event?" Xannan grinned at Edmund's mumbled use of the curse he'd created while giving his stallion a cursory glance. After hooking his bag to the saddle and placing his sword in its saddle sheath, he mounted. "Told you Blazes would catch on."

"You're Blazing frustrating sometimes." Gailin mounted, shifting the reins to guide his mount to the gates where two hundred men, plus a dozen servants to tend to their food and tents, waited.

"I like that combination." Xannan matched Gailin's pace. "Blazing works well before many words."

They slowed to a halt once they reached the gates, and a poor attempt at a silent conversation passed before Xannan sighed and addressed the soldiers. "Quickest path to Falsumbra Forest." He nodded at Edmund, whose selected group of soldiers would scout ahead in rotation. "Stay east of the cliffs so we can keep the higher ground." He tilted his head and looked at Gailin. "And?"

"Time to leave."

Though Xannan squinted at Gailin, his overconfident brother nodded and nudged his mount forward. Gailin hesitated, watching as the gathered group exited the grand castle gates in groups of five. Smooth movements of trained soldiers, ones who had learned all the disciplines his father had. A man of many trades and many lives before creating his own. Gailin's stomach twisted, and he tightened his grip on the reins in hopes to quell the sensations before they reared. But nothing could ever truly stop them.

3

Their journey continued without incident, though Xannan noticed his brother's demeanor descending more into worry than anything else as one day bled into the next. Gailin's sour mood combined with the putrid smell wafting along the breeze made Xannan tense. With orders for Edmund's scouts to circle the forest, the remainder made camp at the southern edge of Falsumbra.

Fire crackling between logs offered a comfortable amount of heat to stave off the chilled winds. Since he knew what to expect, Xannan had also grabbed several pairs of gloves. He'd learned the hard way how difficult it could be to wield a sword with numb fingers.

Xannan rubbed his gloved hands together over the fire, idly recalling the dragons he'd once met. If he wanted to, Xannan could reenter that memory as though it was happening before him once again, though it never extended beyond the dragons' mingling flame of black and white. Rather than let the memory overwhelm his senses, Xannan shoved it aside. Footsteps approaching helped solidify him in reality.

"The men have noticed his"—Mikhael sat next to Xannan, handing him a bowl of warm soup—"his less than enthusiastic expressions."

His friend wore the newest military design. Solid black rather than the dirt-like tones Xannan preferred. Xannan wrinkled his nose and held the bowl, allowing it to warm his hands. "Gailin did say he's confident."

"Yes, well, words and expressions should match in order for all to believe it." Mikhael took a sip of the soup, rubbed a gloved hand over his sparsely growing beard, and sighed. "Try it. Better than last night's mixture."

Xannan grunted and sniffed the bowl, which did smell more flavorful despite the lingering sour tinge. A hint of spices, roasted rabbit, and vegetables. After a small sip, he set the bowl on the ground and searched for his brother. As expected, Gailin was speaking with Edmund. Right now, they waited. No more forward movement until they had confirmation of what awaited them now that Falsumbra Forest was in view. If the scout failed to return within two days' time, they'd advance with the assumption force would be required.

While Mikhael slurped his soup, Xannan watched Gailin. His dark-haired friend was right—Gailin wasn't hiding the worry anymore.

"Remind the men he mentioned confidence." Xannan picked up his bowl and gulped down the remaining liquid. "We are, after all, checking out a settlement."

Mikhael guffawed, loud enough several heads turned toward them. "A settlement?" Mikhael shook his head and held out a hand for Xannan's empty bowl. "I think we both know that's a lie."

"I should have asked, but which scout informed Father?"

Mikhael frowned and stared at their empty bowls for several heartbeats. "No one ever mentioned a name." He met Xannan's gaze, gray eyes clouded with apprehension. "Not to me at least."

"Blazes." Xannan stood and donned the nearby coat. "Double the night guard. I doubt we'll make it to morning without interruption."

After a quick bow, Mikhael jogged off to follow orders, leaving their empty bowls beside the fire. For once, the man said nothing about Xannan's use of the newfound curse.

Xannan approached Gailin and spoke more sharply than he intended. "Wary?"

A slight nod followed by Gailin's common, and frustrating, shrug. "We're already surrounded."

After Gailin gestured at Edmund, the soldier explained further, "Only one of the advance scouts returned, sir."

"How many?" Xannan gripped his sword hilt, allowing its familiar presence to ground him.

"Hard to say, sir." Edmund swiveled his head from side to side, as though he could see where the enemy hid. "The one scout who did return counted five groups of ten before returning. They're waiting."

"Hoping we won't realize the danger and then attack us in our sleep?"

Both Gailin and Edmund murmured their agreement, and Gailin added, "Any thought I have of what to do does not incite confidence, only more wariness."

Xannan's grunt earned him an annoyed glance from his brother that he dismissed. "What if we give them what they want?"

Gailin lifted a brow.

Crossing his arms, Xannan explained. "We pretend to retire for the night, lure them into our camp believing they've been effective, then strike back when they least expect it."

Gailin rubbed a hand along his face and sighed. "Why is it when you mention the same idea I did, I feel differently about it?"

Xannan winked and tapped Gailin's shoulder with the back of his hand. "Because I'm the confident one." He turned to Edmund. "I've asked Mikhael to double the night guard. Have soldiers double up so some tents are empty and others house eight."

Once Edmund was out of earshot, Gailin whispered, "This isn't going to be pleasant."

Xannan tilted his head back and failed to disguise his frustration. "It's our land and it's our duty to protect it." He leveled a glare at Gailin. "And if that means taking the lives of those who threaten us, then so be it."

"That's not what I meant, Xannan."

Several heartbeats of silence passed between them until Xannan rested one hand on his sword hilt and the other on his hip. "You saw something again, didn't you?"

Gailin flinched and glanced away.

"Injuries happen, we've prepared for that possibility." Xannan motioned at the nearby tent of servants and soldiers who doubled as doctors. His muscles tensed, and he hoped he could maintain his record of ending battles unscathed. "We are the best fighters on this continent."

When Gailin's gaze flickered up, Xannan clenched his jaw and followed his brother's line of sight to the sky. Clouds drifted across the stars, and though it wasn't there, Xannan swore he could make out the outline of the beasts which had forced magical abilities on himself and his brother. One breath hitched as the memory knocked loose, explaining why each bowl of soup tasted worse than the last and why Gailin's worry continued to increase.

Xannan pinched the bridge of his nose. "Father said—"

"Because no one ever lies to us, right?" Gailin grimaced as he lowered his head from surveying the sky. "Usually you—"

"I'd intentionally forgotten that smell." Xannan pressed his lips together and frowned. "It has been almost two years since a drokos sighting."

Gailin's forehead creased in thought. "But you aren't denying it, which means they'll come straight for us."

"We could always try comb—"

"No. That is *never* happening, Xannan." Gailin's sharp interruption made Xannan grind his teeth.

"How bad could it be, Gailin?" Xannan motioned between their blades, weapons he'd always believed were meant to be connected no matter how vehemently Gailin denied the idea.

Gailin shifted his sword belt. "You watch the skies, and I'll handle whatever Alkaanians think they can outsmart us."

"Blazing perfect."

They frowned at each other, a quick agreement that the combination hadn't worked well, and Xannan turned on his heel to inform Mikhael of their slight change of plans. He adjusted his gloves as he walked, wishing it was warm enough to fight without them. Xannan wanted to feel the grooves of his sword's hilt as he fought, but he also wanted to maintain control of the weapon.

4

"Follow me," Xannan said as he walked past Mikhael outside the tent which housed the battalion leader's second in command. Xannan heard the quick apologies, and the tempo of his friend's footsteps indicated a veiled annoyance.

"New problems?" Mikhael asked when they'd made it out of earshot.

Xannan scanned the star-filled sky and found naught but clouds flitting across the pinpoints of light.

His friend mumbled a low curse. "Not extinct then?"

With a slight shake of his head as confirmation, Xannan held Mikhael's gaze and hoped his eyes didn't betray the cold fear welling inside his chest. The few prior fights he'd had against droki had led to more deaths than he wished to remember. Memories threatened to surface of friends, soldiers, commoners who wanted nothing more than to live quietly, all with blackened veins as the poison took hold. The only memory he needed to recall was how to kill the mindless, venomous creatures. Stab the heart or slice through the neck. No different from any other attacker. Besides, no reason to make it easier for the magic-hunting dragon-like droki to find them. Not until he was ready.

"Orders, sir?" Mikhael's question pulled Xannan from the threat of reliving his past.

"Take half the battalion and arrange throughout the south end of camp." Xannan's attention returned to the sky. "Leave the droki to me, but make sure none of those idiotic Alkaanians get close."

"And what should I—"

"They all swore an oath to serve and protect." Xannan grimaced at the tone of his voice. The thought of facing the droki again set his nerves aflame. "But I'm not asking anyone else to fight the droki. Just make sure I'm only fighting one type of beast rather than two."

While Mikhael jogged off to gather a group to accompany them, Xannan continued searching the skies. He'd spoken true when he mentioned forgetting their smell. How he had always known they approached, he wasn't sure, but their scent lingered on the howling wind.

A frigid blast of air whipped his blond hair around his face, and he gripped the hilt of his sword so tight the leather covering his fingers creaked. Leather gloves kept the chill from his hands but could not warm the shards of ice settling in his chest. *Not going to be pleasant, indeed.*

After the gathered soldiers arrived, Xannan explained his plan. They would stick to his earlier idea. Overoccupy several tents, leave others empty, and lie in wait for the Alkaanians. If they were lucky, the droki would arrive after the ground threat. But luck often disappeared when droki neared.

As they waited, they exchanged silent hand signals with one another to stay awake. Comical stories, serious ones, reminders of each other's weaknesses to strengthen. "Keep an eye over your left shoulder," he'd signed to Mikhael not long ago. Brilliant in the sparring ring, his friend always forgot to look over his left shoulder in battle.

The Alkaanians' heavy breaths gave them away first, followed by the snaps of twigs some had planted outside tents. Silhouettes of armored men covered the tent walls. A soldier across from him shifted, and Xannan motioned for them to wait. No battle cries had sounded yet. Better to let them make the first move lest they ruin the surprise.

Rather than tear through the canvas as Xannan had expected them to, the Alkaanians approached the tent's entrance. Soldier by soldier, they eased weapons from sheaths, their ringing loud in the silence of night. He sniffed and tilted his head. Only one drokos. So far.

Mikhael tugged on Xannan's arm, frowning when Xannan pulled his dagger free rather than his sword. After another quick reminder for Mikhael to pay attention to his surroundings, Xannan tore a small hole in the canvas and peered at the sky. Not close enough to see, but the scent had grown strong enough to send the shards of ice in his chest plummeting into his gut. There they'd remain until the drokos lay headless on the ground.

At Mikhael's urgent signing of "go," Xannan shook his head and focused on the tent's entrance where the Alkaanians made sharp movements with their arms and ended with one of them hissing at the other "then you enter first." Xannan smirked; they knew and had come anyway.

One finally grasped the tent flap, choking on his own breath as Xannan's dagger found purchase in the man's chest. Chaos followed. A mass of steel. No shouting. Grunts, painful and pallid.

Blade free of its sheath, Xannan stayed near the back of the tent, occasionally glancing through the hole he'd made with fervent whispers for the droki's scent to disperse.

It grew stronger.

The sudden clash of steel dissipated into the stillness of night once more. Five dead. All enemies. Only . . . Xannan paused, realizing he was unaware of how many Alkaanians had arrived. He appraised the eight occupying the tent with him. All now held bloodied weapons, and one sported a profusely bleeding gash down his arm that another hastily patched.

Mikhael turned to Xannan and signed, "Stay?"

Xannan mulled over the idea and shook his head. First blood had been spilled, so now it was time to finish the job. He bent and retrieved his dagger, absentmindedly cleaning the blade on a coat that looked much warmer—and more constrictive—than his own. As he stood and sheathed the smaller weapon his father had gifted him, he searched the skies.

"Stay on the south end." Xannan turned so all could see his hands movement and motioned with his crystalline sword. Shouts erupted from the other side of camp, and he fought between a grimace and a grin. Sword versus sword he enjoyed. A fleeting, distracted glance at the sky and then he winked at Mikhael.

They exited the tent together, Xannan's right shoulder nearly touching Mikhael's left. Another small group of Alkaanians already lay dead. Xannan felt a pang of annoyance; he'd only had the opportunity to fell one so far. In unison, they moved forward, no different from prior battles or practices. But none of those had included the wavering threat of a drokos appearance.

Others tried to inch closer to the center of camp, shifting positions at Xannan's and Mikhael's shouted reminders. Stick to the perimeter. Leave none alive. Perhaps that wasn't Gailin's or his father's plan, but it was his. Each new bead of sweat made him smile, and he submitted to the fray. Swipe after slash after thrust, he killed them before they could graze their weapon against him.

A shoulder bumped his, and Xannan swung, sword halting before it gutted Mikhael.

"You're supposed to warn me." Xannan growled as he turned his attention back to an advancing opponent. Back pressed against

Mikhael's, he felt his friends heavier breathing. "I could have killed you!"

"You're welcome for the assist." Mikhael retorted and stepped away. "Unless you wanted a dagger in your—"

His friend's presence disappeared from behind him. Xannan concentrated on annihilating his current assailant. Two quick moves and he turned around, ducking before a tossed weapon found its mark. Xannan scoured the dark camp turned battlefield. Blocking the swipe of a sword with his own, he listened for Mikhael's commanding cadence of a voice.

"Blazes, Mikhael, talk to me," Xannan gritted out as he dodged another's forward advance. Someone grasped his ankle, and he tugged his leg free, lifting his sword to plunge.

Mouth agape, eyes wide and darting, Mikhael lay prone on the ground. He was attempting to form words, but no sound came forth. A quick survey found the culprit—a knife buried in the base of Mikhael's neck. His friend convulsed, and Mikhael's hand jerked to reach his abdomen where a second wound oozed.

Grimacing, Xannan fell to his knees beside his friend and forced himself to remember the months and years of training he'd received. He curled his fingers around his sword's hilt as he mentally recited. Out of danger, bandage the wounds. First to safety, away from immediate danger so he could bandage the wounds. His grimace deepened; Mikhael had already lost so much blood.

Xannan raked a hand through his hair and growled at the approaching footsteps, swinging his sword against the weapon which dared to infringe on his space. Two more strikes, and another lay dead at his feet. Same as Mikhael would be if he didn't do something soon.

"Missed your heart," he murmured more to himself than to his dying friend. Mikhael gulped and blood trickled around the knife at the movement as the man tried to utter another sound. "No, I'll get—"

An angry snarl behind him made Xannan shift to one side. Sharp pain laced down his sword arm, ripping apart what little tether remained on his own bloodlust. Warm liquid leaked from a deep gash that stretched from his shoulder to his elbow. Moonlight glinted off a raised blade, and Xannan rolled away from the second strike. He tried to lift his sword, but the muscles of his arm burned with a strange ferocity. Cursing, Xannan switched hands and shoved the blade up once he lay on his back. Staring at the tip of his opponent's sword a hand's breadth from his chest, Xannan kicked the man off him and crawled back toward Mikhael.

Xannan stayed low to the ground and relied on his uninjured arm while hoping Mikhael's wounds were bleeding less because they were not as dire as they had first appeared. After a quick appraisal of their surroundings to ensure no one else approached, Xannan sheathed his sword, gritted his teeth, and hooked his arms beneath Mikhael's. He ignored the screeching pain in his sword arm and dragged his friend into the closest tent. Gritting his teeth, Xannan moved as quickly as he could, scanning the chaotic camp. None approached them. They'd all ventured further inward, to the middle of their camp.

"Stay with me." Xannan tapped Mikhael's cheek and leaned in close to where the knife remained embedded in the base of his friend's neck. "I have to staunch the bleeding first. Then get a medic to stitch you up."

He applied pressure as soon as the knife came free. One hand firm against the wound, Xannan glanced at Mikhael's face. Glazed eyes. Skin ashen. Xannan winced as he thumped his free hand against Mikhael's chest, hoping to startle him awake, but all it did was shift his friend's body.

"You need to breathe." A glance down at his friend's wounded abdomen made Xannan press his lips together, and the shards of ice resting in his gut turned to stone. Sticky liquid that should be coursing through Mikhael's limbs coated the soldier's clothing. Xannan lifted the hand pressing against Mikhael's injured neck, anticipating a torrent of blood. Not even a trickle escaped.

Clamors and shouts turned distant as the thought settled. Mikhael's chest no longer lifted, nor did his throat move with the attempt to speak, nor did his arm jerk to reach the gash in his stomach.

Blood leaked down Xannan's wounded arm and filled his leather glove. He ripped the garment off his hand, staring at the drops falling from his fingertips. A reminder that life flowed through him in a way it never would again for Mikhael. Anger chased away logic.

Flashes of what happened coursed through his mind's eye. A tap, an almost deadly blow. Xannan shook his head and closed his eyes, berating himself for turning around. He could have blocked that attack and saved his friend's life.

Xannan stared, forcing himself to breathe while wishing he could make Mikhael's chest rise and fall in a steady rhythm. Or hear Mikhael's gruff voice remind him to pause and think. Pause and assess. His shoulders rose. Fell. Xannan sniffed and thumped his fist on Mikhael's chest, yelling at the man to breathe.

There, a twitch of movement. He hit Mikhael's chest again and sat back on his heels and shook his head, frowning.

It had to be his imagination. A wish for reality not to take its cruel hold. The dead didn't move. He knew that. He'd watched other soldiers breathe their last.

But Xannan stared. Waiting. Thinking. Hoping that perhaps this time would be different. A voice floated on the wind. Mikhael's voice. He frowned at his friend's still body. The dead didn't speak either.

An ear-splitting cry shattered the cacophony of battle. More grunts of pain and death followed, a sign each side had used the other's distraction. Xannan dragged himself to standing, gaze never leaving Mikhael's prone form. His friend's hand twitched, as though refusing death's call. But too much time passed between each movement. No steady pattern. He counted. Five heartbeats. Ten. Twenty. Another jerk. Xannan squinted, gripping his sword hilt. He tensed when a shrill screech consumed his senses. Something was wrong.

Or right.

He shook the latter thought from his head and turned to the tent's entrance. When Xannan switched his sword back to the proper hand, he grimaced. The gash down his arm continued to ooze blood, and his muscles weren't properly responding.

Xannan forced himself to look up, sneering at the drokos swooping down at him.

"Not pleasant indeed." His grip on the sword faltered, so he shifted back to his nondominant hand. One he could take. Even injured. First the drokos, then answers.

5

Chills trickled down Xannan's spine at the shrill scream that lingered in the air above, halting with the thud of its too-large paws on the trampled ground in front of him. He swallowed, grip tightening on his sword. More blood trickled from the gash in his arm. First the drokos, then he'd staunch his wound.

Its stench made him want to gag and vomit more than blood or sweat ever would. He grimaced at the throb in his arm and shoved aside the thoughts of what could go wrong with his favored sword arm incapacitated.

Beady eyes and a snake-like head slithered as another ululating cry escaped its opened maw. Sharp black teeth dripped with a dark substance. Poison. Of the deadliest kind. All he had to do was get his sword into the creature's heart, or slice off its head, and the drokos would be no more.

He shifted his sword and winced when it slipped. His remaining glove was still slippery from Mikhael's blood. The drokos paused, towering over him and pecking down at Xannan, halting inches from his face and sniffing.

His vision blurred, and Xannan told his arm to move. It was close enough to kill. All he had to do was move the sword. He knew the motion but didn't know if his nondominant arm had the strength. Focus became difficult, and his breath snagged on the creature's scent. A mixture of death and life. A combination of fresh blooms and burned flesh.

Though he told his arm to move, it was as if he were frozen and couldn't remember the motions. He blinked rapidly, trying to clear his sight of the encroaching fuzziness. Something was definitely wrong. Had the Alkaanian's blade been poisoned? Unlikely, but it wouldn't be the first time they tried a new tactic.

Blood. He could smell it, taste it, feel its steady stream from his open wound.

He stepped forward, almost falling to the ground. Why wasn't the drokos attacking him? It had a prime opportunity. One little scratch by tooth or claw, and Xannan would die. Given the rapid increase of blood loss, it wouldn't take long for the drokos poison to do its terrible work. Memories surfaced. Farmers, children, babies succumbing to blackened veins.

Xannan swung his sword and found naught but air. He swayed and took another faltering step, switching his weapon back to the proper hand and gritting back a scream as his muscles protested the weight. Holding the sword with both hands, he followed the shimmying movement of the drokos's neck. Back and forth, side to side. The black oil-like poison dripped, and Xannan stepped backward to avoid the droplets.

"Stab in the heart," he grumbled to himself and lifted the sword, growling at the pain as he plunged the weapon forward. The drokos let out an inane screech and lashed out at him with its neck. Its head thumped against his, and before he could finish a prayer its poison didn't infiltrate his bloodstream, the world tipped sideways.

For a moment, Xannan lay there. The scent of dirt and grass were a welcome reprieve from the drokos's stench. Blades of grass prickled against his palm as he searched for his sword. Xannan shook his head, trying to clear whatever fogginess continued to thread its way through his vision.

He rolled to his back, listening. Clashing weapons were far enough away for him to be concerned about their success but not his safety. The drokos lay sprawled atop the grass beside him. No movement. Something silver in the drokos's chest gleamed beneath moonlight. A sword. Probably his sword since his roving hands hadn't located it yet.

Burying both elbows in the dirt, Xannan attempted to sit up. When he lifted his head, the stars in the sky spun. Forgetting his palm was covered both in Mikhael's blood and dirt, he felt along his injured arm. He'd lost more blood than this before and maintained consciousness, but swaths of darkness streaked his vision, and he squeezed his eyes shut.

The tang of blood on his tongue intensified, and he tried to gulp down the surfacing images. He hated reliving the past; it reminded him of how he'd failed the innocents. Pale-skinned children with webs of black lay dead, their parents huddling above with tearful requests to rid the world of the droki. Pain spiked in his temples, sharp enough to make him gasp.

"Mikhael," he muttered to himself. Xannan commanded his arms to move.

Footsteps approached, and he lashed out at the figure drawing near. Neither fist hit its mark, and the movement made the entire world spin. Whoever had found him spoke. Words like help, aid, and his name came through in a vaguely familiar-sounding voice.

The world moved again and next Xannan knew, he was back in the tent where he'd left Mikhael. He reached for his friend, but someone pinned his arm down with a fervent request for him to stop moving.

Xannan didn't listen. When Mikhael's limbs jerked, he tried to focus on staying awake and willing for Mikhael to breathe. One breath, another. Or was it the soldier helping him whose breaths he was counting? Incoherent words drifted to him as the world faded to black.

***

"You know what to do with those two," Gailin reminded Edmund as he wiped his sword clean, sheathed it, and scrubbed his face with his palms. The motion halted at a realization. Enemy soldiers lived. Xannan never left enemy soldiers alive.

His heart hammered in his chest. Wariness and confidence continued to battle one another. What had been the cost of this win?

Someone grabbed his wrist, and Gailin reflexively shifted away from the movement. Lowering his hands, he found Edmund peering at him with both brows lifted. "What is it, sir?"

"I can't sense any more attacks but—" Gailin gestured at the captured Alkaanians. "We have enemy soldiers alive after a battle involving Xannan."

His friend's eyes widened. "Wouldn't you know if he were dead?"

Gailin shrugged and rubbed the back of his neck, wishing he could relive the past as Xannan did. Perhaps he could witness details of the battle he'd not noticed before. "Xannan would have concentrated most of his efforts on killing the drokos. . ."

Any other thoughts about his own soldiers, or even the captured enemy combatants, fled from his mind as he raced toward the felled drokos. Xannan wouldn't be so foolish as to *let* the creature bite or claw him. But that didn't mean his brother wasn't injured.

Gailin slowed his steps, searching the trampled ground. He allowed the thought of his brother to coalesce, and his hammering heart slowed. Gailin didn't know if the slowing meant he'd find Xannan alive or dead. Surely he would know if something had happened. They were connected. Always had been and always would be.

Maimed bodies lay strewn about their camp, dressed in both the livery of Orda'an and Alkaan. He grimaced, wondering how many soldiers he'd led to their deaths at his father's request. All because they had to protect the land they'd claimed as their own. He avoided counting the number of dead on both sides, slowing to a complete stop at the sight of the dead drokos.

Silver protruded from the creature's chest. Gailin frowned. That sword was an extension of his brother.

"What in the Blazes made you forget to retrieve your weapon, Xannan?" Gailin muttered to himself while surveying the area surrounding the dead drokos.

A harried voice infiltrated his thoughts, shouting his name. The white band around the shoulder's upper arm marked him as a battlefield medic. Choosing his steps carefully to avoid the felled soldiers they'd properly bury later, Gailin approached. Black liquid pooled around the drokos and reflected the moon high in the sky. He pressed his lips together and held his breath as he skirted the poisonous puddle.

The soldier led him into a nearby tent barely ten steps from the putrid, dead beast, and Gailin froze at the entrance. Covered in blood with a tear in one sleeve, Xannan was already slick with a feverish sweat. Unconscious, but alive. Of all the soldiers with them, Xannan and Mikhael were two Gailin never worried about. Both were ruthless with weapons in hand.

Gailin's gaze flickered over the tent and his grip tightened on the canvas as he recognized the pallid color of Mikhael's skin, the lack of—Gailin homed in on Mikhael's chest. Had it moved? The commander's skin was too pale, too void of life for any movement to be possible.

"You noticed it, too?" The soldier, Lieutenant Solomon, spoke in a hushed whisper. "Commander Mikhael is dead, but there are occasional movements. Sporadic, usually when—"

Xannan's incoherent whisper made Gailin drop to his knees beside his brother while Solomon tended the wounds. Even though he knew Solomon had already done so and it would be there, Gailin checked for Xannan's pulse. Thready and erratic, it thrummed beneath Gailin's fingers as he held them against Xannan's clammy skin.

His jaw ached as he scanned Xannan for other wounds aside from the one Solomon had cleaned. It seemed no inch of Xannan's clothing had been left unscathed. One glove was missing and led Gailin back to the gash down Xannan's arm.

He leaned over, watching Solomon work, and almost gagged. Chunks of dirt embedded in Xannan's muscle meant the man hadn't paused to take care of it at all. Had the wound been any deeper, Gailin would be looking at his brother's bone.

"Idiot. You can't keep fighting with a wound like that." Gailin continued searching his brother's body for additional injuries. With each section of unmarred skin, Gailin's clenched chest loosened.

Xannan's eyes fluttered, his head lolled, and his lips moved. Another movement occurred behind Solomon where Mikhael's prone form lay. Gailin's focus shifted from his feverish brother to Mikhael and back again as thoughts and feelings and images formed. Mouth now gritty as though he'd inhaled a lump of sand, Gailin pushed aside what he'd seen. Later, once Xannan healed, he would ask questions. He tapped Xannan's cheek as an attempt to wake him, but his brother's head shifted to the other side.

"Blazes!" Gailin scrubbed his face with his hands, not understanding why he wanted to laugh about using his brother's curse word. "What happened, Xannan?"

Gailin tugged off his glove and rested a hand on Xannan's forehead, muttering much more colorful curses than those his brother had created.

The pale-haired younger soldier settled back on his heels, shadows dancing across the sunken skin of his cheeks. "I've stitched the wound, sir. There's a bruise forming near his eye, meaning Prince Xannan may have been hit in the head." Solomon packed his supplies. "He's lost a lot of blood, Your Highness."

"Tell Edmund to retrieve Xannan's sword from the drokos." Gailin couldn't look away from the line of string knitting Xannan's skin back together, flinching at the memory of exposed muscle. Minor scratches happened all the time, but he'd never seen his brother this hurt before. Not physically, at least. There'd been arguments about the swords, jealousy about the differences in their abilities. He cleared his throat, reminding himself to focus on the present. "Then tend to the other wounded, Solomon. I'll take care of my brother."

The soldier grunted as he stood. "Watch for the flailing, Your Highness. He kept trying to hit me."

Listening to Solomon's quick steps, Gailin tilted his head back and balled both hands into fists, pressing them into each thigh. His father would question him about this, ask why he hadn't known Xannan would get hurt, and demand an explanation for why Gailin hadn't protected his brother.

He thought back to the sensations before the Alkaanians had arrived, at the realization a drokos approached. Nothing had made him fear for anyone specific. Injuries and death were the two constants in battle, and they'd been dealt a more serious blow than expected. The Alkaanians had fought back hard, but they'd still won in the end. Gailin frowned, wondering if reading into the sensations would allow him to see more precise images rather than the brief flashes.

Gailin opened his hands, rubbing both palms against his pants to dry the accumulating sweat. "You already have a fever." He whispered as he peered down at Xannan. The man lay still except for ragged inhales and exhales. "Letting dirt in the wound probably made it infected." No reaction from Xannan, and though Solomon had confirmed the commander's death, Gailin squinted at Mikhael's prone form.

When Edmund knelt beside him, Gailin didn't want to say anything. For several long breaths, they sat in silence until Edmund attempted to speak. His voice cracked, and Gailin followed his friend's focus to Mikhael. Though he'd never been a close friend to the commander, many had. Xannan, Edmund, the soldiers of Mikhael's battalion would all mourn this loss. They all considered Mikhael a calm presence in the midst of the storm, the gentle wind that could either prod Xannan's fire into action or snuff it out. It was a role Gailin once held before those magical gifts formed a wedge between them.

Edmund cleared his throat and whispered, "We don't have the supplies to help him heal here, sir."

"I'm aware." Gailin tugged free a fistful of grass with both hands, but his left found Xannan's sword, which Edmund had retrieved. He gripped the blade's hilt—now adorned with an engraving depicting the moment of the sword's creation—thinking and hoping to see something. When nothing happened, Gailin breathed through his nose and pushed to standing. "I'd like you to take them to Violet Grove."

Edmund snapped his head up. "Them?" Gaunt cheeks threatened to turn puffy as Edmund's attempt to prevent tears from spilling faltered. He turned away, shoulders falling as he looked upon Mikhael's body. "With all due respect, Your Highness, Mikhael's dead. No reason to take him to Violet Grove."

Gailin swore he had to have swallowed sand. Had he said them? He'd not meant to. "I meant—"

A feral growl from Xannan made Gailin tense as his chest moved with increasing speed. It seemed crass and wrong, but he had the strangest thought that both needed to go.

"Spit it out, Gailin."

Gailin's eyes flashed at the direct request. He hated and appreciated that Edmund would force him to speak, even when he wanted to refuse. "I don't understand why, but you'll need to take Mikhael to Violet Grove—"

"No." Edmund stood, arms shaking, glossy eyes churning with a level of anger Gailin had never witnessed in his friend before. "We bury our dead. Properly. Not cart them around for some illogical, unknown reason. Sir."

Breaths came heavier and hotter despite the chilling wind. Gailin's grip on his brother's sword tightened, and he studied it again. Once clear crystalline was now streaked with the black ooze of the drokos's poison. He grabbed a cloth from his pocket, careful not to nick his own hand as he worked on cleaning the blade. As he moved, Gailin glanced up at Edmund on occasion. Once the blade was properly cleaned, he held it out to Edmund.

"Take my brother to Violet Grove and give them this message—" He paused, and Edmund lifted a brow, waiting. Gailin gulped down one set of words, then another, and another. "I think Xannan may have more power than we first believed."

Edmund grimaced as he unbuckled Xannan's sword belt, sheathed the weapon, and placed it around his waist. "Not sure the elves will appreciate your forwardness, Your Highness."

"It's been a long night, Edmund." Gailin lowered to a knee, frowning at the uncanny and unfamiliar sight of Xannan knocked unconscious. "Choose who will travel with you, and get some rest. I'll wake you once he and any other severely wounded are ready to travel."

"Order for the captives, sir?"

Gailin lowered his chin to his chest. He wanted answers for how they'd been led here. "Simple dressings if they're wounded. Water only. No one else speaks to them but me."

6

No smell of death and decay meant Xannan wasn't near any droki or a battlefield. A proper bed enveloped him rather than a bedroll in a tent. He grasped the cloth beneath him and inhaled sharply. Pain surged through his arm as memories flooded. Mikhael injured, enemies attacking, the drokos screeching, and then . . . he shoved away the thought. Last he knew, Mikhael was dead.

Though he hadn't opened his eyes yet, he knew light poured into the room. Sunlight or lamps, he wasn't sure. He doubted they'd taken him back to Cantadad, not with how badly his arm had been wounded. Xannan peeked through one eye and sunk into the pillow beneath his head. His arm had been wrapped, which was probably for the best.

Xannan tried to wet his lips and swallow, but his mouth was drier than the Whispering Wilderness desert of Tenoa. With his uninjured arm, he pushed himself to sitting and groaned as the room spun. He lifted his legs and pressed his forehead into his knees, willing the images of the past to abate. Someone's hand pushed on his shoulder, and he lashed out, but his helper avoided the wild swing.

"Blood loss and a blow to the head will make it difficult for you to stand for a time."

49

Xannan allowed himself to be pushed back down, covered his face with an arm, and croaked out, "Arjun."

He peered beneath his arm, flinching at the brightness of the room, to confirm the elf stood beside his bed. He definitely wasn't home; he was in Violet Grove. Shades of wood greeted him, and he covered his face with his arm again. His voice rasped as he asked, "What happened?"

Arjun grunted, and Xannan visualized the younger elf's slight frown with lines etching his mouth and forehead as strands of tawny-colored hair whispered about his face. "I was hoping you would tell me."

"Water?" Xannan managed, wincing as he attempted to swallow.

When Arjun tapped his arm, Xannan lowered it from his face and reached for the cup the elf held. Arjun shook his head once and wouldn't let Xannan lift more than his head, tilting the cup into his mouth for him. As he gulped down the liquid, Xannan glared at the elf. He was a renowned warrior who could take care of himself and didn't need anyone, especially not Arjun, spoon-feeding him anything.

Once Xannan had drained the cup of water, Arjun lifted a brow expectantly, and Xannan turned away to study the opposite wall. He never liked the vine-like engravings that encompassed every elven village and home he'd ever visited nor the fact there was so much wood.

"I can—"

"Please don't," Xannan whispered. He breathed deeply, wishing he could force the pain away as easily as the images. He turned back to Arjun. "Did I at least kill the drokos?"

Arjun nodded once and refilled the cup. This time, thankfully, he handed it to Xannan. After several more swallows, Xannan's throat smoothed from the dry scratchiness, though any quick movements led to the room tilting or twisting.

"Your brother sent a message we're not sure how to decipher." Arjun placed both hands in the pockets of his spacious robes, causing bottles to clink together. The sudden clamor of sound made Xannan wince.

"Gailin enjoys being cryptic," Xannan muttered as he stared into the cup. His brows lifted at his haggard appearance, making him wonder how long he'd been unconscious.

Arjun grimaced and tilted his head forward. When Arjun's deep red-irised eyes turned to Xannan, he looked away, trying to ignore the dizzying sensation the movement caused by squeezing his eyes shut. He had no desire to be forced to answer any questions.

"I know you don't want to be compelled to answer the questions, but Father said—"

"Arjun, how long have I been unconscious?"

Based on the clattering, the elf shrugged. "A few days. I wasn't here when you arrived."

"So possibly longer?"

Arjun shrugged again. "Possibly."

"I can barely open my eyes. When I do, the room turns upside down." Xannan tried to shift further upright, only to hiss through his teeth when he used his right arm. "I need food and more water before you demand answers to events I can't remember."

"Ah, but you experienced them, which means—"

Xannan threw his cup at Arjun, who shifted to one side and narrowly avoided the flying object but not the stream of water. Wiping at his robes as though his hands could dry them, Arjun glanced at Xannan with a smoothed visage.

"I know how it works." Xannan rubbed his temples as the room tilted, digging his nails into his palms in hopes to suppress the pain emanating from his sword arm. "I'm not doing anything until I'm ready." He tried to roll to his side, forgetting that such a movement would make the room spin again. Xannan let his arm fall to the bed, assessing the rest of his body. No other wounds except the arm and head presented themselves, though an ache in his gut made him grumble. "I can't think on an empty stomach."

"I'll return soon." The bottles clinked together in Arjun's pockets as he walked, and Xannan ground his teeth at the noise. "And you are better off staying in bed."

Xannan clenched his jaw. Once the door closed, he sat up slowly. The room continued to sway around him, but he forced himself to remain upright. Even though he knew he shouldn't, he undid the bandage wound around his arm, flinching with each movement. Not surprisingly, the skin had knitted back together, likely a result of one of the many healing potions the elves made. Dark string threading through his skin made an image surface. Mikhael pallid but breathing at random, as though Xannan's thoughts had forced air into the man's lungs.

Eventually, the room stopped spinning while he was sitting, so Xannan risked standing. Before he could reach his full height, he collapsed back to the bed. He sighed and rubbed his face, wondering who had cleaned the blood off and what cryptic message Gailin had sent.

His brother's incoherent voice infiltrated his thoughts, sounding as though Gailin stood next to him. Considering Gailin wasn't in the room, he was hopefully uninjured and had remained with the battalions. They'd need a good leader after Mikhael's death.

Xannan allowed the memory to surface. Something unexplainable had happened. He started to shake his head but stopped before he made himself dizzy again. Whatever images he could recall were likely wishful thinking considering how hard he must have been hit in the head. The only other time he could recall being this disoriented was when he got too close to a rearing horse's hooves.

Xannan attempted to stand again, teeth clattering against each other when he fell on the bed. His silent wish to leave and avoid

Arjun demanding answers was denied when the elf entered with a tray of food. A fist-sized lump of bread, half-full bowl of broth, and more water. Xannan frowned as Arjun set the tray on the bed. "So little?"

"You haven't tolerated food well thus far." Arjun motioned for Xannan to eat and placed himself in a chair beside the bed.

"I'd rather not talk yet." Xannan tore a piece of bread from the roll, chewing carefully and wincing at the soreness of his jaw. "I'm not sure which images are real, either."

"Father believes everything you see is something you experienced." Arjun picked up the bandage Xannan had removed with a subtle smirk. "You're a much better patient when asleep."

Xannan grunted and sipped his water. "Where's Gailin?"

"He remained at Falsumbra Forest. Captain Edmund brought you here." Arjun discarded the dirtied bandage and fished through his pocket, pulling out a vial. He retrieved a small cloth from a nearby table, dabbed the liquid onto it, and applied it to Xannan's arm. Though Xannan flinched, he didn't move and instead continued to force his jaw to function so he could swallow the remainder of the bread. While Arjun rebandaged the wound, he explained, "Your parents and Anna have not been informed of the extent of your injuries yet."

Something tight in his chest loosened at that statement. While he didn't care if his father knew, he didn't want Anna to worry about him more than she already did.

Xannan washed down the last of the bread, frowning at the broth. Roasted rabbit would taste better than whatever was floating in that bowl. "Well, I'd prefer to return home."

Bandage taut around his arm once more, Xannan flinched backward when Arjun grasped his chin. His movement knocked the bowl and cup onto the ground, but squeezing his eyes shut didn't halt the spinning sensation.

"I'll send word they can visit you here." Arjun shifted his robes and cleaned the mess. "There's little we can do for your head wound."

"Doubtful." Xannan stared at the spreading puddle of broth that hadn't been cleaned yet and blinked as its brown hue darkened as though mingled with blood. "I thought elves can heal everything."

"Supposedly." Arjun tossed the broth-soaked cloth onto the tray and met Xannan's gaze, red-irised eyes momentarily captivating. "More?"

"Bread." Xannan mumbled a curse; that answer had been forced from him. "That broth smells terrible."

Arjun frowned, sniffed the dirtied cloth, and shrugged. "Smells like our usual cuisine." He stared into Xannan's eyes again. "What happened in Falsumbra?"

And that stupid tug against his chest he didn't want to experience came again, that aggravating sensation which indicated Arjun was using his ability to force Xannan to speak. Fighting it would only make his head hurt worse. "We foiled the Alkaanians' ambush. Mikhael took a knife to the neck and a gash to the stomach. I tried to tend his wounds, which is when someone sliced my arm open." He gulped, wishing he hadn't inadvertently knocked over his water. "I thought Mikhael was breathing when the drokos arrived. I think it hit me in the head?" Xannan lowered himself back to a prone position. "I kept thinking Mikhael's chest moved, but so much time passed between each breath." He placed an arm over his face and mumbled into his sleeve, "Wishful thinking."

"Hm, perhaps." Arjun's vials clinked inside his robe as he approached the bed. "I'll return with more bread. Rest. I have more questions."

"Wonderful." Xannan closed his eyes, wishing the battle at Falsumbra would stop replaying in his mind's eye.

7

Burying their dead, and their enemy's dead, encompassed several days. As the highest-ranking soldier remaining near Falsumbra Forest, it was Gailin's responsibility to perform the ceremonies, honoring those who had given their lives to help protect their fledgling country. Gailin scrubbed dirt from his sleeve, wondering if his father had been too greedy with the amount of land they claimed was theirs.

In some ways, he didn't mind being sent to the far reaches of their country. It meant escaping the consistent barrage of sharing what he saw and sensed. Since Edmund had accompanied the injured to Violet Grove, Gailin had no one reminding him to share the emotions, thoughts, and brief images swirling inside. At first, he'd found it odd that Edmund would be so forward with him. The same age as Gailin, Edmund held a commanding presence in a way Gailin sometimes envied. But, as his father once explained, the Tremaine family often tended toward the forward and direct. In the end, he'd gained a friend rather than an enemy.

He nodded to soldiers as he walked through the camp. Many appeared tired and a tad melancholic, but their quick salutes were accompanied by shouts of praise. The tent holding the two captured soldiers made him slow in his walk. They refused to share any information. The fact they'd been waiting meant spies had, once more, infiltrated the Orda'anian army.

After a series of hand signal communications with the soldier guarding the captives, Gailin rubbed the back of his neck and decided he would attempt talking to them again later. Dried blood streaked their clothing and faces and they had to be hungry, but neither captive showed fear. Thinking of them gave Gailin a sinking feeling in the pit of his stomach. Smug captives meant another attack was imminent. He continued to the next tent, communicating his concern to the lieutenants who'd been left in charge after Mikhael's death and Edmund leaving.

Once back at his tent, Gailin glanced across the camp to the tent where Xannan should be joking with Mikhael or sparring with him. Gailin rubbed a hand down his face. No one would ever spar or joke with Mikhael again. That thought hurt. Losing soldiers he'd trained with always hurt.

Gailin hoped his brother, who was assuredly at Violet Grove by now, was awake and explaining what he remembered to the elves. Perhaps they'd understand his message and be able to find more answers about Xannan's ability. Those oddly timed breaths and Xannan's murmuring only strengthened the pit of unease in his stomach. The only option that currently made sense to Gailin was that Xannan had to have been forcing Mikhael's body to continue functioning, even in death.

Lowering himself to his bed, Gailin buried his face in his hands for a time. Each time sleep approached, visions jolted him awake. Time and time again, Gailin's mind was filled with the image of a swath of flame followed by a hollow feeling in his chest.

"May I enter, sir?"

Gailin sighed and glanced at the entrance where Solomon was fidgeting with his white arm band.

"What is it, Solomon?"

Solomon entered, offered a quick bow, and appraised Gailin with a calculated expression. "Captain Edmund sent word from Violet Grove. Prince Xannan is awake and healing."

Solomon handed over the message, and Gailin scanned the few lines. The lieutenant had omitted Xannan's lack of cooperation, and Edmund didn't mention the elves' reaction to Gailin's message. Gailin rubbed at his temples with one hand and sighed.

"Trouble sleeping, sir?"

Gailin crushed the paper and studied a few blades of trampled grass, the place Edmund had last stood before him as they argued, once again, about taking Mikhael's body to Violet Grove. In the end, Gailin had relented to Edmund's recommendation after the captain had mentioned how nervous it would make the other wounded.

"I always have trouble sleeping, but I'm not going to take anything for it. Another attack is on the way. Sometime soon." Gailin tossed the crumpled message back to Solomon, who caught it and nodded.

When the younger soldier didn't leave, Gailin lifted a brow. "More to say, Lieutenant?"

"There are other sleep aids aside from medicine, sir." Solomon shifted on his feet, and Gailin crossed his arms. "You hold tension in your neck and shoulders. If I massaged the muscles, it would at least help you relax, Your Highness."

Gailin grunted at the title transition and rubbed a hand along the back of his neck. The lieutenant was right; Gailin held a lot of tension in his shoulders. Easy to do when another army might surround your diminished battalions. He sighed and motioned Solomon over, figuring the brief massage would relieve the ache before the next battle.

As Solomon's fingers dug into his upper back, Gailin tried to shove aside the tingling caution that always precipitated battle. He contemplated what questions to ask the captives or how to convince them to speak. He almost bit his tongue as Solomon found a particularly tense muscle and let his shoulders slump. Thinking of questions for the captives was useless. Another attack was imminent and would lead to more death. Without Xannan, Mikhael, or Edmund, they were at a severe deficit. His soldiers weren't inconsequential, but numbers meant something in battle.

Solomon stepped away from his back, barely hiding his frown. "Would you like dinner in your tent, sir?"

"I'll join the men." Gailin stood and ran his hand through his blond locks, holding them off his forehead as he attempted to focus on what else the future held. Danger, too obvious. Death, inevitable in any battle. Dragons or drokos, unlikely, though he'd have preferred Xannan there to confirm. Victory, possibly. Threads of images coated his vision like strips of cloth, shifting so swiftly it almost made him dizzy.

Solomon caught his arm, his frown deepening. "Were you injured, sir?"

"No." Gailin tugged free of Solomon's grip. "Nothing you could fix, anyway."

The lieutenant waited, as though he expected Gailin to collapse to the ground, and Gailin ground his teeth. "Prepare your supplies, Lieutenant. You'll need them again soon."

After a scrutinizing appraisal, Solomon saluted and left. Gailin almost regretted not asking for his meal to be brought to him. His sword, Futurae, bumped against his hip as he walked, a steady reminder of the ability he could control and the ability he couldn't. One of the soldiers handed him a bowl of soup when he sat down on a log near the fire, and he sipped, wincing when the heated liquid scalded his tongue.

Lifted brows, furrowed foreheads, and constant flickering gazes surrounded him. It made his chest hurt. But if he said he felt confident, they'd believe him. Unlike his father's desire to know every thought that crossed Gailin's mind, the soldiers needed their resolve strengthened. The earlier wariness had waned. Not completely, but it had faded amid the first battle. Probably when Mikhael was killed and Xannan injured.

Gailin lowered his empty bowl to the ground. Arms resting atop his knees, he clasped his hands before him.

"I'm aware we're tired and saddened by the good men we've lost since our arrival. Don't let that despair consume you. Let it fuel your desire to rid our home of its enemies." A hearty supportive shout, followed by sips of broth. One soldier clapped Gailin on the back, and he smiled, trying to channel the confidence which came so naturally to Xannan. "This time, we'll take the fight to them. This forest and these lands are ours, and they will pay for their actions."

Several exchanged wary glances, hiding concerned faces behind cups and bowls. Gailin pressed his palms together, wishing he could hide his worry as well as Xannan always did. Or perhaps his brother simply never worried.

"We'll go in groups of five." Gailin met each soldier's gaze, hoping his own portrayed reassurance rather than the swirling caution. "That will give us about twenty groups." He picked up his bowl and sipped, barely tasting the spiced broth as he swallowed. "We'll release the prisoners and three groups will follow each. They've not had a proper meal in over a week and will be desperate for sustenance. The remaining groups will surround the forest."

After he outlined his plan, the commanding officers saluted and left the small campfire to make appropriate preparations.

Despite their best fighters being absent, or dead, Gailin allowed the fledgling confidence to soar within him. He refused to allow the threads of dismay and despair to thicken, tearing those metaphorical branches from the budding tree of confidence and leaving them on the trodden grass.

Gailin met his group at the edge of camp. Each of the four joining him were soldiers he'd supervised and helped train. They would do well. His jaw clenched as he cracked another metaphorical branch. Confidence, strengthening and growing. He needed it. Desired it.

The four soldiers saluted, and he noticed the white band around one's upper arm. His gaze flicked to the man's face, and he pressed his lips together. *Watchful Solomon.*

He gripped the hilt of his sword. "Follow me. East first, then north. Wait for the signal."

His men nodded and looked to the sky. Moments stretched, lengthening until Gailin tapped his foot against the grass. When his leg tired of the motion, he tapped a finger against his sword hilt. "What in the Blaz—" A low whistle thrummed through the night, followed by a high-pitched note. "Finally."

They traipsed through the forest, weaving through broken branches and falling leaves. As they traveled deeper, the trees grew thicker and taller. Older, immovable. Shouts broke out nearby. Either one of his groups had found the Alkaanian camp or they had found his men. The captain in his group turned to him, brow lifted. Gailin signed a quick series of orders, the captain nodded, and they continued forward as silent as the leaves whispering through the air.

Crackling fires and laughter, occasionally boisterous, echoed through the forest. Each of the soldiers accompanying Gailin pressed their sides against a tree, sharing glances as they peered between the trunks. Revelry abounded. A celebration? Possible. Gailin frowned and tugged his sword free while holding his finger to his lips. Had he lost track of the days during their travels? The next holiday shouldn't be for at least a month.

One of the prisoners stumbled into the camp, mumbling incoherently and collapsing near a campfire. The revelry halted. Men dropped cups and bowls to draw weapons.

"Now," Gailin signed to the nearest soldier.

Lieutenant Solomon slid an arrow from his quiver, nocked it to his bow, aimed, and fired. Blood spilled over the Alkaanian's lips, dripping from the hole in his throat, and he reached forward as he fell. The bars on each shoulder indicated the man's higher rank. And based on the uproar from the camp, that man had been important.

"Again," Gailin signed. "Ranked soldiers first. Hit true."

Solomon nodded, aimed, and fired. This time his arrow speared an Alkaanian's chest. The soldier stumbled backward, dead before his back met packed dirt.

"Nice shot." Gailin nodded his approval to Solomon, whose smirk didn't replace the worry in the lieutenant's gaze. "Cover us."

Jaw set, Solomon nocked another arrow, lips pursed in concentration. Gailin's grip on his sword tensed, and he donned the blanket of unfeeling callousness he'd perfected after years of doing his father's bidding. One border skirmish after the next. Consistently protecting land they claimed was theirs simply because they wanted it. This land had once been no one's. Not under human control, at least. The elves and dragons had shared it once. Now both of those races hid, while Gailin and Xannan fought to establish Orda'an's borders by killing any who encroached upon it.

Void of emotion, Gailin stalked forward. An arrow whizzed by his ear, thudding into an Alkaanian attempting to draw his blade. He dared not look back at Solomon but said a silent thanks to the young lieutenant.

Soldiers poured out of tents and rose from campfires. Once-packed dirt swirled around them. It coated his pants and threatened to blind him. Gailin coughed and held his arm to his mouth, watching for enemy soldiers.

He ducked from an arrow and swung out at a golden-clad soldier. A tree of confidence, growing stronger with bold green leaves coating every branch. Gailin used that sensation and cut a path through the campfire.

Simmering anger he had suppressed trickled up as the fighting continued. These men had almost killed his brother. They had killed several of his friends. Good men who deserved the chance to marry, have children, and grow old with others. Instead, they lay beneath dirt Gailin had moved with his own hands. Hands he now used to destroy any who came near.

Anger fueled him forward until one of his men shouted his name. Gailin jerked, momentarily surprised at the lack of title. His sword, usually a clear crystalline hue, was so red it was almost black.

For once, he was grateful for the solid black coat his father had designed. It hid the blood better.

One of the captains led an enemy combatant forward, shoving the golden-clad soldier to his knees before Gailin. He stared down at the man and tilted his head, tightening his grip on his sword. Liquid squelched through his fingers, and he had to swallow his own revulsion.

"We don't take kindly to others attempting to take what is ours." Though Gailin knew he said the words, he barely recognized his own voice. "Spread the word of what awaits those who try."

He turned away, shaking his head and blinking as images attempted to surface. More death. More fire. He made it to the tree line, resting one hand on a trunk while the other lifted the sword covered in gore.

"Your ability is increasing as well, isn't it, sir?"

"Go away, Solomon." Gailin gritted out. He needed cloth to clean his sword and reached for where he kept some, but he hadn't brought his pack.

"The sword was doing . . . something, sir." Solomon pulled a cloth from his pack and handed it over. As Gailin cleaned, Solomon explained, "It seemed to glow. Faint, but it reminded me of a lantern whose flame is about to die. I wonder if Prince Xannan's did something similar?" Solomon handed Gailin another cloth and shrugged. "Sorry. I'm aware it's not for me to worry about, sir."

"No, it's not." Gailin frowned at the two dirtied rags, wondering if Solomon had a third, but the lieutenant had walked away. Instead, Gailin unbuttoned his coat and cleaned off what little remained on his sword. Tendrils of white tumbled from hilt to tip in time with a low hum. It wasn't glowing, as Solomon thought, but it was changing. For good or for bad, Gailin wasn't sure.

8

"You can't keep me holed up in this room," Xannan growled at Arjun. He gripped the edge of the bed with both hands, focusing on the room *not* spinning. If not for the dizzy spells, Xannan would have marched himself back to Falsumbra days ago.

Arjun crossed his arms, face blank as always. "I'm not keeping you, Prince Xannan." The elf shrugged, the slight lift in his shoulders creating that aggravating clamor of glass from the bottles he kept in the pockets of his too-large robes. "You can't stand without assistance yet."

Desperate to prove differently, Xannan shoved himself to his feet and immediately regretted the motion. "Blazing frustrating," he gritted out as he collapsed back to the bed, the uncontrolled thud rattling his teeth. "How is it none of those obnoxious glasses in your pockets can assist? Surely you have some way to help me see straight again?"

Arjun contemplated Xannan for a moment. "We can heal injuries, yes. Even head wounds." The elf pursed his lips and clasped his hands behind his back. "The dizziness is not from the blow to your head?"

"Not this again." Xannan tensed and forced himself back to his feet. One hand propped against the wall to remain upright, he glared at the elf who was about to force him to answer questions again, momentarily forgetting that Arjun's ability required eye contact to work.

"What were you thinking when you noticed Mikhael's chest moving?"

"That I wanted my friend to live." Xannan studied the light-colored wood flooring. The scent of it grated on him. Stone or grass smelled better, or a day's-old battlefield. He recalled the souring deathly odor of the drokos. Maybe not a battlefield but definitely grass. "I could have blocked the attack. He's dead because he blocked an attack for me. And I didn't do the same for him."

"You should try—"

"I have no desire to relive that battle, Arjun." Xannan curled his right hand into a fist, thankful no twinge of pain accompanied it.

"If we are to understand your ability, then you must attempt to use it, Prince Xannan."

"To what end?" Xannan straightened to his full height and tested lowering his hand from the wall. Back rigid, he grunted. "Why relive what we already know occurred?"

Arjun pinched the bridge of his nose and grumbled beneath his breath. "Shall we attempt a walk?"

Xannan shifted his feet for better balance and crossed his arms while making sure not to move his head. It would be worth the attempt, even if it didn't last long, simply to get out of the stifling room. He gestured with his arm for Arjun to lead the way, bracing for the movement. Something as simple as walking should not require so much effort.

"We won't go far." Arjun opened the door and shoved his hands into his pockets. "Movement might ease some of your anxiousness."

"Anxiousness?" Xannan lifted a brow as he took a tentative step forward. "I don't get anxious."

"Hmph, so you say." Ajrun matched Xannan's painstakingly slow pace. "But you've been mumbling in your sleep."

"You've been watching me sleep?" Xannan almost turned his head, stopping before the quick motion made the hallways of vine-etched wood twist in his vision. "Sounds rude."

"Or necessary." Arjun lifted a shoulder, causing a cascade of clinking. "Prince Gailin believes you may have more power than we first believed. Thus the close observation."

"Yes, well, Gailin is overly cautious and worries too much."

"But it makes me believe he saw something, too." When Arjun met his gaze, Xannan forced himself to study the floor beneath their feet and concentrate on placing one foot in front of the other.

"I don't remember Gailin finding me." Xannan paused, waiting for the momentary dizziness to dissipate. "Someone dragged me back inside that tent though." He ran a hand through his hair and closed his eyes. "Whatever I saw must have been my imagination."

"Perhaps." Arjun tucked an escaped strand of his tawny hair behind his ear. "But you've always been able to view the past as it truly was not as you wished it to be, correct?"

Xannan strode forward, one hand trailing the wall both for support and to give him a reason not to look at the elf. At a crossway, Arjun motioned to the right, and Xannan frowned. Based on his previous visits, additional guest rooms were located along that hallway. To the left would be the main thoroughfare of meeting rooms and kitchens. He flattened his palm against the wall. "My parents arrived, didn't they?"

"Queen Dana and your betrothed did, yes." Arjun frowned and rubbed his chin. "King Seth informed us of Gailin's win at Falsumbra. The northern lands are, once again, under Orda'anian control. He awaits your brother's return to Cantadad."

Xannan studied his bare feet. The words did something strange to him. He was the brother who won battles; Gailin was the brother who got answers. "Gailin's win, huh? And how many captives did he take?"

"None."

Xannan snapped his head to Arjun's before he could remind himself not to. Holding his head in his hands in hopes to stop the hallway from swaying, Xannan asked, "None?"

"Save the one he sent back to the Alkaanian capital." Arjun shoved his hands back into the pockets of his billowing robes and pressed his lips together. "It should be enough to prevent additional attacks for a time, I would think, but I do not always understand the stubbornness of humans."

A door opened, and a familiar pale face framed by black hair peered at him, worry and happiness warring with each other as her brows couldn't decide whether to knit together or raise. "I knew I heard your voice." Anna raced toward him, pausing before she reached out to touch him. "I don't want to hurt you."

"My arm is healed." Xannan leaned his back against the wall and reached for her hands, heart warming at her touch. "But my head has been a . . . different story."

"That's an understatement," Arjun mumbled, and Xannan shot him a glare over Anna's head.

Anna wrapped her arms around his waist and leaned her head against his chest. "You said you'd be careful."

"I was." Xannan sighed and rested a hand on her back, thankful she had greeted him before his mother did. Or his father. "It all happened so quick once the drokos—"

"Drokos?" She lifted her head, hand pressing against his chest as her breaths became shallow. "But they're. . ."

He grimaced. "Not extinct, apparently." As her face turned ashen, Xannan focused on meeting her gaze and displaying the strength he knew he had. "I won't let them hurt you."

Anna turned away, sucking her lower lip between her teeth. She'd lost several of her family to the last droki attack, had seen, same as he had, what the creatures' poison could do to perfectly healthy individuals. The day he met her two years ago was the last time he'd seen the droki attack anywhere, until Falsumbra.

She pressed her hand into him, as though she needed reassurance he was real and breathing, and turned to face Arjun. "Have you told him?"

"About Gailin's victory, yes. Nothing more."

"As if Gailin winning a battle without me wasn't enough, there's more?"

Anna turned back to him, eyes crinkled with worry. "His Majesty wishes for you and Gailin to remain here until both you and the elves understand, in full, what your swords are doing."

"But we—" Xannan lifted from the wall to pace along the corridor, planting his feet as the floor lurched at him. He rested his shoulders against the wood panels and tilted his head back. "We've studied the swords. Used that magic. Arjun has asked me enough questions to last ten lifetimes. With that order, Gailin and I will be stuck in this Blazing stifling wooden-paneled . . . prison until we die!"

"This is far from a prison, Prince Xannan." Arjun clasped his hands behind his back and sighed. "Told you he wouldn't take kindly to the news."

"Which is why you waited for me to deliver it," Anna grumbled. "I need him back at Cantadad. We have preparations to make."

A harrumph came from the doorway Anna had exited, indicating his mother, Queen Dana, had joined the conversation. White gloves adorned her hands, reaching to her elbows and matching the cape clasped at her neck. She tugged on a glove and said, "More like Anna wants you close by as she's finished most of the preparations." His mother's brown-eyed gaze studied him, brows creasing as she murmured, "How long has he been here, Arjun?"

"At least one full week, Your Majesty," Arjun said, his tone softening. "I believe the dizziness remains because he's avoiding using his ability. If you would like me to insist—"

"You wouldn't," Xannan interrupted. He opened one eye to ensure the hallway was steady, then used both to glare at the elf. "Could you force me to relive the battle?"

Arjun shrugged. "Possibly."

"You should at least wait until Gailin is here." His mother's gaze found his again, somehow soft and hard at the same time. It was as if she tried to show concern while admonishing him for having been injured. "Your father insisted he return home first, probably making a show of protecting our northern lands."

Though Xannan tried to tamp it down, the claws of jealousy tugged at his insides. He was the renowned warrior, Gailin the pensive prince who analyzed every piece before giving some vague statement of what was to come. Xannan ground his teeth, wishing he had not been injured. Images flashed at the thought, threatening to consume his vision, but he focused on those before him.

His fair-skinned brown-haired mother, in a deep blue dress reminiscent of the sea, stood with her appraising demeanor that turned him back into a fifteen-year-old boy who didn't know any better than to pick up a sword on a cave's floor.

Xannan shifted his gaze to Anna, whose dark eyes searched his as she kept her hand on his chest. He was glad she did, as the weight of her hand and her presence provided more comfort than he'd had since leaving Cantadad. Rather than risk Arjun attempting to control his actions, Xannan chose not to look at the elf.

Resting his hand atop Anna's, Xannan asked, "So is Celena speaking with Magna again? Asking more questions of the one who is partly to blame for whatever these weapons became?"

"She is." Arjun must have moved his arms because the ridiculous number of bottles in his pockets made a racket of sound. "She should return by the time Prince Gailin arrives."

Xannan sighed and leaned his head against the wall, wishing he'd bathed at some point in the past few days. "I really hope I can see straight by then." He cleared his throat and steeled his nerves for whatever emotion he would see etched across his mother's face as he asked, "Was Father angry?"

A sympathetic smile meant yes, but his mother was about to lie instead. Xannan knew his father cared about his children, but the man also held high standards, many of which Xannan was good at ignoring.

His mother smoothed her skirts, making them ripple like the waves of the ocean. "Your father is happy you're alive, Xannan. The message Gailin sent us made your injuries sound significantly worse than what I see now."

"But I should have been able to handle this group." He gritted his teeth, thinking back through what orders had or had not been given. All it did was dredge up what he had last seen of Mikhael.

"Xannan." Anna rested her hand on his cheek, and he sank into its warmth. "You did your best, as you always do." He looked down, chest clenching at the depths of emotion swimming in her dark eyes as she whispered, "Sometimes things go wrong."

9

Gailin clasped his hands behind him. The door to his father's study was, in many ways, more frightening than an enemy soldier. Brief congratulations had greeted his return in the courtyard, combined with appreciation he'd returned home uninjured and a quiet dinner where his mother and father discussed matters to address across the nation had all led to this moment.

He doubted his father wished to rehash the conversation he'd mostly listened to between his parents the previous evening. Trade routes to approve, treaties to craft, and borders to protect. The only new matter of business was outlining the proper line of succession. Logically, if Xannan and Anna had a male heir, Gailin would be bumped down the line. An odd prickling sensation nettled at his nerves, and he shook himself. He might not become the next king, but he believed there would always be a place for him beside his brother.

Grip tightening on his fingers, Gailin glanced at the two soldiers who guarded the bare wooden door. Neither said more than a murmured honorific, providing no indication if his father would remain pensive and calculating or angry.

Though Gailin wanted to feel proud of his actions, he couldn't. Their goal had been to "check out a settlement." Instead, Gailin had buried twenty of their own soldiers between the two skirmishes. He muttered an internal curse. Those weren't skirmishes. Those were planned battles. Battles that no amount of diplomatic discussion would have prevented.

He knocked once and entered at his father's muted voice. Cramped and warm, the study was decorated with rich shades of brown. Two leather chairs sat near each wall while a round etched wooden table in between them made pacing impossible. Shelves of books lined the walls, broken only by a small window opposite the door and the roaring fireplace whose heat licked Gailin's back, adding to the beads of perspiration trickling down the nape of his neck.

It was ironic, considering how much of Cantadad's castle was extravagant and almost comically large. All except where their father spent most of his time. Though he'd never seen where his father had been raised, Gailin wondered if this small study was reminiscent of the cramped spaces Seth used to tell them about.

Quiet conversations grew sparse as the years trudged on. All because Seth was more than their father—he was their king, too.

Gailin studied his father's posture as the man leaned over the small table.

"I've read Captain Edmund's report. And yours." Seth flicked a finger against the parchment curling into itself on the table now that Seth wasn't holding it down.

"Then you know my concerns, Father. We have a spy in our ranks." Gailin assumed the position of a soldier, hands clasped behind his back, shoulders rounded, spine straight. "I fear it's someone who has managed to get close to myself or Xannan."

Seth grunted and frowned at the curled message. Even travel-worn, the parchment was bright against the dark lacquered wood. "Keep tabs on those near you." His lips thinned. "Even Captain Edmund."

"But Edmund—"

"Is a Tremaine, from the next most powerful family in this nation aside from ours, Gailin." Seth lifted his head to Gailin, brows knitted together with worry and concern. "Since he helped discover the last two spies, I'm wary he may have already known who they were." He pressed both hands against his knees and stood, wincing from the effort. Based on the stories he'd once told Gailin and Xannan, their father was lucky he could walk. Seth ambled to the shelf holding empty glasses and a full decanter of wine. "Though for your sake, I hope Edmund is not a spy. He's been a good friend to you, but my earlier advice remains nonetheless."

Gailin tensed and nodded once, shoving down the desire to continue that argument. "Any news from Violet Grove?"

"All I've heard from Eonar is that your brother is *recovering*." Seth poured a glass of wine. "You'll be headed there soon yourself."

Gailin raised a brow, eyeing the second cup his father was filling. He accepted it, grateful to have something to do with his hands and for liquid to coat his parched throat. Gailin sipped the wine, swallowed, waited for five heartbeats, and said in a moderated tone, "Surely Xannan can return without me once he's well enough."

Seth lowered into one of the four plush seats, motioning for Gailin to do likewise. "It's about more than your brother's recovery."

Sitting opposite his father, Gailin sipped the wine again, wishing the liquid wasn't such a dark red or visible through the clear glass. Everywhere he looked, he saw reminders of the slaughter he had caused. All but one wiped from existence, at his order. He grimaced. Not just his order, but by his own sword.

An exasperated sigh made Gailin lift his head to meet his father's studious gaze. The man missed little and understood too much. "Captain Edmund mentioned the message you gave him for the elves, about Xannan having more power than first assumed." Seth leaned back in his seat, face shadowed by the sun's fading light and the remnants of a beard he could no longer grow. Too much scar tissue, according to the healers.

Seth drummed his fingers along the padded armrest, the fire reflecting in his steel-gray eyes. "Are you seeing visions again?"

Gailin choked on the wine, pounding his fist against his chest to loosen his throat. Only Xannan had guessed he'd seen a vision. The last time his father had known about them, an odd conversation with Eonar had occurred. "I'm not seeing anything other than what's before me."

While Seth shook his head and drained his wine glass, Gailin cursed the observant battlefield medic.

"I have many significant landowners breathing down my neck for explanations." Seth leaned forward, forearms braced against his legs, empty glass dangling from his hand. "They fear what you and Xannan can accomplish. For ridiculous reasons, they believe your children will also have magic." Seth peered into his glass, the frown deepening the wrinkles and scars marring his face like a web. "I need to dispel this belief, to prove that what you can do is solely because of those swords. Without that confirmation, others will undermine what I have created. Tear this country to pieces to form a new one under their rule and make sure neither you nor Xannan would be able to rule."

"So you wish to ensure your children will inherit the crown you made for yourself?" Gailin blurted the words before he could take them back, cursing himself for asking the question. Seth had offered so much to the people of these lands. Protection from others, a chance to live without oppression, a place to create homes. Rather than rely on slave trade as other countries did, Seth had created a land where people traded product for product.

A muscle in Seth's temple feathered rapidly, and he stood. Setting his glass aside, Seth crossed his arms and stared down at Gailin.

"I'd rather not learn what they'll try and do to either of my sons to knock me from this position, Gailin." He leaned against the shelf holding the decanter of wine. "You've no idea the number of threats I've had to subdue to protect you. And especially your brother. I fear diplomacy will not be enough to keep their blades from your throats."

"You subdue threats?" Gailin almost shouted the words, a shocked laugh exploding from him. "Or do you create them?" Gailin grunted and drained his glass. "We've already had blades at our throats, Father. Or approaching them." He motioned at the map of the continent pinned to the wall above his seat. "Less than a week ago, I was gutting Alkaanians before they could end me."

Seth winced and wiped his face with a hand, halting the motion at his chin. "Alkaan is one small obstacle."

"Small?" Gailin lifted a brow and could almost hear the annoyed chuckle Xannan would have given in response to their father's statement. "I know of twenty families that would beg to differ, Father."

Seth slapped his open palm against the shelf, rattling the remaining empty glasses beside the wine decanter. "Their deaths were honorable, son. You need to remember that or your soldiers will no longer follow orders."

Jaw slacked, Gailin bottled up his rising frustration. Seth was worried. Gailin could feel the emotion emanating off his father in waves, hitting him like the rise and fall of the ocean tide.

"So what do we do?" Gailin asked as a singular thought floated to the surface, one Gailin couldn't allow to formulate. If it ever became true, there would be no repairing what little relationship remained between him and Xannan. At his father's prolonged silence, Gailin added, "Anna is Alkaanian. Surely her union with Xannan can help sooth some tension."

"While I wish such a union could assist, I fear it may only make matters worse. She's not of noble blood. They'd sooner kill us all." Seth approached the fire, stoking it with a metal rod. When Seth's back went rigid, Gailin leaned forward in his seat. He knew that sign, knew what often came next and how it made him feel like nothing more than a tool.

Almost verbatim to the last time they had spoken, and so many times before that, Seth said, "I ask about your ability because it can be used not just to my advantage, but yours as well."

Gailin contemplated throwing his empty glass as he knew Xannan would in this moment. Their abilities were the only thing of importance anymore. Since Gailin's often showed so quickly on his face and in his mannerisms, he couldn't get away with tucking it into some small corner of his mind as Xannan did.

"What if I don't want to use it?" Gailin studied the last dredge of wine coating the bottom of his cup. A singular red drop that he let consume his vision. "What if I want to forget this magical sword ever entered my life?"

An argument followed, though all Gailin remembered was his own rising anger matching his father's, ending in a quick dismissal with a reminder to leave for Violet Grove in the morning. He wasn't opposed, it would be better than staying in the castle.

One step followed another as Gailin skulked through the hallways. He'd been victorious. Won. Defeated the Alkaanian encampment until only one soldier was left to share the news that Orda'an did not take kindly to the encroachment on their land. No questions on strategy. No wondering what move Alkaan might make next. No more than a magical gift.

"What is it you always say to your brother?"

Gailin halted, and the tension eased from his shoulders at the calm cadence of Ella's voice. "Stop scowling?"

"That's the phrase," Ella said as her hazel eyes pierced his soul with comprehension. "No commendations then, I take it?"

His scowl returned. "Not that I wanted them, but at the very least an acknowledgment of my success. Not more Blazing questions."

Gailin kept his hands clasped behind his back, even as Ella held both of his arms. He wondered if she could feel his muscles trembling or if she knew what he'd done. It wasn't like him to be so thorough. Maim and take as prisoner was more his style. Annihilate was Xannan's code. Usually they balanced one another, able to gather the necessary information and weed out whatever spy had wormed their way into Orda'anian ranks. His scowl deepened until he could feel the creases in the skin of his forehead. Another spy needed to be ferreted out.

Ella's hands tightened in their grip. "I think it's time for that ride you promised me last month."

His arms fell to his sides, and his shoulders drooped. "I must prepare to leave in the morning." Gailin shook his head at her inquisitive expression. "Not with a battalion. Father wants me to go to Violet Grove. Apparently, we need to complete another round of answering the elves' questions."

"I tried to make them let me go with Anna, but your mother barely agreed to let Anna go." She grasped his hand and tugged him along the corridor. "You're being stubborn. We have time for a nice quiet evening in the fields."

Gailin stiffened at the sudden sensation of cold washing over him. Accompanied by a flash of black flame, it made his mouth feel dry. "Fear," he whispered. "Father fears for our future. And I feel fear. But mine is . . . different from Father's."

"Logical," Ella murmured as she crossed her arms and canted her head, loose blond hair cascading over her shoulder. "Bring the sword." She gestured at the weapon hanging at his hip and lifted her chin, jaw set in a way he knew her next words would be ones she didn't want to say but would to appease him. "And Edmund can come too if you'd feel better having someone watching over us."

Gailin tapped her nose and chuckled as she rubbed at it. "Good idea. I'll get Edmund from the barracks. Meet you at the stables."

"Fine." Ella smoothed her skirts and wrinkled her nose. "I would've preferred us to be alone, you know?"

At Gailin's lifted brow, her smile turned mischievous. "You have been gone for over a month, my love."

His cheeks and chest warmed, until the cold well of fear bubbled up inside again, making his smile falter. "Any particular requests for sustenance?"

"Food." Ella winked as she swished her skirts, lifted them, and descended the stairs leading directly to the stables.

"Helpful," he murmured as he watched her, chest tightening at the thought that others might wish her harm to get to him.

10

Grass threated to coat the once well-worn path Gailin and Edmund traveled toward Violet Grove. Odd patches poked up, occasionally distracting the horses and providing a distinct sign of how much had changed in the past five years. Few humans trusted the elves anymore, fearful that interacting with them would result in the sudden onset of magic as it had for Gailin and Xannan.

That event, Praesidio's breaking, had been memorable, and though only a select few were present, many learned the story. It had been difficult to hide their abilities from those who traded in gossip and secrets. Even with a steady exchange of maids and guards, the stories spread. Eventually, Seth allowed it to happen. "Better for them to fear you," he'd decided. And now that fear was being turned back on them.

"Do you need me to remind you again?" Edmund asked through chattering teeth. Winter had taken a firm hold, and even though the ground was not yet covered in white and some of the grass still clung to life, the biting chill of the air made for an unpleasant journey.

"To stop scowling?" Gailin focused on the path. Rocks and tree branches littered the area, and he wanted to make sure his mount didn't step on any. Not that the stallion would, but Gailin figured it was a decent way to distract himself until someone, like Edmund, forced him to think aloud. "It's so cold your teeth haven't stopped knocking against each other for the past two hours." He spared a glance for his friend and they both tugged their coats closer. "And, if you recall, the last time my brother and I were sent to the elves, it didn't particularly end well." Gailin breathed through his nose. "So I think I'll stick to scowling."

Edmund's small chuckle turned into a curse as his teeth resumed their apparently uncontrollable chattering. Puffs of Edmund's breath lingered in the air before him. "I have a vague recollection. Mikhael was the one who talked Prince Xannan down, yes?"

A brief sadness twinged in Edmund's voice as he said Mikhael's name, and Gailin's grip on the reins tightened. Gailin had spent years trying to help his brother see reason. But when Mikhael would tell Xannan the same thing Gailin just had, his obnoxious barely older than him brother would listen.

"As per usual," Gailin murmured. Their mounts plodded along the path, their breath obvious in the cold. At this pace, they should arrive in the village by nightfall. He hoped, as he didn't want to spend another night on the frigid ground, especially since the threat of snow appeared more prevalent with each survey of the darkening sky above them. Even the freezing wind carried a new scent on it. Not death or decay, but that heavy wetness which promised a quiet blanket for the ground.

Edmund rubbed his palms together with a surprising force. "It doesn't usually get so cold so quick this far south, does it?"

"Why is it the chill bothers you so much? You grew up in the far north."

"I've been spoiled. Cantadad is close to the desert. I'm not sure if I prefer the heat or the cold though." Edmund rubbed his hands together a bit more and shrugged. He gave Gailin a sidelong glance, nudging his mount closer. "What will it take to make you stop scowling? If you keep doing so, you'll look angrier than Prince Xannan does all the time."

Gailin grunted and tried to force his brows to a neutral position. Instead, they furrowed further as he sifted through his emotions. His last visit to the elves had involved a mental exercise, where he had to place different thoughts into different boxes, locking them away until he needed them. That was what he did with the visions. Most of them. The most recent encounter with that portion of his ability flirted with the edges of conscious thought and overwhelmed his dreams.

He shoved the vision aside and chose to ponder if being within the elven village would be more pleasant without his brother there. Delicious food, warm wooden atmosphere, and a group who sought to understand him as a person rather than a magical tool sounded like a dream compared to some of his days at home.

Edmund's gasp was Gailin's only warning before his mount reared and neighed. He grasped the saddle horn and reached for his sword.

"Did you not see them?" an angry woman's accented voice asked as Gailin's mount lowered to all fours and he was able to assess his surroundings. A familiar white-haired, red-eyed elf, Celena, and a dragon with mingled brown and white scales stood before him and Edmund.

While Edmund gaped at the sight, Gailin's heart sank. "Why is Magna here?"

"Because I told her to come see whatever it is that caused your ridiculously cryptic message." Celena brushed dirt from her pants and tugged the wool fur coat about her shoulders. "Could you not have told us *why* you think your brother has more power suddenly? Last we spoke we determined you had both accessed all the swords have to offer." The elf-woman glanced above her, frowning at Magna who huffed and folded her wings into her body. Celena sighed. "All she'll share is that I'm not wrong. But I don't think that means we're right, either."

"So he hasn't explained then, has he?"

Despite being in awe of the dragon, Edmund snorted a short laugh. "Prince Xannan does hate talking."

"And Father sent me to make sure he does." Gailin sighed and nudged his mount forward, skirting around where Celena stood amid the path.

"Then no need to waste time." Celena glanced back up at the dragon, who snapped her wings as though frustrated. "We need you to help us understand what happened."

A huff, another snap of the wings, and Celena waved her hand in a sharp, dismissive gesture. Magna lifted in one fluid motion, wind circling and buffeting against Gailin, nearly knocking him from his mount.

"Will she return?" Gailin asked as he watched Magna's form fly away, shrinking with each beat of her wings. "Does she even understand what happened?"

Celena huffed and crossed the bridge.

Edmund cleared his throat at Gailin's side. "She makes for pleasant company, I see."

"That she does," Gailin murmured, wondering if Celena was hiding something from him as he nudged his mount over the bridge that allowed them to cross the Guadelaide River. It was narrow here, barely wider than his mount's length. On the other side was the tree line to the Shendaran forest, the evergreen leaves a comforting sight against the biting cold.

He nudged his mount forward to ride alongside Celena, who didn't even react to his approach, though his mount did. He'd never seen her be mean toward horses, but he had to constantly nudge his mount closer to the elf. "How is Xannan?"

"You'll see yourself soon enough."

"I'm aware, but—"

"Then why ask me?" She shifted her shoulders and tugged her coat in closer, veering a sharp left onto a smaller path that led to her family's home rather than the village center.

"Celena?"

The elf-woman waved her hand and continued walking.

After a stop at the stables, Gailin led Edmund to the central-most building, grateful for its warm embrace as they stepped inside the delicately carved wooden hallway. Flurries had begun to fall during their final trek, and while the snow was beautiful to watch, Gailin preferred to be inside when observing that phenomenon.

Though the interior was significantly warmer, both Gailin and Edmund kept their coats on. First matter of business: find Xannan. Gailin twisted his lips with a sharp inhale and decided it would be better to eat and rest before speaking with his brother.

When Edmund cleared his throat, Gailin jolted from his thoughts and froze, then the scowl returned. He figured his brother would be stuck in bed, laid up from the blood loss and head wound, even after almost three weeks had passed. Instead, Xannan strolled hand in hand with Anna. Smiling, laughing, back to his usual self. Or at least the version that appeared with Anna at his side.

"I see your recovery is going well," Gailin grumbled and crossed his arms. At the motion, Edmund buried his face in a hand and muttered something about brothers.

"I heard you're owed congratulations," Xannan said with that ever-present lilt of annoyance. "One left alive, according to whatever report Arjun got his hands on."

Gailin inclined his head. "Arjun speaks true."

A muscle in Xannan's jaw ticked. But he nodded. "Good. That group deserved annihilation for their actions."

When Xannan tensed, Gailin's bubble of fear surged, reminiscent of before he'd found Xannan on the battlefield. Whatever the connection, Gailin didn't like it. He gripped the pommel of his sword, and the strange fear eased into a slight warmth at his brother's words. Logical that Xannan would give him more commendation about the success than their father had.

"Let's hope it doesn't happen again," Gailin said as he released his sword's hilt.

Anna looked between them, tight lips dipping further into a frown with each back and forth. She patted Xannan's arm, almost thrust him forward, and held out a hand for Edmund.

"Talk," she said with a wave of her free hand between them as she dragged Edmund down the next hallway and out of sight, saying something about finding food that wasn't pure liquid.

"What did Father have to say?" Xannan winced as he leaned his shoulder against the wall.

Gailin squinted at his brother. "You haven't fully recovered?"

"No." Xannan lifted a shoulder. "But the hallways spin less the more I walk. That thing must have hit me in the head pretty good."

"Must have." Gailin scrutinized Xannan's arm, the one he had last seen with a gaping gash running down it. "The arm?"

"Better than the head."

At least his brother was acting somewhat normal, Gailin decided, though it was odd to not hear an attempt at using his newest curse somewhere in any of those phrases. "Do you—"

"No, I don't want to talk about it. Not yet at least." Xannan lifted from the wall and ran his hand through his shoulder-length blond hair. "Besides, didn't you literally just arrive?" At Gailin's nod, Xannan chuckled. "No wonder they went after food. Join them?"

They walked down the corridor several paces, and after removing his outer coat, Gailin said, "If you need—"

Xannan rounded on Gailin. Face pressed close to his, Xannan gripped Gailin's collar. "Don't. Please. I've tried to figure out what happened." Xannan dropped his voice to a whisper, as though worried the walls might have ears and tell on him. "I've relived the battle several times now. And it hurts. I don't know what I need, and I don't know what I tried to do."

Xannan straightened and grimaced, chest expanding with a controlled breath. "I doubt Father will let us return until we have answers, and I'm trying. But I still don't understand if or how. . ." Xannan grimaced, voice lowering again. "Mikhael is . . . was—"

"We buried him, Xannan." Gailin fixed his collar, brows pinching at Xannan's confused expression. If Xannan had relived the battle, then he had seen what had occurred with Mikhael. Possibly. The way he spoke of it was odd.

As they continued their trek to the kitchens, Gailin added, "He may have had some life left in him before you were knocked unconscious, but he was gone by the time Solomon found you."

His brother's face paled, but Xannan nodded. "Figures nosy Solomon would be the one to find me with a gash in my arm."

"Probably kept a worse infection at bay."

"Perhaps."

Once they stood at the entrance to the kitchens, Xannan froze and audibly swallowed, whispering, "Mikhael should be here, too."

Gailin remained in the doorway as Xannan sat at Anna's side, opposite Edmund. He'd been a fool to bring Edmund along. His brother was right: the image wasn't complete with Mikhael missing.

Part Two

"I only *considered* setting things on fire."

11

That scent made Xannan flinch. Even in memory, the deathly, decaying smell of the droki curdled his insides. He inhaled and exhaled slowly, remembering the importance of shoving aside that taste.

It was a memory. One he hadn't relived for some time, but he wanted to see if the gaps remained. Throughout the years, those small gaps in his memory had become more frequent. Xannan crossed his legs beneath him and rested his sheathed sword across his thighs, wishing he'd been able to find at least one room in this village without wood paneling.

After another deep breath, the scene from barely two years past unfolded.

Burning buildings surrounded him, accompanied by several whimpers and screams. Not human screams, but those of a drokos as it died. Xannan heard Gailin's grunt as he cleaved his sword through a drokos's neck. That kill brought their hunt down to one. One drokos left to annihilate from this attack. All because someone in this village had used magic, likely without knowing.

Xannan stepped carefully and cautiously through the debris, pressing his lips together and wishing he could pinch his nose closed to avoid the stench. A pale-skinned arm reached through the debris, waving frantically, and Xannan moved almost without thinking. He grasped the hand and pulled, cursing himself for inhaling through his mouth. The stench of the droki would sour his taste buds for weeks.

The person he pulled from the debris tumbled into him, hands clawing at his shoulders, his arm, his chest, his waist.

"Whoa, whoa." Xannan tugged himself out of the person's reach, focus flitting to the sky at the loud, careening cry of the drokos as it circled above him.

"It's after me," a woman's voice whispered nearby. It belonged to the person he'd pulled from the debris. Xannan looked from her to the drokos and back again, brows furrowed.

"Doubtful." Xannan watched the drokos's flight path, trying to assess where the beast might land. "Can you walk?"

She gasped and whimpered. "Orda'anians." When she collapsed, Xannan fought the urge to roll his eyes as he bent down to ensure the woman breathed. He shifted her hair—which was darker than a starless night sky —and grimaced. Dirt and grime covered her skin, ashes coated strands of her hair and lips, and small streams of blood snaked along her bare arms.

"Xannan!" Gailin hollered, and Xannan stood, rounding his shoulders.

He opened his eyes to the present, greeted by the dull brown wood panels, and sighed. The gap in his memory remained. Xannan resituated his grip on his sheathed weapon, shifted his shoulders, and closed his eyes to reenter the scene.

Three droki lay dead, headless, amid the debris. Xannan and Gailin helped the soldiers search the destroyed town, though Xannan's focus kept shifting to the woman. Wrapped in a blanket, she stood surrounded by several soldiers. That had been Gailin's idea, though his brother claimed he felt nothing for or against the woman.

"They're all dead, aren't they?" she said when he was close enough to hear. A shudder racked through her when her gaze fell on the beheaded beasts. "Would you have let those things kill me?"

Xannan canted his head, holding out a hand for a cloth to clean his blade.

"She looks Alkaanian, sir," Mikhael said as he handed Xannan a cloth.

Xannan gave Mikhael a sidelong glance and focused on the pale, dark-haired, dirt-covered woman. Tossing the soiled cloth into a nearby flame, Xannan asked her, "Well, are you?"

The woman's dark eyes flitted from him to Mikhael several times before she spoke in one breath. "If I say yes, will you kill me?"

Mikhael's laugh cut short at Xannan's glare.

"Why would you ask that?"

"Because it's your reputation."

Another gap. Xannan ground his teeth, trying to recall any other moment from that evening. But next he recalled, they were in Cantadad and he already knew the woman's name.

"Apologies, Your Highness." Anna curtsied, allowing a brief smile to grace her features. "I was unaware this wing housed the royal family. Her Majesty said I could explore and—"

"Then let us explore." Xannan held out his arm, patting her hand once she placed it in the crook of his elbow. "What would you like to see?"

"The training yards, Your Highness."

His brows lifted. Anna blushed and turned away. "I'd be a fool to rely on a dragon-blessed prince rushing to my aid every time I'm in trouble, Your Highness."

"Then to the training yards, Miss Anna."

Xannan scrubbed his face with his hands, grateful Arjun hadn't entered the quaint room yet, and stood. He moved through several sword forms, hoping the motion might knock loose why his memories had gaps. Based on everything he had ever learned about his connection to the blade, those gaps were impossible. But they were there.

The day he'd met Anna wasn't the first appearance of those gaps, which meant she couldn't be responsible. He winced at the strain in his arm, cursing whatever soldier had managed to wound him, and paused in the middle of the bare room. Xannan rubbed his arm and shook his head, dismissing any possibility that Anna could be a spy. Not after how he'd found her. Alone, fearful for her own life. So he offered her a new one. A better one.

He resumed the sword forms and struck the door, unaware it had been opened until it was too late.

Ever resolute and immovable, Arjun followed the length of the sword and looked at Xannan with those mesmerizing red eyes. "Her Majesty has requested to return home today, and your betrothed has decided to accompany her."

Xannan stalked past Arjun, buckling the sword belt around his waist and ignoring Gailin's brief shout. By the time he reached Anna's room, she was already packing what few items she'd brought.

"Stay," he said, and she jolted, tossing him one of those sad smiles. The same she offered each time they returned from any battle.

"You need to learn more about yourself, Xannan." She turned back to folding a dress. "Besides, I have more preparations to make."

"More?"

Anna glanced over her shoulder, a mesmerizing twinkle in her dark eyes. "Your parents aren't the best decorators."

He chuckled, wrapped his arms around her waist, and shifted her to face him. Anna smirked and tapped his chest before turning back to her packing.

"I would prefer you stay." Xannan held her shoulders, lowering to whisper in her ear. "Wait until I can escort you home."

After another soft whisper directly in her ear, Anna gasped and dropped the last of her dresses on the bed. A bright green, almost too bright against her pale skin. She retrieved the dress, tucking the sleeves within the folds of its skirts. Anna laid it atop the others and turned to him with a tense smile.

"I'm a distraction here." Anna tugged on her bottom lip, gaze heated as it took him in. "And the quicker you solve whatever happened, the sooner we can be wed."

"Solve." Xannan made a noncommittal sound and threaded his fingers through his hair, shoulders tensing. "You don't seem worried about the journey."

"Gailin did send quite the message to the northern tribes, so I imagine they won't try anything for a while." She smoothed her dark skirts and cleared her throat, placing each dress with delicate motions into her traveling case. "Especially if His Majesty continues his hunt for that spy."

Xannan tucked a lock of her long, black hair behind her ear. "Oh, we'll find the spy."

She tilted her head up to him and made a light tsking sound as she pursed her lips into a subtle smirk. "Always so confident."

Xannan faked a wince. "I'm afraid the continuation of that sound may make it impossible for me to kiss you again."

That earned a laugh, loud and deep. Full and whole, unlike the version of Anna he'd first met. Surrounded by her dead neighbors, she'd hid to avoid the droki. Lifting to her toes, she threaded her fingers through his loose blond hair and pulled him close for a long and thorough kiss. When she pulled away, her teeth tugged at his bottom lip, and she whispered, "A taste of what awaits." She smoothed her skirts, the tense smile returning. "Be kind to your brother. And Arjun."

At his annoyed grunt, Anna pinned him with a glare, though the hand she placed on his cheek was gentle and kind. "Mikhael's death was not their fault, nor was it yours." Anna tapped his chest in time with the words, holding her hand against him as she added, "Stop blaming yourself."

Xannan released a long, slow breath, noting the concern and care emanating from Anna's dark eyes. He would always consider any death of an Orda'anian soldier while under his watch his fault. But since that was a burden he refused to allow anyone else to carry, he nodded and kissed her again, groaning with displeasure when his mother's voice preceded a distinct knock.

"My parents and their timing," he murmured, resting his forehead against hers. "I would've loved more time away with you. There are some gorgeous groves surrounding this Blazing aggravating town center that would've been perfect for an afternoon escape."

Anna peered around his shoulder for a blink. "I'm sure we could delay our journey for one more afternoon?"

"I fear there are approaching storms which claim otherwise." His mother's voice was gentle but firm. When he turned to face her, she was tugging on the bold white gloves that ran the length of her forearm before meeting the shortened sleeves of her solid black dress. Layers of cloth, which Xannan assumed would assist with warmth, surrounded her in a way that, unfortunately, reminded Xannan of the dark scaly skin of the droki. She frowned at the tips of her fingers, wriggling them as though the gloves were a nuisance. "Eonar recommended we leave before the sun reaches its peak, and even then we risk the storm catching us. Besides, I've spent too long away from the castle."

Straightening, Xannan asked, "Who are your guards for the journey?"

"Lieutenant-Captain Solomon and Captain Ishmael," his mother said with a raised brow. "Your father does not believe either of them to be the spy."

Xannan grunted. "Nosy Solomon got himself a promotion." He shook his head and smirked. "For finding me?"

With a small nod, his mother said, "We appreciate his service and wanted to acknowledge his role in keeping both of our sons alive."

"Logical." Xannan turned back to Anna, muscles of his jaw tensing. "You have the dagger?"

Anna patted her sleeve, where he'd helped her learn how to keep his first gift to her hidden. "Always."

***

The wooden floor was even more uncomfortable while sitting on it than standing with bare feet. No matter how Xannan shifted, the floor didn't budge, and his butt was going numb. He wanted to stand, to move, to run, to spar. Anything except sit here with his eyes closed while Arjun walked him through a series of mental exercises. Supposedly they would help him remain calm while reliving his past. Whoever claimed such must have been lying in order to get others to be quiet. So, while Gailin and Edmund conversed with Celena about her journey beyond the mountains, Xannan sat there.

"Your thoughts are straying again," Arjun said.

The floor creaked, so Xannan opened his eyes to confirm the elf had stood and did likewise.

"I thought you couldn't read minds." Xannan pressed his hand into his lower back and stretched his neck from side to side. Despite the dizziness dissipating, both the elves and Gailin had determined Xannan should wait longer before returning to any type of physical exercise.

Arjun put both hands in his pockets, tilting his head so a lock of tawny hair escaped its loose hold, and frowned. "I can't. But I can read your facial expressions. There's a scowl of concentration and one of annoyance. The latter has been planted on your face for the better part of an hour."

"I don't need mental exercises to help." Xannan rubbed the back of his neck, wincing at how it stretched the muscles of his upper arm. "I need to regain strength. Make sure I can still fight."

"You wish to fight to avoid finding answers."

"And?"

Arjun rubbed both of his temples with one hand. "Do you make everyone repeat conversations like this with you?"

Xannan shrugged and strapped his sword around his waist, situating the belt so it wouldn't dig in at odd places. "Are we done for today?"

"The more you fight it, the longer you'll be here."

Xannan snorted. "Like you could stop me from leaving."

"So why haven't you?"

Arjun's red eyes churned a deeper shade, and Xannan fought the urge to step back. He'd asked himself that very question this morning, when Arjun found him in the kitchens and insisted they resume the mental training. No one was truly stopping him from leaving, except himself. Since he'd spent years avoiding anything related to reliving the past, Xannan didn't want to admit that he, too, was curious.

As an answer, Xannan tugged on his boots, concentrating on following his movements rather than give Arjun a chance to force another answer out of him. When Xannan exited the small room—whose purpose he had yet to ascertain—Arjun followed him, and his scowl deepened.

"I thought we were done for the day."

"It would be foolish of me to stop my observations. I know you've relived the battle a few times now."

"What's so important about this Blazing battle?" Xannan shouted, lifting his arms to either side. "I was injured, almost killed. My closest friend *died*." He let his arms fall and curled his fingers into fists.

If he wasn't careful, he'd end up breaking Arjun's nose again. "Why would *anyone* want to relive those moments?"

Arjun lifted a brow, glass clinking in his pockets as he moved his hands within. "I never expected you to *want* to relive the battle." The robed elf's red eyes searched Xannan's. "But we need you to understand what happened before we can understand it ourselves."

Arjun's lack of reaction only stirred Xannan's anger further.

"What else is there to understand, Arjun?" Xannan moved to the wall, clenched fists resting on it. "We've spent an entire week with those ridiculous mental exercises of yours."

He leaned his head against the back of his hand. Images surfaced, visions of his past, events he had lived. The moment Mikhael spoke with him, followed by the sharp silence of his friend's speech. And then the piece he knew they wanted him to discuss, but he couldn't make sense of it himself.

"You thought Mikhael still breathed, even after Lieutenant Solomon was aiding you, correct?"

Xannan's throat clenched, and he nodded, grateful the motion didn't make him feel like he was being tumbled about by the sea anymore. "More than thought," Xannan admitted quietly. "His chest moved. Shaky, uneven. As if in time with my own thoughts."

Usually Arjun not speaking meant glasses clinking, but when Xannan turned to face the elf, Arjun seemed frozen in place.

"More power than we initially assumed," Arjun murmured, brows furrowing as the bottles in his pockets clinked together. "And now I know what to ask you to do next."

When the elf's red-irised gaze met his, Xannan groaned. "I've been through it four times—"

"No, no, not the battle." Arjun rubbed his chin and shook his head. "I think you may be able to wield some control over the dead."

At first, Xannan's lungs emptied of air. Unused to the feeling of shock, he leaned his back against the wall. Since Arjun's idea was preposterous, Xannan laughed. It started as a soft chuckle, growing until the missing air was from the constant laugh. One far from contagious as Arjun merely lifted a brow.

Summoning his resolve, Xannan quieted. The elf flinched as Xannan's arm approached, but he merely slapped Arjun's shoulder. "Didn't think you were one for jokes, Arjun."

"I'm not." Arjun crossed his arms, gesturing with one hand, and resumed the tense position. "Your words were that Mikhael seemed to breathe in time with your thoughts."

"But that's not—I can't—I wouldn't—I don't control people, Arjun. Dead or alive."

"You kill them, though," Arjun muttered while searching Xannan's gaze again, adding a simple, "Don't hit me," as Xannan lifted his arm.

Xannan tensed, nails digging into his palm, and lowered his fist. He could try to ignore the elf's command. It would hurt. Not as badly as the recently recovered head wound, but bad enough that Xannan flexed his hand at his side and breathed deep. His anger was getting out of control. He needed to walk, to roam, to move, to do something other than talk.

Nothing more to say, Xannan sped through the hallways. To him, they were identical. Different shades of wood stacked atop one another, complete with torches. Maybe he should knock one down and set it on fire; then he wouldn't be sent back here for a time. That or they'd make him and Gailin sleep in a tent while it snowed.

He wasn't sure when his brother found him, or where, but when he came to a dead end and no more hallways to turn into, Gailin was there. Same look as everyone else. Brows furrowed. Worried.

Xannan made a sharp gesture. "Tell me your version of this Blazing battle everyone needs to stop asking me about."

Gailin's furrowed brows managed to deepen. He crossed his arms, obviously mulling over whatever words he was about to use, jaw clenching when he'd settled on a decision. "Mikhael only moved when you mumbled in your half-conscious state. Thus the message." He paused and turned away, so Xannan couldn't read Gailin's expression. "I told Edmund to take Mikhael's body with you. Logically, he refused."

The hollowness of shock consumed Xannan's insides again. "What would that have accomplished?"

Gailin shrugged, pressing the toe of his boot against an errant floorboard trying to escape its hold. "It sounded right to me at the time."

"And now?"

For the span of too many breaths, Gailin continued pressing his boot against the floorboard, frowning as it bent back up each time he shifted his foot. Pensive, thoughtful, ever careful of what he would say and how it would be perceived. Eventually, right before Xannan contemplated marching back home, Gailin said, "I think we need to start asking questions instead of answering others."

12

Though Gailin pressed the floorboard down again, he knew it was useless. No different from how he'd felt for several days. Neither Arjun nor Celena questioned him about his abilities. Edmund, who quickly tired of traveling back and forth, chose to stay. That choice made Gailin believe his friend trusted the soldiers escorting his mother and future sister-in-law, though his own trust remained tenuous.

"Ask questions, you say?" Xannan rested on a window ledge, hands gripping the small piece of wood protruding from the wall while his fingers drummed along the edge. "Let's start with why in the Blazes you would ever tell someone to travel with the dead?"

Rather than face his brother's accusatory stare, Gailin continued pressing on the errant floorboard. "It honestly wasn't a conscious thought." Gailin leaned his shoulder against the wall. "I didn't realize I said it until Edmund questioned the order."

"And why did you bring Edmund here with you?"

Gailin shoved both hands into his pockets and tipped his head until his temple rested on the wall. "I can send him home, if that would help."

"I'm not sure," Xannan whispered. He leaned forward, hands remaining tight on the window's ledge as he took a deep breath. "It's odd to see Edmund without Mikhael."

"Agreed," Gailin murmured as he studied the sky through the window. The jerky movements, the even shorter than usual retorts, all pointed to Xannan having pent up energy which needed to be released. "It stopped snowing."

Xannan lifted his head slowly and smirked. "You up for a sparring match?"

"Are you?" Gailin asked quickly, wincing when Xannan scowled at him.

"Let's find out." Xannan moved swiftly through the hallways until they were at the main entrance. He opened the door, shivered at the cold blast of air that blew in a drift of powdery snow, grabbed a nearby coat, and motioned for Gailin to follow suit. Clad in a fur coat with the higher collars and fewer buttons of elvish design, Gailin followed.

Their boots left prints as they walked through the light coating of snow dusting the pathways. Open space abounded in the elven village, and though no specific training rings existed, Xannan led them along the usual path. In the past five years, they'd spent a decent amount of time in Violet Grove. Whenever the questions and assigned tasks became too much, they came here. It no longer functioned as a place to hide, but at least they could escape the interior of the meeting house.

When Xannan paused and lifted his head to the sky, frowning, Gailin mumbled a soft curse. "We forgot practice blades. I'll get them."

"Or we can use our swords," Xannan said without removing his focus from studying the sky. Despite being midday, it appeared no different from dusk. No visible sun or moon. Clouds upon clouds, murky and indicative of additional flurries falling from the sky at any moment. Same as it had in the week since their mother and Anna had left. "Or our fists."

Gailin grunted. "You know how much I dislike both of those ideas."

With a sigh and shrug, Xannan pulled his sword free of its scabbard, hefting the blade as though he hadn't spent almost two weeks bedridden.

"Wait—" Gailin stepped closer, scrutinizing his brother's sword. "When did those appear?"

Black streaks marred the white hue of Xannan's blade. Each seemed to move of its own accord, akin to two black-furred squirrels chasing one another up and down a tree.

"I'm not sure." Xannan moved through a series of forms using his nondominant hand, and Gailin almost rolled his eyes.

"You've been practicing when they told you not to?"

"Better to strike a random bit of wood in a dark room than an elf's face." Xannan switched hands and winced. "The wound itself is healed, true, but the muscle—"

"Was ripped in two. Or looked it." Gailin crossed his arms, watching as his brother grunted and continued through one form after another.

"Remember what Celena said the day we got these?" Gailin squinted at Xannan's movements, noticing the slight falter to his brother's grip on the sword.

"'Such power inside one,'" Xannan quoted, mimicking the elf's typical accented monotone.

"Father and Eonar always thought that indicated mine." Gailin focused on the moving black streaks. "What if they're wrong?"

Xannan struck a young tree with his blade, almost cleaving it in two. He left it there and faced Gailin. "Your ability is the more powerful."

"I didn't try to bring someone back to life," Gailin murmured as he approached the sword stuck in the tree. "You did."

A few faint flurries swirled in the breeze around them and landed. After threading his fingers through his hair, Xannan scrubbed his face with his hands. He lowered both arms, frowned at the falling snow, and turned back to his sword. Hovering one hand above the blade, Xannan seemed like a snake ready to strike. His frown deepened as he traced one of the black streaks with a finger, shaking his head.

"I laughed when Arjun said something similar."

"Unsurprising." Gailin rubbed his hands together, hoping the quick friction would warm his fingers. The coat he'd grabbed wasn't as warm as he had hoped.

"Why in the Blazes are you two out here?" Edmund called out to them. Hands shoved into his armpits, the soldier visibly shivered once, shifting his shoulders as he continued his approach. A thick cloth hat rested on his head of barely there hair.

"I'll go back inside." Xannan tugged his sword free of the tree trunk and sheathed it, rounding his shoulders and sparing a quick glance toward Gailin as he stepped away. Gailin grabbed his brother's arm, lightly biting his cheek when he realized he'd grabbed the one that had only recently healed.

"You don't have to leave, you know?"

Xannan shrugged off Gailin's hand and rubbed his arm. "Why bother making friends if you'll just lose them?"

Any words Gailin could think to say lodged somewhere between his brain and his mouth, so rather than speak or move, he stared at his brother with an idiotic expression of confusion. Or shock or some other strange mixture of whatever emotions were trying to coalesce at the time. Any time his own emotions took a hit, those of his ability reared their ugly heads as well. Fear, frustration, worry, shock, amazement—all of them swirled together until the image of the blinding flame pierced his mind's eye and made him gasp.

Rubbing his temples, Gailin briefly thought about the flames again. The image itself did not change. Red flames mingled with black, ending with a glint of gold.

"Gailin?" Edmund whispered nearby, almost in his ear. "Apologies, Your Highness, I'm not used to seeing that expression on your visage."

Gailin shook his head once. "I'm fine."

Luckily, Xannan hadn't continued back inside and instead stared at Gailin with one brow raised. "Visions again?"

"I'd rather not—"

"See?" Xannan made a sharp gesture, glowering. "It's Blazing *awful* when everyone wants to know what you can or cannot do." Though he didn't need to, Xannan pulled his sword free of its sheath again, holding it upright so all could see the tendrils roving through it. Up and down. "Power, huh? But how to access it?"

Gailin shifted his head backward, blinking against the snowflakes landing on his lashes. "We already do."

"Do we though?"

Xannan hefted his sword and continued through forms again, almost cutting Edmund in the process. The soldier cursed and jumped backward, eliciting a small smirk from Xannan that made Gailin roll his eyes. A few more shifts through the air and Xannan halted the blade right before it would have dug into Gailin's arm.

Meeting Gailin's gaze, Xannan said in a level voice, "I wasn't wearing or holding the sword when I last held on to consciousness after Solomon moved me. But, if my memories are to be believed, I still tried to revive Mikhael through thought."

Edmund made a noncommittal sound that became a cross between a laugh, a cough, and a strangled shout. Holding a fist to his mouth, eyes seeming to bulge from their sockets, Edmund croaked, "Revive?"

"You've relived it how many times now?" Gailin gently lowered Xannan's sword.

Having the two weapons so close together made his skin itch. The blades wanted to connect. They called to each other, desperate to be reunited. And yet, considering their combining made Gailin's stomach tie itself in more knots than any other thought he'd ever had since that night in the cave.

"Enough to know you and Arjun are likely correct." Xannan grumbled and motioned for Edmund to follow him into the clearing. The soldier, who knew Xannan's moods as well as Gailin did, glanced between the brothers. Xannan sighed. "I haven't had a proper sparring match in weeks. I won't hurt you. Not intentionally, at least."

"Not very comforting, Your Highness."

Xannan shrugged, Edmund did likewise, and then the two both had swords in hands, circling one another in the clearing as Gailin observed. Most concerning now wasn't Xannan's admission of what he'd tried to do, but the changing aspect of the weapon.

"Magna warned me of the changes."

Celena's sudden proclamation made Gailin swear and almost stumble into the elf-woman.

She chuckled. "Trained soldier and I can sneak up on you. Perfect." Celena held out a finger to catch a snowflake. "The dampening effect of the snow assists, too."

"Changes?"

When Celena offered no additional explanation other than to gesture at his brother, Gailin resumed his observation of Xannan and Edmund's back and forth exchanges. Every attack Xannan attempted to land, Edmund easily avoided. With each pass, Xannan's brows furrowed and his breaths shortened. Both happened quicker than Gailin had become accustomed to.

Sighing, Gailin said, "He's going to do something foolish soon."

"I thought we agreed Blazing foolish would be a thing," Xannan called out over the clang of weapons.

"I thought we agreed those didn't go together."

Gailin's chest clenched as the sparring continued. Though a level of caution precipitated each movement, he worried his sometimes too-hasty brother would cause an unnecessary accident. No different from Edmund's habit of toying with his daggers throughout the day. After several more hits, Edmund disarmed Xannan, sending the sword of mingling black and white clattering to the ground.

"No, that was 'Blazing perfect' that didn't work." Xannan placed his hands on his hips, staring down at his sword. "It would be Blazing perfect if the swords could just speak to us, though."

13

Xannan retrieved his sword, wincing at the slight strain in his muscle. Weapon sheathed, he shifted his hair from his forehead and appraised Edmund. The soldier didn't seem winded, though both his and Gailin's brows knitted together in concern while Celena's shifted with a slight hint of amusement.

With one hand, he motioned for the elf to approach. It wouldn't be the first time they'd sparred. And Celena's close combat skills challenged him more than Edmund's, especially when weaponless.

She obliged his silent request, red eyes churning a deeper shade as her slow steps formed a circle around him. Hands in her pockets, it appeared as though the elf-woman was out for a stroll rather than about to whack him upside the head.

Xannan tensed, shifting to keep her in view. Larger flakes of snow filled in the prints left by her boots until she stepped there again. Almost. Her slow circling decreased in size with each pass. Soon she would be close enough he could strike.

"I thought you despised using your fists," Celena said, finally removing her hands from each pocket. "Or are those simply for how much your dear elven friends anger you?"

He lashed out, cursing when his fist swung through empty air. Pulling his arms back into his chest, he glanced down where Celena had lowered to a knee and looked up at him, smirking with those mocking red eyes.

When Xannan kicked, intending to strike her shoulder, she caught his boot. His balance compromised, he cursed again and stumbled to the side, grateful she released his foot without his having to fall to the ground.

"Celena," came Gailin's warning voice from a nearby tree. Xannan didn't dare glance at his brother, not when the elf-woman had begun her slow, methodical circle once more.

"I know the prince's temperament." Celena shuffled a step to the side to avoid Xannan's quick flurry of punches. None landed. "I'm more adept than Arjun." Celena ducked beneath Xannan's next punch, gripped his sword belt with one hand, shoved her shoulder into his abdomen, and pulled his sword free. She flaunted the sword and offered a mocking smile. "See?"

Muttering a stream of curses, Xannan reached for his weapon, lost his balance, and fell. Growling, he pushed himself to his knees.

"That's mine," he gritted out.

"As we are all aware," Celena said as she hefted the sword, briefly triumphant in a way that made Xannan contemplate tackling the elf-woman to the ground.

Rather than give in to his anger, Xannan focused on taking calming breaths. "Now that you've proven you move faster than I ever will, give me my sword back."

Celena ignored his outstretched hand. "I wanted a closer look." Her red eyes brightened for a moment when her gaze flicked to the sky and back to the sword. Lips twisted between a grimace and a frown, she inhaled deeply enough Xannan noticed her shoulders lift. Similar to the last image he had of Mikhael. A single breath. A fleeting thought.

"Magna's here?" Gailin scratched at the stubble on his chin that never fully grew in regardless of how long the man forgot to shave.

Celena offered an absent-minded nod, shifting the blade to inspect it from a different angle. Neither Xannan nor Gailin had ever learned precisely how Celena's ability to communicate with the dragons functioned, and all simply took her word that she told the truth of what the dragons shared with her. Sometimes Magna would share information with them as well, but that was exhausting and painful. Even then, it didn't happen as often as Xannan would have liked.

"Access," she murmured. Red eyes held Xannan's stare, captivating him. "You've been accessing the stored magic."

"That's how our abilities work." Gailin scrubbed his face with his hands and lowered his arms. "And why both Father and Eonar claimed mine had the larger store of magic."

"Curious." Celena ran a cautious finger along Xannan's blade, following the tendrils of black.

Gritting his teeth to prevent himself from saying something he'd likely regret, Xannan pushed to standing and reached for his sword. She backed away a step. "Celena, I'm not in the mood—"

"Try it, while Magna's here."

"Try what?"

"You know what." Celena cocked her head, a single line etched in her forehead. "You've been angry enough about what you see between Gailin and Edmund."

When he reached for the sword, she stepped to the side. "Alone. Stuck with Arjun for days on end. An unpleasant experience for you both, I'm sure." He swiped for his sword again, and Celena said, "You don't need the sword, Xannan. Neither does Gailin."

None of the men spoke. Celena snapped the fingers of her free hand in each of their faces. "Think!" Another snap right in front of Xannan's eyes made him shake with the effort not to lash out. "Why would the two of you need dragon-blessed weapons while Arjun and I don't?"

"Simple, you two already had magic."

She shook her head emphatically. "Ours would have manifested long before that moment. All of our abilities are a result of that day, but yours were *enhanced* by the weapons." She gestured for Gailin's sword, and he flinched away. Sighing, Celena motioned with an open palm at Xannan. A slight indication of her expectations of his actions.

Confused if the cold or anger caused his shivering, Xannan clenched his jaw to prevent his teeth from chattering. Chilly winter winds presented a problem when he had to stop moving through the forms.

He'd considered attempting the process before. For several nights now he'd lain awake, staring at a wooden ceiling, wondering what would happen if he wished his friend alive again. Fear of what might appear had quieted those thoughts, preventing him from allowing the idea to come to fruition.

Xannan turned from the studious gazes. Concern and curiosity mingled on both Gailin and Edmund's visages while Celena's boasted a cross between amusement and annoyance. Try. He could try. For whatever it would be worth, he supposed.

Arms crossed, he focused on the space between Gailin and Edmund. The place where, had his friend not been mortally injured, Mikhael would be standing. Not that any of them would be stuck in Violet Grove if Mikhael had survived the battle. Hair the same shade as his eyes, akin in many ways to mud. Skin a tinge darker than Xannan's own. The newest design of the soldiers' coat—the solid black with none of the white cuffs or buttons others had to display. A proper commander. A well-trained soldier with a sword Mikhael had crafted himself wrapped around his waist. Xannan visualized his friend and, with a deep inhale, imagined breathing life into that form.

A clouded image flickered in the space where he focused. Gailin gasped, and Edmund held his fist to his mouth, eyes bulging. The faint manlike form disappeared, leaving naught but frigid empty air once more.

With a silent swear, Xannan immediately regretted the attempt. It would hurt. Emotionally. Those feelings shouldn't bother him, yet the idea of creating what could never be reality again made his insides turn cold.

The cold made him pause for another reason. That sensation was so similar to. . .

"No droki can enter Violet Grove, Xannan." Celena offered his sword. Though he scowled at her and opened his mouth, the elf-woman continued speaking. "Obviously you managed something without Praeteritum, but my guess is you both use your swords to focus."

At Gailin's grunt, Celena pressed her lips together and motioned toward the once again empty space.

Xannan shook his head, fingers curling around the hilt of his sword. "I shouldn't— I'd rather—" He curled his hand around the hilt. "Blazes."

"Blazes?" Celena sounded incredulous. "Why in—oh." Her brows knitted together, and she pinched the bridge of her nose, mumbling in the elven language Xannan occasionally wished he had asked to learn. "Magna circles above. If anything goes wrong, she will contain it."

"It?" Xannan pointed with his sword at the space where a ghostlike image of Mikhael had flickered into existence for a single breath. "We're more than an 'it', even in death." He lowered his weapon, grip tightening. "But what purpose does conjuring the dead have?"

The elf-woman shrugged, Gailin lifted a shoulder, and Edmund appeared frozen in place.

"Don't. Please don't, sir." Edmund's fist muffled his whisper further, making it so Xannan almost didn't hear the soldier's soft plea. "This is worse than Gailin telling me to travel with Mikhael's body."

"If you don't wish to witness this, then return inside," Celena said with a wave of her hand as though she meant to dismiss Edmund from their presence. Her focus remained on Xannan. "You want to understand, no?"

A brief exchange of glances and Edmund folded his arms while lowering his chin, obviously steeling his nerves for whatever was about to happen. Xannan's chest hurt from inhaling the frigid air. Snowflakes had coated his hair and clothing in a fine layer of moisture, and his thoughts raced in a way that made him question if he was himself in that moment. He often didn't think through his actions. If something needed to be done, Xannan did it. Decisive, as a future ruler of a country should always be. So why did he hesitate now?

Rather than view whatever emotions the others now portrayed, Xannan focused on his weapon, following the moving lines as he slowed his own breathing. The longer he concentrated on visualizing how his friend had been in life, the more his head ached. A dull throb turned into a piercing pulse, culminating in a flash of blinding pain that made Xannan lower to a knee lest he fall to the ground again.

"Fascinating." At Celena's murmured word, Xannan lifted his head and the motion made the world spin.

Pressing the point of his sword into the ground, Xannan used it to pull himself to standing. He really wished the sensation of shock would stop occurring. Lungs devoid of air, heartbeat rapid, throat closing, tongue thick and dry—all piled on top of the throbbing in his head.

One hand gripping his sword, he leaned on it slightly as his other hand strayed toward his temple. The motion paused when he realized what stood before him. Not a faded image of his friend. If he hadn't known Gailin had buried the man, he'd believe Mikhael had joined them. Except for the dull look on the man's face. Emotionless and ashen. Though Mikhael's physical form stood before Xannan, his friend's essence was absent.

"He looks—" Xannan swallowed and cleared his throat, wishing he could take a swig of something strong enough to dull his thoughts. "How can he look so real?"

Celena ignored his question, circling the . . . fake Mikhael. She snapped her fingers behind Mikhael, and he turned his head at the sound. At the elf's quick glance up and subsequent frown, Xannan wondered what she and Magna had shared but feared the answer.

After completing a full circle survey of the fake Mikhael, Celena asked, "What happens if you lose focus?"

"How in the Blazes would I know the answer to that?" Xannan sheathed his sword and folded his arms, ignoring the desire to rub his temples while wondering if he could manage to massage the back of his eyeballs since they now hurt the most.

"You—" Celena snapped at Edmund, gesturing for the soldier to do something, but Edmund's focus snagged on the newest figure occupying their space. Sighing, Celena said, "One of you needs to start sparring with Xannan again so we know if this creation is a permanent existence or one connected to his thought process."

When neither of them moved, the elf mumbled in her own language again with several quick glances to the sky. "Stay here. I'll return with Eonar and Arjun. They'll want to see this."

As soon as Celena was far enough away not to hear, Edmund whispered, "You made him appear from nothing."

"Still think your ability is the lesser of the two?" Gailin questioned.

The ache in Xannan's head increased until he swore a thousand needles pierced his scalp at once. Holding both fists to his forehead, he muttered a curse. Cold winds with flurrying snowflakes faded into blackness as he fell to his knees and lost consciousness.

14

Despite moving as soon as he realized what was happening, Gailin didn't manage to catch Xannan before his brother crumpled to the ground. He knelt beside Xannan, and a quick appraisal confirmed Gailin's suspicions. "Unconscious," he said aloud to Edmund.

The soldier's fist hadn't moved from in front of his mouth since the first flicker of Mikhael's form had appeared. Gailin couldn't blame Edmund for his reaction. The thought of the dead being conjured churned his insides. Yet, a part of him accepted this growth in Xannan's ability. Fear existed, as it always did.

"Guess that answers the focus question," Edmund mumbled into his fist, motioning to the once again empty space where the too-real image of Mikhael had stood until Xannan lost consciousness. "But why did doing that make him pass out?"

Gailin gritted his teeth, remembering what had happened the first several times he'd experienced full visions. "He's not accustomed to it." Gailin tugged at his collar, contemplating how they would get his unconscious brother back inside. "No different than I used to deal with."

"You? But you've never—"

"Not since you've known me." Sighing, Gailin motioned with his head for Edmund to join him in lifting Xannan's limp form. He

114

shifted his brother into a seated position, resting one of Xannan's arms across his shoulders while Edmund did likewise. "In the year before you joined the army, I would get dizzy each time the emotions surged. Even now, those feelings which are not my own twist my insides." Both men grunted and lifted, arms wrapped around Xannan's waist.

The movement elicited a moan from Xannan. "Wait—Mikhael—he's—Blazes, no, stay with me."

The murmured phrases ended with a snarl as Xannan regained use of his limbs and swung at Edmund. Too shocked to react, Edmund took the full brunt of Xannan's fist to his chest, stumbling backward several steps. When Xannan's second swing came for Gailin, he grabbed his brother's fist and held firm.

"We're in Violet Grove," Gailin said calmly, refusing to relinquish his hold of Xannan's hand, though none of the rest of his body felt at ease. It had been years since Xannan had lost himself in reliving the past. Not since the first few battles. It was why Xannan killed all who got in his way, claiming that with all enemies dead, none could haunt his thoughts. "The battle is over and has been for several weeks."

Gailin ducked beneath Xannan's next swing, not releasing his hold on Xannan's other fist. Unable to shift Gailin's grip, Xannan lashed out with a knee, then a foot, then tried to press with his shoulder. At the last, Gailin wrapped Xannan's arm behind him and held, reminding himself to speak in a level and measured cadence. "The battle is over, Xannan. None here wish to harm you."

"They do," Xannan spat as Arjun, Celena, and Eonar came into view. His brother struggled, tugging until Gailin lost his grip. As soon as Xannan's fist was free of his hand, Gailin ducked, expecting the swing. But it didn't approach him. In fact, Xannan didn't move except to clench his fists at his sides. "Everyone here would be happy to punch me." He tilted his head to the sky, jutting his chin out. "Even that one, I bet."

"Xannan, you're—"

"Don't tell me how I feel."

When Xannan turned around, Gailin stepped back and his heel landed on the toe of Edmund's boot. "Should I. . .?" Edmund whispered. Gailin shook his head. They needed to talk to Xannan, help him, not knock him out again.

"So the creation disappears when you lose focus, I see." Celena tapped a finger against her arm, lips twisted and brows scrunched as they always were when she spoke with the dragons. Granted, the changing color of her eyes gave away when she used her ability as well. "Distraction or unconsciousness?"

"The latter," Xannan gritted out.

The moment Gailin met his brother's gaze, he regretted it. The man's anger radiated from him. Or frustration. Gailin struggled to determine what his brother felt in that moment. Or how he himself felt about his brother's ability to conjure that which no longer lived.

"The head wound," Xannan spoke over his shoulder, addressing Arjun. "You did heal what was caused by the drokos but couldn't counteract me using my . . . this magic?"

"That would be an accurate assessment now." Arjun shifted his stance, and Xannan turned away.

"We all have questions." Gailin flinched at his brother's glare. "But we don't have to answer them when the snowflakes falling on our clothes grow thicker with each breath." He gestured at the meeting house. "A warm meal, a normal conversation—"

"Normal?" Xannan guffawed. "Nothing about this past month has been normal! And now—"

Mikhael's form reappeared. Though Xannan wavered, he maintained his balance, one hand gripping the hilt of his sword like a lifeline. More figures appeared around Mikhael. Soldiers. Orda'anians who'd lost their lives fighting to protect the fledgling country their father claimed was in danger because of their abilities.

Five, twenty, thirty. Some more distinct than others. Older, younger, middle-aged, Gailin recognized many by name. Xannan faltered to one side, legs trembling with the obvious effort to remain upright. As one, the figures disappeared. All except Mikhael, whose features remained the most distinct.

"Told you this was worse," Edmund murmured next to Gailin, low enough that others couldn't hear. Though Gailin acknowledged his wariness of Xannan's newfound ability, he wasn't sure if it was his own emotions or those forced upon him.

When Gailin stepped closer to his brother, Xannan tensed, hands flexing. The shadowlike form of Mikhael flickered, winking out of existence as Xannan stumbled. Gailin caught him, lending support with a grimace as he met the studious stares of the three elves. "The goal in coming outside was for *me* to speak with Xannan, not for you all to bombard him." He shook his head, failing to quell the surge of anger climbing his insides. "I think we have enough answers, for now." Frowning at the weight Xannan relinquished to him, Gailin glanced over his shoulder and told Edmund, "Make sure everything's ready for us to return home in the morning."

Gailin stepped forward, pausing when Eonar held up a hand and said, "I'm not sure—"

"None of you are ever sure!" Gailin shouted. "We've been away from home for a while and I, for one, am tired of being here. And if I'm tired of it, Xannan must be beyond frustrated."

His brother tensed again but said nothing.

"Fine." Eonar's red eyes which rarely changed hue flickered between Gailin and Xannan. "I'll return to Cantadad with you."

***

While Xannan sat on the bed and stared at the floor, Gailin paced the room the elves had offered. He should say something, anything, yet no words seemed appropriate to convey exactly what he thought or felt.

The bed creaked beneath Xannan's weight, and Gailin paused. A single exchange, enough for Gailin to know his brother didn't want to speak but would. With every year, Xannan gained more of the commanding presence expected of him as the crown prince. That fleeting thought surged again, the one Gailin pushed down and pretended had never occurred before. Foolish to even consider the implications of what it could mean.

"I can conjure the dead," Xannan croaked, voice dry and monotone. He lay on the bed, one leg dangling off the edge, the other foot planted so his knee jutted up and placed an arm across his face. "What in the Blazes am I supposed to do with that?"

Gailin grunted and resumed his pacing. "Learn other perspectives." He rubbed his temples with one hand and shook his head. "Think of the truths you could learn."

"If I can make them speak," Xannan mumbled into his arm. "My head is still spinning."

"Or the room appears to be or you would be—ow!" Gailin flinched and rubbed his arm where a small book had hit him. "Guess the spinning doesn't affect your aim."

A hint of a smirk appeared as Xannan lifted to his elbows and breathed slowly through his nostrils. "It's like what used to happen with you, isn't it?"

"Appears that way," Gailin murmured as he retrieved the book and paced again. "I'm to the point I no longer know what questions would even be worth asking since the moment we achieve one answer, a dozen more questions arise."

"So we break it down." Xannan squeezed his eyes shut and lowered his back to the bed, forearm covering his face again. "What about your visions? The ones you've been lying to Father about for how many years now?"

Though tempted to toss the book back at his brother, Gailin resisted. If Xannan's head truly hurt as much as it appeared, striking his brother with a book would accomplish nothing. "What about them? Quick flashes, nothing concrete."

"Dizziness? Loss of consciousness?" Another controlled breath. "Blazes, why would using our abilities cause such physical pain? My head feels like a thousand daggers are boring into it at once."

"I could get—"

"I really don't want any of those elves in here right now. Spinning room or no, one of them *will* get a broken bone. Or more." Xannan peeked at Gailin from beneath his arm. "And they couldn't help it the first time so no point in trying."

"At least take something to help you sleep?"

Xannan laughed, soft, low, and short. "How, precisely, do you feel about these elves, Gailin? You discuss how you feel about other enemies but never say anything about these three."

"That's an . . . odd question to ask." Gailin replaced the book in its spot on the bedside table, where he'd left it the night before. The pages were filled with his handwriting, detailing events of the past several weeks. The battle, Xannan's ability, everything Gailin learned or thought he recorded in those pages. "I've honestly never thought about it. Had no reason to wonder."

"So if we picked one to return home with us. . ." Xannan resumed a seated position, grimacing and turning pale as though he might be sick.

"Celena," Gailin said and, at Xannan's arched brow, added, "She's the quickest to speak her mind and the one you're least likely to punch in the face."

With a half chuckle, Xannan pushed himself to standing. "Valid point." He placed both hands on his hips, nose and brows scrunched as his gaze darted from the door to Gailin and back again. "Tell Eonar she's coming instead of him." Another quick glance, an audible swallow, and Xannan took a hesitant step toward the door. "And hopefully I don't bring these things to life in my sleep."

"Hopefully." Gailin shuffled forward, lifting both hands in placation at his brother's angry glare. "I'll make sure Edmund has everything ready to leave first thing in the morning. Or should we plan on breakfast first?"

"Eat on the way." Xannan opened the door and gripped the frame. "I'm sick of this place and its bland, disgusting food."

15

Sunlight made the blanket of snow covering the ground shimmer, and though it shone boldly, it offered no warmth. Xannan shifted his shoulders, trying to focus on something other than what he had managed the previous day. Wind whistled around them, seeping through his coat and swirling his shoulder-length blond hair, sometimes strongly enough he worried the gusts could knock him from his mount.

As requested, Gailin and Edmund had made sure everything was ready for them to leave first thing that morning. Including a grumpier than usual Celena who continuously searched the skies. She hadn't taken kindly to being dragged along with them.

Xannan nudged his mount closer to the elf-woman. "Is Magna following us?"

"Close enough to be of assistance if need be." Celena held the back of her hand to her mouth as she yawned. "Magna dislikes being away from home but fears what you using this new aspect of your gift will attract. She placed protection around Violet Grove so the droki cannot enter." Celena squinted at the sky, shook her head, and sighed. "No other droki have been sighted since the one which attacked you."

"Good," Xannan resituated himself in his saddle, grip briefly tightening on the reins. "I really hate the droki."

"You hate everything," Celena retorted.

"I second that statement," Gailin said as he guided his mount to ride alongside Celena opposite Xannan.

Several paces ahead, Edmund maintained the lead, observant of their surroundings with the occasional shiver. For the most part, open plains surrounded them, with the sporadic sparse tree-lines whose bare limbs would offer minimal cover. Though he hated the cold, Xannan preferred traveling during the winter months since the land offered fewer places for enemies to hide.

"I don't hate everything," Xannan said with a sidelong glance at both the elf and Gailin. "Just things which are frustrating and cause problems."

"Which is many things." Gailin rubbed the back of his neck. "I'm surprised you haven't complained about the cold yet."

"I've been distracted."

"Do you two want to ask me questions or talk to one another?" Celena swiveled her head back and forth, brows lifted.

Xannan shrugged, Gailin pressed his lips together, and Celena nudged her mount forward with an annoyed harrumph.

"Distracted?" Gailin asked as their mounts moved closer together. "With what you managed to accomplish yesterday?"

"It's more than that." Xannan surveyed the land around them, glancing over his shoulder. Based on the grayness of the approaching clouds, several more layers of the powdery nonsense that had managed to find its way inside his gloves and down the back of his shirt would fall soon. "Anna has almost everything ready for the wedding, which both excites and frightens me."

"Frightens?"

After switching the reins to his other hand, Xannan nodded. "The closer it gets, the more I think about the commitment I've asked Anna to make not just to me, but to the country."

"Logical," Gailin murmured, falling into his common pensive silence that sometimes made Xannan's hair stand on end.

The interim was his to view the plains. Edmund remained ahead, pointedly avoiding looking at Celena. The thought made Xannan smirk and then frown as he remembered how Mikhael reacted to the elf-woman in the same manner. *Had* reacted, Xannan reminded himself.

Clearing his throat, Xannan asked, "How was your welcome home parade?"

Gailin's grunt and sad shake of his head made Xannan raise his brow. "No parade." Gailin's shoulders slumped. "No commendations other than an argument."

Before he could stop it, Xannan's brows climbed further. He'd always thought Gailin and their father understood each other, that they got along. "You argued with Father?"

"To be honest, I don't remember most of it. Pretty sure a shattered wine glass may have been involved at some point." Gailin shifted in his saddle, and Xannan's jaw slacked at his brother's admission. While Xannan was often quick to anger, Gailin always seemed resolute and calm, but apparently even he had a limit. Sighing, Gailin added, "Father claims additional threats have been made. Mostly from Alkaan."

"We can handle them. Obviously."

Gailin grimaced. "Father's worried your marriage to Anna will make relations with Alkaan worse, not better. And he fears for our safety."

"But she's—"

"I presented the same argument, Xannan."

When Gailin's green eyes, which were several shades darker than Xannan's own, met his, Xannan recoiled. If he could read the fear on his brother's face, then it had to be bad. A series of unfortunate situations rose to the surface of his mind, each more depressing than the last. For as long as Xannan could recall, they'd had to fight to keep what their father had created. Without him and Gailin protecting their borders, Orda'an would have fallen long ago. But if more than one country attacked simultaneously, they'd have a difficult time fending off their foes. Whatever his brother feared, the emotion seemed to be securing itself in Gailin's visage.

"What do you fear?" He hadn't meant to say anything, but Xannan's words hovered in the air between them. "More droki? Someone else's death? Me injured again?" Each of Xannan's questions made Gailin's grimace deepen. When his brother's gaze flicked toward Edmund and back, Xannan added, "You can tell me, you know?"

Gailin sighed and tilted his head to the sky. Following his brother's movement, Xannan noticed the first flurries drifting through the air, almost as if they'd always been hovering around them rather than slowly falling from the sky. Gailin whispered, a soft breath, "You see me as a tool too, don't you?"

"That's not—I wasn't—" Xannan gritted his teeth, jaw clenching. "Blazes, Gailin, you can't keep all of that bottled up inside and you know it." Xannan's mount neighed and pranced to the side, but Xannan maneuvered the horse back to ride alongside his brother. "We're brothers, not a prince and his soldier."

"Aren't we though?" Gailin pulled his mount to a halt and leaned forward to rest his hands on the pommel. "Once you're crowned, I'll be placed in command of the army." He waved a dismissive hand when Xannan attempted to speak. "Maybe you'll be able to create a few treaties to stop the seemingly never-ending need to attack one another. And yet, I fear even that thought." After fishing for his water flask, Gailin took a long sip. "I cannot explain what it is I fear, other than that the emotion exists. It's accompanied with a flash of flame. A roaring fire that grows in intensity each time the vision forces itself into my mind."

"Droki or dragon?"

"Droki don't have flame," Celena commented.

"Blazes, Celena!" Gailin regained his balance atop his mount, but the elf only smirked.

"What else was in your vision?" She cocked her head, red irises churning in a way Xannan knew had to be her communicating with Magna. Or any dragon.

Gailin shrugged. "Nothing more than the flame."

Another set of hooves approached, much louder than Celena's mount had been, and Edmund signed a quick series of signals. Someone, likely Alkaanians angry after Gailin's victory, lay in wait up ahead. Several more silent exchanges occurred, confirming the number of enemy soldiers and how far, as well as their thoughts on what the weather would do in the next few hours. Celena remained silent in her observation, lips pursed as she watched Gailin and Edmund communicate with quick flashes of their hands, accompanied by Xannan's occasional interjection.

Once they resumed their slow plodding walk along the path—Xannan riding alongside Celena with Gailin and Edmund taking the lead—Xannan said, "Would be nice if Magna could give us a dose of her flame and annihilate them."

"I'm sure you'd appreciate that, but she's returned home for now. Well, almost home. She's checking the magical boundary at the cliffs again."

"Again? Is she worried something will get in?"

"Or out." Celena shrugged. "I'm not at liberty to say more until Magna deems otherwise."

"Not at liberty?" Xannan repeated slowly, smirking and shaking his head. "Didn't realize you followed any orders other than your own."

"Mostly. Technically I could tell you, but it will be of little use to you other than to know Magna is also strengthening what she used to make the droki dissipate. She's been trying to annihilate them."

"Good. I'd be happy to kill them all myself."

An amused grunt came from the elf, followed by a sharp intake of breath when Edmund and Gailin halted their mounts. Movements barely visible over his shoulder, Gailin signaled where the enemy soldiers were and which he and Edmund would take. Xannan nudged his mount closer to Celena's and whispered, "Time to use those knife skills of yours Arjun's always threatening me with."

"I'd prefer to observe your famed swordsmanship." Celena folded her arms and lifted a brow. "Or was that exaggerated?"

Xannan pulled his blade from its scabbard. "Praeteritum is what you call it, yes?"

She nodded. "A pathway to the past."

He grunted and dismounted, vaguely acknowledging the distant clashing of blades as Gailin and Edmund engaged others. True to her words, Celena remained mounted, and when he turned his back to her and approached a nearby tree line, Xannan could feel the pinpricks caused by her observation of him. Jaw clenched, he rotated his sword and lifted his arms.

"Here to destroy Orda'an's future?" He heard the shifting footsteps, the barely audible whispers, the branches cracking, the snow crunching, as those he spoke to contemplated what to do. Xannan smirked. "I'm sure you've heard what happens to those who attempt to take what is ours. Go ahead, try and prove us wrong."

At the whistle of an arrow, he sidestepped while swishing his sword to knock aside the next projectile, wincing with a mental reminder to not overexert himself.

Memories attempted to dredge to the surface, reminders of how his last high stakes fight had ended with him unconscious and severely wounded. He gripped the sword tighter, thankful the chill air helped cool his clammy palms, and focused on the task at hand.

Four men wearing the dull Alkaanian brown hid within the nearby tree line. Sword, twin daggers, spear, and a bow. *Archer first, then daggers, followed by spear, and leave sword for the last.*

16

An idea tickled, but Xannan chose to ignore it. Based on recent events, that attempt would end poorly. Xannan reached inside his vest and retrieved a dagger, hoping his aim with his nondominant hand wouldn't falter.

He approached the tree line, visualizing where his weapon would find purchase in the archer's frame. As the archer craned around the tree and aimed his bow, Xannan released his dagger, allowing himself a small smile when it sank into the center of the man's neck. The archer stumbled backward, dropped his bow, and grasped at the small weapon. Based on the amount of blood, Xannan knew the archer would no longer present an issue.

The spear and dagger-wielder, however, had different types of projectiles. Snow crunched softly beneath their shifting feet. Xannan paused several paces away from the trees where they hid. Puffs of air gave away their positions. He lifted his free hand, readying a phrase to sign, but lowered his arm when he remembered no one stood at his side.

"But he could," Xannan whispered to himself.

He visualized his friend. Sword drawn, eager grin, Mikhael would take the spear-wielder and would have already felled the man with two daggers. Xannan clenched his hand into a fist and mentally shattered the image. Since he had no desire to prolong this fight, or knock himself unconscious by recreating a man no longer alive, Xannan stalked forward, leaning away from an errantly thrown dagger.

Weapon raised, the spear-wielder ran toward him. Xannan smirked when the Alkaanian tripped on an uprooted branch hidden beneath a mound of snow. A stream of angry curses indicated the man had hurt himself, so Xannan focused his attention on the final two opponents.

Behind him, the clash of swords grew distant. He approached the dagger-wielder, torn between a grimace and a smirk with how much the man's arm trembled. Even the daggers themselves shook. Perhaps the soldier's obvious nerves were due to the cold winds whipping through the plains, or because of Xannan's "famed swordsmanship" as Celena had called it. Either way, he almost felt guilty ending this Alkaanian's life.

Xannan lifted his sword to strike, pressing his lips together at the roiling black clouds streaming from tip to hilt of the weapon which had molded itself to him. The blade yearned for him, and he for it.

An Alkaanian sword flashed in the sunlight with a series of fancy forms Xannan's father had learned, but he'd never quite understood their purpose. All the intricate moves served to accomplish was to tire one's arm more quickly than necessary, and most moves were simple to sidestep or back away from. When the Alkaanian's sword finally reached for him, Xannan twisted away from the motion and struck his weapon into his opponent's side. The tough leather coat prevented Xannan's sword from delivering a dire wound, and he grimaced when the Alkaanian smirked.

Surrounded by three opponents since the spear-wielder had regained his bearings and approached, Xannan lashed out at the nervous one first. Disarmed and shaking like a leaf caught in a breeze, the Alkaanian ran. With two others in his way, Xannan had no choice but to allow it.

"Sword and spear," he grumbled. "Interesting odds."

Neither opponent spoke, the tips of their weapons approaching from opposite sides at the same time. Xannan dropped to a knee and swiped below the swordsman's abdomen, across his thighs where the thick leather was absent. The Alkaanian gasped and collapsed while one leg spurted an insane amount of blood. Xannan held his sword at his side, the tip facing behind him as the blood seeped into the white powdery blanket of snow.

Cold metal pressed against Xannan's neck sent a chill down his spine.

"Your country will not thrive," the remaining Alkaanian said in a deep, thick drawl indicating he had been raised in the far northern lands, near the border that supposedly not even the dragons dared to pass. He pressed the tip of his spear against the back of Xannan's neck with enough force that Xannan knew the man would impale him soon. But, as many opponents who almost bested him tended to do, this man took the opportunity to gloat. "We will not—"

Xannan shoved his sword backward, reveling in the satisfying give of skin as he pierced the last opponent through his stomach. After twisting his sword, Xannan tugged it free, standing to avoid the Alkaanian falling on top of him.

Though he believed the archer long dead, he checked the body to confirm and retrieved his favored dagger. Satisfied none would rise to attempt to attack him again, Xannan returned to his mount beside Celena's, finding both comfort and annoyance in the absent sounds of weapons clashing. The elf stood beside her mare, and Xannan motioned at her singular bloodied knife.

"Took care of the runner." She nodded at the lifeless frame near the barely visible dirt path. Amusement danced across her visage as she cleaned the blade and waved it at the three he had killed. "I expected more from you, based on the stories."

"Out of practice." He retrieved a cloth from his saddlebag and cleaned his sword, revealing the roving clouds. Their movement was more consistent now, less erratic than it had been when he'd thought of Mikhael fighting alongside him.

Xannan cleaned the dagger he'd retrieved from the felled archer, tossed the cloth aside, and swung into the saddle of his dappled gray mount. His brother and Edmund approached, mounted with weapons sheathed.

Gailin pulled his mount to a halt with a face that made him look etched from black storm clouds. "They knew I'd been sent to Violet Grove."

"Or followed us," Edmund grumbled as he shifted his shoulders to resituate his coat. "Though I saw no one."

"Nor did I." Gailin met Xannan's gaze, a muscle in his jaw ticking. "We have to tell Father."

"The more who know there's a spy, the quicker he learns and disappears." Xannan gripped the reins with both hands, wishing it was warm enough to remove his gloves. And his heavy fur coat. "If this is the same one who led us to Falsumbra, then we need to arrest and question him."

"And that's Father's—"

"I have almost as much authority as Father does." Xannan glared at both Gailin and Edmund. The latter lowered his gaze, but Gailin met Xannan's stare with equal ferocity.

"Almost." Gailin ran a gloved hand along his head and winced. "Father's experienced this before. We should at least seek his counsel."

"So he can berate us for not doing this"—Xannan gestured at the dead soldiers surrounding them—"his way?" He shook his head. "In two months, I'll be of age to receive the crown, and we'll find a way to get these targets off our backs."

Edmund grunted, and his cheeks reddened when he glanced up at Xannan. "Apologies, Your Highness, but you and your brother will always be targets. As will your future families. Thought you knew that by now."

"We can change our future." Xannan shifted his grip on the reins and almost asked Gailin about their future until he remembered doing so would make his brother feel like no more than a tool.

"I really hope that's true," Gailin whispered. He leaned forward in his saddle, patting his mount's neck. "I keep having that same vision, which could mean we haven't done the right things to change it yet." He shook his head and turned his horse to continue down the path.

Sighing, Xannan followed suit, surprised his brother hadn't insisted they bury their enemies as he usually did.

***

Xannan paused outside the entrance to the dining hall. The remainder of their journey home to Cantadad had been uneventful, if he didn't include the frustrations of the cold. He tugged at his collar with a sidelong glance at Gailin.

"We're not telling Father what I can do." Xannan pulled on each sleeve and tied his shoulder-length blond hair back with a small string. "We returned out of concern about finding the spy when Alkaanians were spotted near Violet Grove, agreed?"

Gailin lifted a brow. "I dislike lying to Father. And especially to Mother."

"But it's not a lie," Xannan said with a wink. "It's an omission of a *part* of the truth."

He pushed the door open, smiling when Anna rose from her seat to greet him. Before she moved, Seth cleared his throat and motioned at the empty chairs to either side of where he sat at the head of the table. Resuming her seat beside their mother, Anna was tight-lipped.

Between cleaning off the grime of travel and caring for his mount—a rare distraction he needed since Mikhael wasn't there to talk through what he did and did not know about the spy—Xannan hadn't been able to speak with Anna for more than a few moments.

Opposite Anna and at their mother's left sat Ella. Gailin whispered something to her as he took his seat that made Ella almost choke on her sip of wine.

"My last communication from Eonar claimed you likely had months to go before understanding what, precisely, happened at Falsumbra." Seth dabbed his mouth with a napkin, hiding both hands below the table when a slight tremor appeared. "And yet, a week later, you are home and the Elder Elf did not escort you. Do explain."

"Seth, dear," their mother, Dana, said from across the table in a veiled tone of warning only she would be allowed to have with Seth. "I think we should be grateful to have our whole family home, don't you?" She lifted her glass, a slight twinkle of pride masked by worry alight in her dark eyes. "To your safe return, my sons. May you always return home whole."

With a slight tilt of his head, Seth lifted his glass and drank.

"We were worried—" Xannan began at the same time his father said, "Where is Eonar?"

Xannan scowled and stabbed his fork into the slab of meat covering half his plate. He sawed at it, methodically moving the knife back and forth as he lifted his gaze to his father's. "Eonar remained at Violet Grove." With a lift of his chin toward Gailin, Xannan added, "We prefer Celena's company to the crotchety elf. Though, based on how quickly she left here, can't say she thinks the same of our company."

"Xannan, careful how you speak of your elders," his mother warned. A warning accompanied by Anna resting a hand on his forearm and searching his gaze.

Xannan mouthed "later." He bit off a chunk of meat from his fork and spoke around the bite. "Alkaanians knew we were in Violet Grove."

"Still think your friend Edmund is innocent, Gailin?" Seth reached for his cup of wine and frowned as Xannan stuffed another bite into his mouth. "I may need to revise his position in the army."

"Edmund is loyal. And if you wanted to revise his position, you should have done so before allowing him to choose Mikhael's replacement."

Though he tried to stop the reaction, Xannan stiffened at the mention of filling Mikhael's position. After honoring those who'd lost their lives, Edmund had settled into reviewing the lieutenant-captains' accolades. He'd even asked Xannan for a recommendation, but Xannan couldn't give one.

Xannan met his brother's gaze and glanced away when Gailin added, "If Edmund is the spy, then he's killed many of his friends to remain close to me." Gailin twirled his fork in one hand and had yet to touch the meal before him. "It could be anyone who fought at Falsumbra. Any who heard what happened—"

"Any who helped annihilate the Alkaanian battalion there?" Xannan asked, washing down the meat with half a cup of wine. Though it was a terrible idea to consume too much wine too soon while at dinner with his parents, he couldn't help but enjoy the fine cuisine after weeks of the bland nonsense the elves considered food. Sustenance, yes; enjoyable, no.

"True. Several heard my orders." Gailin's gaze grew distant, eyes darting about the room. "But only a handful upon my return knew where Edmund and I were headed." He gave Xannan a pitying glance. "And Edmund and I spent most of the time at Violet Grove together. Or making sure you didn't set anything on fire."

In his periphery, Xannan saw his mother's angry glare and raised a hand to halt her admonishment before it began. "I only *considered* setting things on fire. I wouldn't actually do so." Xannan downed the remainder of the wine and motioned for more, frowning when his father signaled the servant away from the table. Standing, Xannan took his cup and fetched the decanter of wine himself, pouring as he said, "Solomon and Ishmael should be questioned."

When silence greeted his words, Xannan sighed and swirled the cup of wine, inhaling appreciatively and wishing the elves could at the very least make a decent drink to enjoy. "Aside from Edmund, they were the only two who knew for certain that Gailin and I were at Violet Grove. Since Edmund remained with us, he could not have orchestrated the ambush; therefore, question Solomon and Ishmael."

Seth snapped, and a guard by the door approached the table. After a lengthy whisper to the guard, Seth motioned him away and shifted his plate, allowing enough space to rest his clasped hands on the table. He pinned Xannan with a stare that made his insides plummet. "Do you have magic of your own, son?"

A muscle ticked in Xannan's jaw, and he avoided glancing at Gailin as he said, "No. What all reported at Falsumbra was due to exhaustion after the journey."

An interminable silence stretched, broken by the quiet scrapings of cutlery against platters as the women continued eating. Xannan resumed his seat at the table, chewing thoughtfully on one bite after another with brief glances at his brother and father. Where Gailin emanated confusion, his father radiated tension.

"Would it be so bad, Father?" Xannan asked after the servants gathered the plates and the table was clear of naught but their cups of wine, once more refilled. "We wield the magic of Praeteritum and Futurae. Certainly wielding magic of our own would be beneficial."

"Some might consider it so." Seth stood, knuckles pressing against the table. Following his father's arm, Xannan noted the visible scars, the evidence of the life he'd not known that his father had once endured. "Others would kill you for it." The tremor of the man's arms began again, and Seth clenched his fists tighter as though that could stop it. "The Orda'anian nobles which support me as king, and therefore you as my heir, are of the latter group."

Xannan drummed his fingers along the side of his wine cup, his nails creating a soft ringing reverberation. "And if we did have magic of our own?"

"Though we cannot remove the connection the weapons formed to you and Gailin, there are methods by which the Izari Tribe of elves could assist in removing one's innate magic." Seth gestured at the table. "Maintain caution but for tonight, enjoy the wine, my sons, and celebrate your continued success at protecting our noble country."

Once the doors closed behind their parents, Anna blurted out, "You lied to His Majesty. Again. How does he not know when you lie to him?"

Xannan paused the motion of lifting the glass to his mouth, brows furrowing in the reflection he saw in the liquid. He shook his head, took a sip, and set the cup down forcefully enough that liquid sloshed over the side. "Perhaps you're better at reading my expressions than Father is." After tugging his hair free, he stood and made an elaborate bow, holding out his hand for Anna. "Forget the lies. Forget about the spy." Xannan snapped several times and beckoned one of the servants. "Musicians. And desserts. As many as you can find."

The servant bowed, and though Anna tried to frown, she couldn't stop the smile from overtaking her disapproval. "Dancing?"

"To distract us all," Ella said. Her chair scraped as she pushed away from the table and stood, crossing her arms and mirroring Gailin's expression in a way that made Xannan laugh.

"Oh come now, show us these exquisite dresses that"—Xannan twirled Anna around and whistled softly as the light blue skirts spread in a wide circle. He followed the skirts up to where they accentuated her waist and chest—"will definitely stop my heart before any blade will." Tugging her closer to him, he tucked several wayward strands of her black hair behind her ear and whispered, "You, my dearest Anna, are more stunning than a sunrise on the ocean's horizon."

Grasping the solid black jacket which had been the only clothing option in his room upon returning home, Anna pulled him close, halting the motion before their lips met. "And you, my insatiable prince, are almost drunk."

"You try living with the elves for two months," he grumbled and reached for his glass, which Anna grabbed from the table before he could. "That only worked because you were closer."

"Magic?" Anna asked, sipping from the glass she had stolen. "Aside from the sword?"

The door opened to a stream of servants carrying platters of sweets, followed by a smattering of instruments.

"No dancing . . . yet," Anna released her hold of his jacket and straightened the bodice of her dress, but her gaze followed the musicians. "I knew you lied because I saw the look on Gailin's face."

At his name, Gailin jolted from where he and Ella had been speaking softly and squinted at Anna before shifting his attention to Xannan. "You might as well tell them." His gaze raked over the influx of servants. "Perhaps with fewer ears to listen, though."

"First, we dance." Xannan grasped Anna's hand, pulling her toward the open space while plucking a small cake from a platter. "And I eat something with flavor."

An hour passed, offering enough time for the initial fuzziness of several glasses of wine to wear off. And enough time for him to thoroughly appreciate how well Anna's sky-blue dress fitted her person and demeanor. It matched her laugh with its thin sleeves and ruffled skirts, accentuated her skin tone with its not too light and not too dark color, and still allowed her to move through each dance with an ease his mother's favored design, with its too tight bodice and too wide skirts, did not.

"It's getting late, Xannan," Anna whispered, resting her cheek on his chest. He held her there, savoring how comforting it was to hold her in his arms and the heat of her breath each time she exhaled. "We meet with the Tremaine family tomorrow, and I'd rather not be fighting the urge to nod off while Edmund's father drones on about specific trade routes again."

Resting his chin atop her head, he tensed and whispered back, "I have something to show you." He gripped both of her shoulders and leaned her back to gaze in those dark, captivating eyes. "Promise me you won't tell anyone. Especially not my parents."

She pursed her lips, studying him, and nodded. Though he expected to feel relief at her agreement, it felt like something took hold of his lungs and squeezed. As they weaved their way through quiet hallways, Xannan glanced back to note Gailin and Ella followed—Gailin with that permanent scowl and Ella with pinched brows.

"Xannan, this is—" Anna paused when he held a finger to his lips and led them into the abandoned bedroom. It was buried deep enough in the castle that few came to this hallway anymore. It made for the perfect hideout when he wanted to ensure his time alone with his betrothed wouldn't be interrupted.

Once all four were inside, Xannan leaned against the closed door and tilted his head back. He met his brother's furrowed stare and asked, "Do you think Magna still maintains Cantadad's barrier from the droki?"

"I certainly hope so," Gailin said, his words muffled as he dragged his hand down his face and shimmied his shoulders. "You could simply tell them, you know?"

"What would be the fun in that?"

At Gailin's grunt, Xannan smirked, but his muscles tensed, nerves steeling for the potential dizziness that creating his friend's form might bring. He pressed his palms against the wooden doorframe behind him, allowing the striations to ground him as he focused on the space between them. For a moment, he wondered if his sword hummed as well. Opposite Xannan, his brother watched with that too studious gaze. Arms crossed, lips pressed into a thin line, Gailin held Xannan's stare. He could feel both Anna's and Ella's gazes on him too. The weight of that expectation almost made him change his mind.

To his right, Anna tucked her black hair behind one ear. Xannan ignored his betrothed's raised eyebrow and swallowed.

"Xannan, will you please just—"

Mikhael's form flickered into existence between them, joined by a pulsing ache in the back of Xannan's head.

Pressing a hand to her stomach, Anna paled and whispered, "Impossible."

Ever logical, and never afraid to speak her mind, Ella added, "Mikhael is dead." She glanced at Gailin and back to the ghostly figure. "Gailin said Mikhael was among those he had to bury in Falsumbra."

Gailin stepped around Mikhael's figure, hand hovering almost close enough to touch. He frowned at Xannan, who remained leaning against the doorframe. Xannan straightened and briefly massaged his temples, tugging at the ends of his jacket and wishing he was wearing his preferred vest. Brushing his hair back, Xannan sniffed. It was his first time using magic in Cantadad, and he wanted to ensure Magna's protection of their home hadn't faltered. No faint scent of death meant, hopefully, no droki would come hunting for him.

Though Gailin was taking a closer interest in his ability than before, Xannan watched Anna's reaction. One hand pressed against her stomach, the other wrapped around her neck while her eyes flickered to and fro as her skin paled further with each breath.

"How?" Anna's arms dropped to her sides and stared at him. The look of shock coating her visage reminded Xannan of how he felt the first time Arjun claimed he could reanimate the dead, and he grunted, tipping his head back against the doorframe.

Xannan rounded his shoulders and focused on maintaining the figure. "All I know is this can happen." He clenched his fists at his sides. "But if I can speak with them, reanimate their physical forms—" Xannan met Anna's gaze. "Perhaps I could help you speak with your parents again. Or your friends."

Her growing shock disappeared into anger. "Parents and friends," she scoffed, "who left me to die in a droki attack?" Anna shook her head and approached Mikhael's figure. "I have no need of such a conversation with them." She hovered a hand above Mikhael's arm, flinching when she laid it on the figure that was somewhat solid. "This will become useful in overtaking Alkaan, won't it?"

17

Prior trips to the nearest beach along the Vadamon Sea hadn't required sneaking out in the middle of the night. Now, after multiple threats to their lives, both Gailin and his brother chose to leave at a different time than originally planned. As with any idea that seemed foolish and brilliant, this had been Xannan's plan. His brother was tired of the speeches, the talks, the plans, the preparations and wanted to escape to have a quiet moment without being surrounded by an entire battalion.

Gailin had agreed with one caveat—that he and Edmund would come along. His brother had hesitated to agree with Edmund's presence but acquiesced with Gailin's reminder that an extra pair of eyes would do more good than harm.

Even after riding for an hour with none in pursuit, Gailin continuously glanced around them. If it had just been himself, Xannan, and Edmund, perhaps his own anxiousness would have eased. But when Xannan requested a "quiet" moment, he meant time with Anna. Anna had then told Ella of the plan, and Ella demanded to come along as well. Since the two women remained close friends after Ella's parents became the castle staff's supervisors and spoke constantly, there was no way to change Xannan's initial plan with Anna so that Ella wouldn't know.

Idly, Gailin wondered if Xannan felt Mikhael's absence as starkly in this rendezvous as he had in others. The mentions of the late soldier's name had grown sparser over the past two weeks. As had Xannan's presence in the sparring rings. Others assumed Xannan was busy preparing for his nuptials and the slowly approaching coronation. Some deemed it illogical for their father to choose to relinquish his crown once his eldest turned twenty-one years of age; others supported their father's decision.

But Gailin knew too much pain hid within those practice rings. He noted Xannan's fading smiles after jokes, the additional hits others got in, and Xannan's terse comments to the soldiers. Where his brother disappeared to, Gailin wasn't sure. And he had no desire to repeat finding his brother and future sister-in-law partially clothed in an abandoned bedroom.

Gailin shook that memory from his mind and appraised those around him, grimacing. Mikhael's absence was felt more in these small groupings, especially since they'd appointed a new commander to Mikhael's battalion. Now it was Patrick's battalion. At least Solomon hadn't been promoted. Though Gailin was grateful for the soldier's medical assistance and sharpshooting skills, the man often spoke out of turn in a way that grated on both him and Xannan.

"Please don't make me say it," Ella said in a harsh whisper loud enough to be heard over the slow plod of the horses' hooves. "We made it away from the castle without notice and you said it would take them at least two hours after we left before they'd realize we're gone, yes?"

Gailin sighed and glanced over at her. "It's not this little jaunt that has me scowling."

"It's the entirety of our future," Edmund said, waving an arm with an extravagant motion and winking at Gailin. "She's right, sir, enjoy the moment."

With another wink, Edmund nudged his mount forward, saying something to Xannan and Anna that Gailin couldn't decipher as a gust of wind carried the words away. Based on Xannan's quick motion and inappropriate hand-sign, however, Gailin could make a decent guess what the soldier had said before spurring his mount to scout ahead again. Edmund had remained in constant movement forward and behind, checking to see if they were being followed and ensuring none lay in wait as they had on the journey home from Violet Grove.

"Do you ever think it odd"—Ella frowned and urged her mount closer to Gailin's—"that as princes of the kingdom, you have to make this much effort to enjoy a morning, maybe a day, on the beach?"

Gailin grasped Ella's reins and helped keep her mount closer. "It's not that we'd be told no, it's how many would have been instructed to come with us if we'd told Father." He attempted a smile that made Ella roll her eyes at him. "Or would you have rather traveled with another fifty soldiers?"

She whisked the reins away from his hand with a tsk, tapping his arm when he attempted to retrieve them again. "Xannan tells Anna more than you tell me." Ella straightened in her saddle. The wind tugged several of her blond locks free of the singular braid she wore while riding. "Discussions are failing and more war is coming?"

Gailin swallowed a silent curse. Castle workers really did hear everything. "Hopefully not full-scale war." He focused on his brother's back ahead of them, noting the added tension that hadn't dissipated since the aftermath of Falsumbra. "Xannan has a plan."

"So I've been told," Ella murmured, face wrinkling as the wind tugged free several more strands of her hair. "A proper trade agreement? His Majesty tried that once before."

"That was with King Leopold," Gailin acknowledged. "He and Father had a history. Leopold's son, Ephraim, has never met Father. We're aware none of our messengers have returned. Logical considering the damage we've done to their troops." Gailin grimaced, remembering his hand in that annihilation and how his future would likely involve the death of many more soldiers before his own end came. "Xannan wants to make them listen."

"Should be interesting to watch." She smirked at his shocked expression. "I know, I'm not coming along for that discussion." Ella returned her gaze forward, inhaling sharply as the open expanse of water became visible. Brown dirt dotted with the earliest twinges of springtime grass transitioned into the sinking granules of soft sand. As they led their mounts to a nearby tree line that Edmund had already inspected, the soldier trotted past them and behind once more.

"You know"—Ella frowned at the tie she'd done for the horse's reins, tugging against them to redo it—"you and your brother once said you would teach Anna and me how to wield weapons."

Gailin froze, hands stuck in the midst of creating a loose knot to keep his dappled stallion at the tree line. "I never want you to have a reason to run toward danger."

She harrumphed. "And what if danger runs toward me and none are around to assist?" Ella's visage darkened, and she folded her arms. "Unless you plan to send me back home and never see me again in order to *protect* me?"

He busied himself with the knot, focusing his attention on the motion of his hands while inwardly cursing Ella for being so incredibly intuitive. Her mind was quicker than a falling raindrop sometimes.

"I won't deny I've thought about it," he whispered as he tested both his knot and the one she'd done, smiling softly at how it stayed firm. Gailin grabbed the pack of food he'd prepared for them for the day and wrapped his arm around Ella's shoulder. "But I'm pretty sure you'd dig your heels deeper in the mud than a mule would."

Ella laughed, a harmonious sound that had been the first thing he'd ever noticed about her. Per his mother's instructions, he'd always treated the castle workers well. So when Ella began assisting her mother, it was only logical for him to introduce himself. That laugh. Gailin would do anything to hear it time and time again.

She patted his arm, chuckling. "I'm not the mule in this pairing, my love."

She swished her skirts, tossing him one of those mischievous grins of hers before climbing the small hill that blocked their view of the ocean when not mounted. After tugging each of their knots once more, Gailin followed, smiling at how Ella's laughter created a perfect addition to the waves lapping against the shore. Turtles, recently hatched, scurried toward the water. While Ella and Anna followed the small animals, Xannan and Gailin found a clear area of the sand and spread out one of the blankets Xannan had been tasked with bringing.

Pouring each of them a glass of water, Gailin peered through his cup at his brother. "Didn't realize you were so desperate for a quiet moment like this."

"You weren't?" Xannan downed his glass and leaned back on his elbows, legs crossed at the ankles and loose blond hair swaying in the breeze. Gailin had chosen to keep his hair tucked tight at the nape of his neck with a string; he hated when the strands invaded his vision.

Gailin sipped his water and smiled. Both Ella and Anna waded through the high tide, skirts lifted and shoes abandoned. "You've been telling Anna your plans."

"I thought we agreed not to discuss politics on this outing."

"Anna tells Ella." Gailin tapped a finger against his glass. "And then she worries about me even more than usual."

"Get used to it," Xannan mumbled as he lowered to his back and interlaced his hands behind his head, making his arms look like wings. "I didn't want to tell Anna, but I swear she's better at getting me to speak than Arjun is, and she has no magic like he does."

Chuckling, Gailin finished his glass and filled the next two as Ella and Anna retrieved their shoes. "That's because you care about Anna more."

"I would hope so."

"Hope what?" Anna asked as she sat cross-legged near Xannan's head. She accepted the cup Gailin offered her, threading her fingers through Xannan's blond locks with the other.

Xannan smirked and gazed up at her, pure love etched across his face. "That I like you more than Arjun."

Laughing so hard she spilled her water in her lap and on Xannan's head, Anna controlled her breath long enough to say, "I would hope so, too."

His soon to be sister-in-law's laughter was contagious, and when Gailin met Ella's gaze, a familiar twinkle there made his smile widen. For one day, he decided, he could put aside the worry.

Ella grabbed the second blanket Xannan had left folded and jerked her head away from their current position. After a quick glance at the path they'd taken to confirm Edmund had not returned with a warning, Gailin stood and offered his hand. Ella placed her hand in his, and he pulled her to standing. When Gailin turned to his brother, he chuckled. Those two rarely wasted time in locking lips and almost ignoring their surroundings. The only indication Xannan knew they hadn't left was a wave of the man's hand, motioning them to find their own space.

Bag slung on his shoulder, Gailin gripped the strap with one hand and Ella's hand with the other. When he didn't hold his sword's hilt while walking, it alternated bumping against his side, then his thigh, and back again. He thought after five years of wearing the weapon, that motion would no longer annoy him. The rhythmic thuds reminded Gailin that even a quiet day on the beach could turn catastrophic.

Ella tugged him to a halt. "That's a hundred steps."

Close enough to be within shouting distance, far enough away to have a modicum of privacy. The roar of the waves crashing into the shore covered the thud of the bag as he dropped it to the sand and helped Ella lay the blanket neatly before they sat atop it.

"Sorry I didn't tell you more about our discussions with Father," Gailin said as he tried to shift his sword so it didn't dig into his side.

Ella released an exasperated sigh, leaned forward, and undid his sword belt. When he tried to protest, she laid a finger on his lips and nodded at where she'd placed the sword. "It's right there if you need it."

"I feel naked without it," he said around her finger.

She smirked. "I'd be quite content to make that a reality rather than a sensation." She replaced the weight of her finger with her lips, pressing against him until his back met the blanket. Straddled atop him, she began unbuttoning his coat.

"Ella, we—"

"Shush and kiss me." Ella tugged his coat free of his arms, and a chilled wind rolling off the ocean waves made his skin tingle. "Shove aside those emotions, like they taught you." She clasped his head in both of her hands, holding his gaze. "Threats don't scare me, not completely at least. Losing you does." Ella lowered her forehead to his, tapping his nose with hers as she whispered, "Take advantage of the quiet moments when you can."

Gailin did as she asked.

18

Smiles and laughs came easy when he and Anna lay on the blanket, reveling in the smooth cadence of the ocean's waves. The longer they lay there, the more concerned Xannan became that Edmund would shout they'd been followed. But the soldier's warning never came.

So they passed the day in blissful peace, enjoying each other's company. No different from some of their earliest quiet moments together, cautious questions turned into honest conversations. With Anna, there had been no expectation. He'd offered her a home, a place of safety, and in return, she'd given him an even calmer voice of reason than Mikhael once provided. With Anna, he could remember that he fought for much more than glory. He fought to protect those unable to protect themselves.

At Anna's urging, they had first snuck out to this beach together, barely two years past. Xannan lifted her hand, brushing his thumb over the ring he'd given her on this same beach several months ago. Lying on his side and propping up his head, he looked at Anna. She inhaled the scent of the ocean, eyes closed with a small smile gracing her lips.

"What are you thinking about?"

Anna's smile widened, and she met his gaze. "How nervous you were the last time we sat on this beach together."

"I was not—"

"Oh, don't try and deny it." Her dark eyes danced with amusement. "You can slay a hundred men in a day, but asking me one simple question made you"—Anna traced the path a lone bead of sweat had taken down his face with her long-nailed finger—"sweat."

Xannan lowered her hand from his face, grinning. "At least you said yes."

"I can't believe you thought I'd say anything else." Anna sat up and crossed her legs beneath her, tracing the scar running the length of his arm, and he grimaced. "I know," she whispered. "I was scared, too." The path of her hands left shivers behind. "Every time you leave for another skirmish, I fear the list of buried will include your name."

"I wasn't scared." Xannan sat up and grasped a fistful of sand, letting it slowly slip through his fingers. "I'm still angry it ever happened." He glanced in the direction his brother and Ella had gone, letting his attention linger long enough to confirm they were there. "Blazing spies."

"Too bad Arjun refuses to question them," Anna murmured, searching the bag and pulling out a flask of water. She studied him as she tipped it back. "Did you participate in—"

"Father didn't allow it." Xannan picked up another fistful of sand, releasing the entire batch into the wind. "But I spoke with both Solomon and Ishmael afterward."

She waited, tipping the flask over her lips once more, and Xannan debated how much she needed to know. Xannan also wasn't sure if either soldier now being held in the dungeon was telling the truth. Each claimed the other was the spy, refusing to name anyone else.

"I'll need to speak with them again." Xannan held out his hand for the flask, devouring a decent amount. "After reviewing the conversations I had with them. Alone."

"Do whatever it takes to keep you, to keep us safe." Anna leaned forward and kissed him. She shifted and sat beside him, wrapping her arms around his and whispering, "It's okay to admit you miss him."

He followed her gaze to the ocean. Unsure of what to say, Xannan rested his hand atop hers and watched the sun drift closer to the horizon. Once the sun touched the ocean's edge and emblazoned the dark blue water with a myriad of colors, Xannan figured it best they journey home, though he'd have preferred to remain in this day forever.

After collecting a discarded sock and an empty glass that had drifted along the sand with the ocean breeze, Anna said, "We should do this more often." She frowned for a moment and added with a smirk, "The more . . . enjoyable parts at least."

Xannan grunted and strapped his sword belt around his waist, grateful he'd had no reason to use it that day. "This took over a week of planning to pull off."

She shoved the two items into the bag and tugged at his vest before he could finish buttoning it. "And once you're king, you'll simply tell them what you wish to do."

"I'm afraid it's not that simple, Anna." He shifted his sword belt and shook out their blanket, wincing as sand tried to blind him.

"You forget to shake it away from you with the breeze *every* time." Anna smiled, set the bag down, and helped him fold the blanket. "And once you're king, you can make it that simple."

Xannan shoved the blanket in the bag and glanced in the direction his brother and Ella had gone, smirking at how disheveled they both appeared. "Let's worry about what I can and cannot do as the king of a country once I have that title."

They crested the sand dunes, carrying the supplies they'd gathered to where the horses remained tethered. Edmund leaned against a tree, tossing a dagger in the air and snatching it with the opposite hand, grinning. "No activity on this side of the dunes since we arrived." His grin widened, and Xannan glanced back and noted Gailin and Ella had also crested the hill. Edmund glanced between Xannan and his brother. "You all obviously had an excellent time on the beach."

Xannan rolled his eyes and hooked his bag to the saddle. He turned to offer Anna a hand to mount, but she was already in her saddle, guiding her mare into the path. He grinned up at her and said, "So capable." She winked and nudged her mount forward as Xannan turned toward Edmund. "Scout ahead. I'm sure Gailin can add if I'm right or wrong, but my guess is we'll get a welcoming party from Father long before we reach the gates."

After mounting, Xannan met his brother's gaze. Gailin sighed, shrugged, and mounted. The journey home continued quieter than the one to the beach. Chilled winter winds were diminished this close to the wide-spread Tenoan desert several days south, but the change in seasons only meant a change in the type of liquid falling from the sky. He was undecided which he preferred to travel in: snow or rain.

Edmund galloped back to them, pulling up short with a quick series of signs that Anna and Ella might have understood. While Xannan had never taught them to Anna, she was observant. And smart. Sometimes too smart. What Edmund shared made Xannan's jaw clench. No large welcoming party waited for them, just their father and his personal guards.

"Blazes," Xannan grumbled and glanced at Gailin again, seeing his despair mirrored in his brother's visage. The thought of speaking to their father shouldn't make him feel like a child, but it did.

When neither Xannan nor Gailin spoke, Edmund cleared his throat. "I can escort the ladies back home while you speak with His Majesty."

"That won't be necessary," Anna said as she urged her horse back into a walk. "This day was as much my idea as yours, Xannan. Besides, you're old enough to not need your father's permission to come and go as you please."

"Will you say the same to our future children?" Xannan surprised himself by asking the question aloud, but he motioned for an answer.

"Within reason, yes."

The thunder of several horses' hooves meeting hard dirt not yet soaked by the threatening rain clouds made the five of them halt their mounts.

"Let me do the talking," Gailin said as he weaved his mount through the others to be beside Xannan.

"Your last conversation with Father ended with a shattered plate, Gailin."

"Mine was an accident." Gailin swallowed, as though convincing himself the lie he'd just told was the truth. "Yours was intentional."

"We'll make a great pair, you and I, won't we?" Xannan's smirk faded at Gailin's grimace and the sudden flash of confusion his brother was quick to mask.

"What were you two thinking?" Their father's voice thundered over the pounding hooves, and his mount pranced around their small group. "Leaving in the dead of night, taking naught but *one* soldier with you, and risking their lives?" He motioned at Anna and

Ella in turn, while his deepening glower moved from one person to the next.

This wasn't their father speaking to them; it was the king of a country concerned about its future.

"Father—"

"I know this wasn't your idea, Gailin." Seth turned to Xannan.

Rather than shrink into himself as a part of him wished, Xannan straightened in his saddle. "My betrothed requested a quiet day on the beach, without fifty-some-odd soldiers roaming around us and eavesdropping to report back to you what they saw and heard."

"Don't blame your actions on others, son."

The lack of name stung more than Xannan wanted to admit.

"I'm not, Father. This was a joint plan Anna and I created. Between myself, Gailin, and Edmund, we could protect ourselves."

"Even if a troop of five hundred arrived? A thousand?" Seth moved his mount closer to Xannan's. "Your arrogance will be your undoing if you don't contain it, son."

"It's not arrogant to be confident, Father." He managed to keep his tone level, which was more than he could say for his vision or his trembling muscles as his grip on the reins tightened. It had been his hope they'd at least make it back to the castle before this happened. He hadn't anticipated their father coming this far out himself.

"Call it what you will, you need to think before you act."

Xannan craned his neck, pushing down the multitude of angry retorts eager to release themselves from the tip of his tongue. When a hand rested on his arm, he almost lashed out, until he recognized the quaint fingers.

"We did think, Your Majesty," Anna said with a slight dip of her head. "I wished for a day free of planning and believed Xannan needed a day to relax."

Despite Anna's calming hand on his arm, he tensed at her words, fearful of how his father would receive them.

Seth grunted. "Your mother thought you'd been kidnapped and wanted me to create a search party. But if I mobilize any troops right now, that spy we haven't ferreted out will report back to our enemies and then a thousand soldiers will be marching to our doorstep. If not more." The king's mount pranced to the side, and he guided the stallion with the reins, glaring at each brother in turn once more. "The issue isn't where you went, it was who you didn't tell."

"But—"

At Seth's raised hand, Xannan quieted, a muscle in his jaw ticking painfully. "The mantle of any crown does not come without hardship, Xannan."

"I understand that, Father." Xannan quickly appraised the guards flanking his father. Both had been in the army for over a decade. "Do you think the spy is not currently in the dungeons?"

"Where one spy exists, more follow," Seth grumbled. His scrutiny lasted longest on Edmund before sliding back to Xannan. "You may soon be of age to receive this crown, but I will not relinquish control to one who doesn't properly prepare for a day away. No one in the castle knew of your whereabouts. Finding you here was a hunch. I figured there was a reason you proposed to her on that beach."

When Xannan opened his mouth to speak, Seth raised a gloved hand, and Xannan clamped his lips shut.

"You have six months to prove your worth, son."

"Prove?" Xannan spat the question as his father turned the stallion away. His father's back stiffened, but Xannan could handle the man's anger. "Gailin and I have done more than prove our worth, *sire*. We have fought and killed. We have won battle after battle. *We* are the ones who have shown our worth. It's time you recognized such."

Seth didn't turn to face Xannan, back remaining stiff. "Prowess on the battlefield does not a leader make, Xannan." With that, their father kicked his stallion into a trot, flanked by the two guards.

"Well, no broken bones or dishes counts as a successful conversation, right, sirs?" Edmund asked with a plastered fake smile.

Jaw clenching, Xannan nudged his mount into a slow walk, glaring at his father's back shrinking into the distance.

Gailin matched his pace a few moments later. "Do you think Eonar or Celena told Father about what you can do?"

He shrugged. "Would it change anything?" Xannan glanced over his shoulder, ensuring Edmund followed at the rear of the group and turning around before either Anna or Ella could see his furrowed brows. "I could save a hundred cities from annihilation and he'd find something wrong with it."

"Or he's more angry because you *haven't* shared what you—we—learned?"

"He doesn't need to know." Xannan twisted in his saddle, trying to smell the air around them without sniffing. "And I have no plans to attempt that again right now."

Gailin leaned over and lowered his voice. "Droki?"

"None of us have been using magic; they'd have no reason to travel this far south."

"They?" At Xannan's nod, Gailin cursed. "Now we'll both get a lecture. Father always assumed droki would follow us because I can't control when I do or don't use my ability."

"Pretty sure your mind has been otherwise occupied for the better part of the day." If his brother blushed at the comment, Xannan didn't see. He was too busy studying the skies. The scent of the droki lingered, drifting in waves of increasing strength but tainted with the crisper scent of their much kinder kin. A swath of flame confirmed his suspicions, and the deathly scent of the droki dissipated almost as quickly as the fire.

"That would have been useful a few months back," Xannan murmured.

"We were busy then."

The elf-woman's voice should have surprised Xannan, but it didn't. Gailin, however, nearly fell off his horse. "Blazes, Celena, do you transport like a dragon does or just not touch the ground while you walk?"

Celena flipped Gailin a gesture that would have made Xannan laugh if she wasn't staring at him with eyes a deeper red than he'd ever seen. "It's taken us a while, but that was the last of the droki who managed to escape the prison Magna created for them. So long as she or one of her chosen survive, the droki will remain contained. Granted, there's the issue of power transference and—"

"The droki are gone?" Xannan interrupted, and she nodded. "Permanently?"

"Magna has many more years of life in her and wishes to spare humankind the terrible deaths wrought by her distant relatives. So long as she lives, the droki will no longer be a threat." Celena spoke in such a matter of fact tone that Xannan almost asked the woman to repeat what she had said. She canted her head, "What did you think has been keeping Magna busy since you got those swords?"

His chest emptied of air as he allowed the thought to settle. The poisonous fiends wouldn't attack him again; they wouldn't try to harm Anna, or Gailin, or Ella, or his parents, or any of his people. "We can use our abilities outside the castle and Violet Grove?"

"Correct." Celena nodded once and frowned. "Though Magna claims the many threads of magic have dissipated. Droki are thorough in their quest for sustenance."

"Thank you." Xannan almost nudged his mount forward but peered down at the elf instead. "Do you need a ride?"

"I have one." She winked and walked into a nearby field, leaving both Gailin and Xannan to shake their heads.

"She needs to wear a Blazing bell," Gailin muttered, gritting out a worse curse when he met Xannan's gaze. "What are you thinking now, Xannan?"

"Father wanted us to bring more protection." Xannan closed his eyes and breathed deeply, no different from how he'd practiced in his room over the past several weeks, where he knew a drokos would not come swooping down and attempt to consume whatever this magic was that he could use. The initial pain in his head dulled to a faint throb, harsh enough to be a nuisance but not to make him will the forms away yet. When he opened his eyes, an army of conjured soldiers stood before him. "And I can create an army."

"I don't know if the right response is Blazing incredible or—"

"Blazing insane," Edmund finished for him.

19

Gailin smoothed the collar of his solid black coat, clasped each cuff, and slowly buttoned it. With the first button, he recalled how their father had glowered at them, admonished with so few words, reminded him and Xannan that so many more lives were at stake than their own should something happen to them. At the second button he remembered each gentle caress of Ella's lips against his and how thorough she was in distracting him. A quick glance back at the bed confirmed she remained fast asleep, and as much as he'd prefer her distractions to a conversation with his father, he let her rest.

The third button clasped, he unlocked the mental boxes where he'd placed the surging emotions. Flames lingered at the edge of every thought, coating his vision in hazes of red and orange, ending in the charred black that fire always left behind.

Gailin swallowed the visual and acknowledged each emotion before mentally shoving it aside. Fear. Anger. Desire. Adoration. The anger was hardest to ignore. Anger at their father. Anger at both Solomon and Ishmael, both of whom refused to speak since being imprisoned and accused of treason.

As he did the fourth button, he froze. Same as before, the image reared, unmistakable. He shook the visual from his mind, tucking it away. The only way that would become a reality would involve more death surrounding him. Perhaps if he ignored it, then it wouldn't happen.

Gailin finished the last several buttons quickly and surveyed his room. Extravagant, spacious, with Ella asleep on the too-large bed where she'd curled up next to him the night before. A day on the beach, it turned out, could be exhausting.

He moved over, shifting her blond hair from her face. She stirred as he gently kissed her forehead, and he smiled. "I'll return soon, my love," he whispered when her eyes fluttered.

Ella gave him a sleepy nod, yawned, grasped the covers, and rolled over. For a moment, he soaked her in. They'd been together longer than Xannan and Anna, but Gailin feared taking that next step before his brother was wed and crowned would be rude of him. It wasn't stubbornness that kept the ring hiding in his desk drawer from Ella's fingers. He approached the desk, contemplating once again when would be the most appropriate time to ask the question.

His focus turned to the sword leaning against the desk. Sheathed, it appeared ordinary. But power emanated from it. Once Gailin removed the scabbard, a clear crystal with the deadliest edges of any blade would greet him. It seemed to throb in time with the emotions he sensed. The hilt, pommel, and guard had been designed by their father, engraved with the symbol which had become their family crest. Two dragons, each holding a sword, with a strange cloud in their midst. Ironic, considering the elves had brought one sword. And now the blades had latched to him and his brother, gifting them abilities that brought both hope and despair.

Gailin checked each button of his coat and reached for his sword, hand hovering above the pommel before grasping it, hoping the images wouldn't force their way to the surface. Two tried, the first overwhelming his vision with red flame before sunlight gleaming against a golden crown made his jaw clench.

Grimacing, he buckled the weapon around his waist and opened the door, glancing back at Ella with a sad smile. If she knew his father wanted another private meeting with him, she would advise against it. But he wanted to repair the damage done by their last conversation.

Walking through the breezeway, Gailin nodded at the servants beginning their days. The months spent waiting to spy on Ella going about her duties had allowed him to learn how much the castle servants did. Without them, this massive building his father had commissioned would barely function.

He glimpsed Ella's mother down the hall and felt his cheeks flush when the woman lifted a brow. Gailin tilted his head back down the hallway, and Ella's mother nodded and continued her tasks.

After a quick jaunt up the stairs and down a quieter hallway than the one below, Gailin knocked on the door to his father's study, making it a point not to cram his hands in his pockets, clench his fists, or cross his arms. Instead, he rested his hand on the sword, which made the flame-filled image surface as the door opened, and Gailin mumbled a soft curse.

"Your mother hates those words," Seth said while gesturing for Gailin to enter. "She'd never admit it, but she uses them as well. Usually in reference to her sons."

Gailin grunted and lowered to a chair. "I imagine you both curse in reference to more than Xannan and me." He shifted his sword and rubbed both hands along his thighs. "Any updates on locating the spy?"

Tapping the door shut with his boot, Seth tugged at his lapels and shook his head of cropped blond hair. "Both Solomon and Ishmael remain silent. I fear we may have to resort to torturing them for answers."

"We should remain above such means."

"And if neither of them are the most recent spy?"

"You said before, Father. Where one spy exists, there are more. Even if both Solomon and Ishmael are spies, there must be others." Gailin rubbed the back of his neck and almost closed his eyes. "As long as we lay claim to the lands from Falsumbra Forest to the Cliff of Lycene, we will have spies within our ranks."

"I'll speak with them again after our conversation. Alone." Seth moved to the small table near the door and lifted an empty glass, replacing it when Gailin shook his head. He wasn't thirsty, not for wine at least.

"So am I here for myself or my brother?" Once the words left his mouth, Gailin wanted to take them back. Part of the reason he'd come was to repair the rift growing between him and his father, which that question would not do.

"Both," Seth said as he sat in the chair next to the one Gailin occupied. "Eonar told me what Xannan managed in Violet Grove. I would like to know why neither of you shared this information and if this"—Seth frowned and waved a hand as though the word was wrong—"ability has increased since then."

Leaning forward to rest his forearms on his legs and clasp his hands together, Gailin modulated his tone and said, "What Xannan can or cannot do is his to share, not mine, Father. And it's wrong to question me on him when he's not even present."

Seth grunted and stood, opening a secondary door hidden near the study's fireplace. As Eonar and Arjun entered, Gailin's heart raced. Usually speaking with the elves did little to his emotions. Today it set them scrambling. Based on Arjun's apologetic expression, he'd been asked to come here for a specific reason. Like Gailin, the younger elf had an ability that defined him, making others see him for what he could do rather than who he was.

Gailin pressed his palms together to prevent himself from lashing out. He met Arjun's gaze again, jaw clenching when the elf looked away first. As Seth lowered into the seat next to Gailin, the two elves took the seats opposite them. Arjun sat directly across from Gailin, the glass bottles he always carried in the pockets of his billowing robes clinking together.

"You feared your brother's ability," Eonar said, pulling Gailin's attention to him. Unlike his son, Eonar's robes did not emit clinking sounds as he moved. Eonar sat on the edge of his seat, pale red eyes appraising Gailin as though the elf could read his mind. "Do you still?"

Gailin shrugged, squeezing his fingers. "I'm always worried about what Xannan might do." He spared a glance for his father, but Seth's face gave away nothing. "He's decisive, sometimes too quickly. And we've already established how his ability has changed in recent months." Gailin clenched his jaw, surveying those surrounding him. "Send for him so you can ask my brother directly if you're truly curious what he can do. I'm not sure he's even shared with me all he is now capable of, especially after—"

He halted, not wanting to mention how Xannan had breathed life into what had to have been a thousand soldiers. Maybe more. Xannan had barely wavered atop his saddle when he did, and though Gailin had wanted to feel shock or despair or something negative at the sight, all he'd truly felt was awe and the slight twinge of jealousy.

"Gailin, finish your thought." Seth motioned with his hand.

The visual of his father's hand before the roaring fireplace gave Gailin pause, especially as the image of naught but fire flooded his mind again. It was becoming more difficult to push away, meaning whatever would cause that image to come to fruition was nearing.

He stood, pausing at the door. "I'm more than a tool to use for answers, Father."

As Gailin grasped the door handle, his father said, "Eonar presented a solution." Seth's chair creaked with the sudden absence of weight. "It's evident Xannan's ability reaches beyond what the weapon itself gifted. We must contain it lest it consume him."

Each time Gailin spoke with his father, the man seemed older, as though each day withered his skin into dozens of ripples. That thought reminded Gailin of the ocean, of the quiet day he'd had on the sandy beach, Ella warm against his side as he traced patterns along her bare arms, laughing when the wind blew her hair into his face. Or his mouth.

He wanted more moments with the four of them. Picnics on the beach, their future children chasing birds, laughing with the unabated joy only children seemed to possess. Those were the moments he cherished. Not these. If only he could will himself into that future, away from the death and destruction that came with being royalty.

His grip on the door handle didn't loosen, but he didn't open the door.

Seth's voice broke the silence. "I would like you to retrieve a crystal which can store magic."

The flame-filled image reared its ugly head and Gailin almost lifted a hand to his temple. But if he did, his father might know he'd seen something. Instead, he tensed and stared at the door, waiting.

Behind him, Eonar cleared his throat. "I will provide directions but am afraid I cannot journey with you, Prince Gailin."

Gailin swallowed, throat drying as he croaked out, "I haven't said I'm going anywhere."

"This isn't optional, Gailin," Seth said.

The man's voice was closer now, and Gailin could feel his father's presence near his shoulder. He tried with climbing desperation to shove aside the image engulfing his mind's eye.

When his father's hand gripped his shoulder, Gailin tensed and shifted to face the others. "A crystal which can store magic? Like the swords?"

His gaze flickered between Eonar and Arjun, making sure to avoid staring into the latter's eyes for too long lest the younger elf insist he do something. At Eonar's nod, Gailin escaped his father's grip and leaned against the door. "And you could take mine or Xannan's ability and store it inside this new crystal?" The Elder Elf nodded again, and Gailin sneered. "Since that worked so well with the swords?"

"Your role is to obey, Gailin."

"My role is to protect and serve the people *you* brought out of, as you say, captivity and torment." Gailin held up a hand when Seth tried to approach. "Will you do the same to me? Trap my ability to sense hints of the future into some random crystal? If memory serves, once inside a crystal, anyone capable of wielding magic can use it."

"From our—" Arjun cut short at Seth's motion.

"You didn't create an army of the dead in a single breath," Seth murmured, and Gailin's heart plummeted.

"Edmund told you?" Gailin ran a hand through his blond hair and half-laughed. "Blazes, never thought he—"

"Anna," Seth interrupted.

Holding his sword, Gailin slumped against the wall. If Xannan ever learned Anna had mentioned that stunt to Seth . . . Gailin didn't want to consider the implications. They were made for one another, but he had to admit that he understood Anna's fear. His gaze raked over the small room again, lingering on Arjun's apologetic demeanor.

"Anna didn't tell you of her own accord, did she?" Gailin turned around and stepped closer to his father. Pointing at Arjun, he added, "He *made* her tell you."

"She wanted something which could allow a peaceful future. One she fears will never arise given what Xannan can do." Seth paused and glanced back at the two elves, a muscle in his temple pulsing.

Gailin shook his head and huffed a breath. "You're a terrible liar, Father."

"This isn't a discussion, son."

"Then what good does it do to have Arjun and Eonar here? Hmm?" Gailin threaded his fingers through his hair, tugging it away from his scalp. "The sword's magic is as much part of Xannan and me as breathing is. It has been for years and, as far as I can tell, it will always be a part of us."

"And since that magic is in the swords, rather than innate, it cannot corrupt you," Seth acknowledged, pausing when Eonar cleared his throat.

"I understand many believe magic itself cannot corrupt, but it is the person who wields each gift who controls how it is used. If you wish magic be used for good, then you must gift it to good people," Eonar explained. "The Elder Elves of each clan have requested Xannan's ability be further tethered based on his proclivities."

Gailin winced, the realization coming full circle. "Logical reaction when one who enjoys killing his enemy can also revive the dead."

"Precisely." Seth folded his arms, concealing the increasing tremor of his limbs. The longer Seth stood, the more he shook, as if his body no longer cooperated. "Once Eonar tells you where to look, you will take Anna under the guise that she is to help you pick a crystal as a gift for her betrothed to give during the ceremony. To assist with this ruse, your mother will also attend." Seth lowered to a seat, clasping his hands before him. His father was weak, perhaps too weak. "You'll leave in two week's time."

"Father, I don't think—"

"If you were truly concerned about this trip, you would have said something sooner."

"I'm saying something now, Father!" Gailin gestured at Eonar and Arjun in turn. "Why did you ask them to come here? To strong-arm me into going Blazes only knows where? To retrieve something that could be as catastrophic as this sword?" He gripped the pommel of the weapon and was hit with a wave of emotions that might have made him collapse had the wall not been close behind.

Eonar leaned to one side, arm resting on the edge of the worn leather chair. "Futurae and Praeteritum were not initially designed to hold such magic." Light from the warm hearth danced along the armrest's seams, helping Gailin focus his vision. "The cave near the Cliff of Lycene contains many crystals from which to choose. Some may call to you, similar in stature to the crystal which comprises Futurae. It will not be catastrophic, as you claim."

"Last I checked, I'm the only one in this room who can know what such a quest may or may not cause." Gailin shoved both hands in his pockets and shook his head. "It's not a good idea, Father."

"And allowing Xannan to have armies of dead waltzing around is?"

"Maybe you should speak with Xannan about that before choosing to take it from him." Gailin removed his hands from his pockets and folded his arms. "So far he's done nothing more than show he is capable of forming them. I've not seen them do anything aside from stand there."

"I'd recommend retrieving the crystal," Eonar said softly, almost apologetically. "And, as previously agreed, I will bind Prince Xannan's memories so he no longer attempts to revive anyone."

20

"Why are you so on edge?" Xannan asked for the third time as they walked deeper into the castle's depths, closer to where Solomon and Ishmael were being held prisoner. Since he'd heard nothing, he wanted to check on the prisoners himself. And question them.

A shrug and a sidelong glance, Gailin remained silent but his glower deepened.

"And you swear you didn't hear anything about Father speaking with the spies?"

His brother shrugged again. Xannan gritted his teeth, grasped Gailin's arm and turned him so they were facing each other in the middle of an unoccupied hallway. No dignitaries were visiting yet, and servants had barely begun to make this corridor seem welcoming.

"Spit it out."

"No." Gailin continued walking until Xannan tugged on his shirt.

"Not an option. Something is wrong. I can tell. Something you can't shake. The spies?"

"No," Gailin repeated and continued down the corridor, forcing Xannan to jog a few paces to catch up.

"I'm positive one of these two is the spy, considering they're the only two who could have shared our path home from Violet

Grove." Several paces of their footsteps echoing passed, until the silence grated on Xannan again. "Don't make me use my rank against yours, little brother."

No smirk or snort. Gailin continued walking, tensing as they neared the entrance to the dungeons. He paused and leaned against a wall, hands crammed deep into his pockets. "I spoke with Father this morning."

"Shatter another wine glass?"

"Maybe I'd feel better if I had," Gailin murmured with a significant rush of air. "Father wanted to speak with these two alone again, so I'm worried he's still there."

Xannan folded his arms across his chest, brows pinching together as he studied his brother. "I still want to speak with them. But that isn't all, is it?"

Gailin grimaced and averted his gaze. "Eonar and Arjun were with Father."

"Excellent." Xannan sighed. "What did they tell—"

At Gailin's wince, Xannan said, "He knows I can create Mikhael's form?"

"What does Father not know may be the better question," Gailin murmured and continued toward the dungeons.

Following, Xannan tugged at the awkward sleeves of their newest jacket design. The solid black was fine, but the shoulders were too snug, and the buttons rose too high, making him feel like he was choking. While matching Gailin's pace, Xannan asked, "Have I done it before it happened with Mikhael? Revived the dead?"

Gailin paused in the middle of the hallway, turning his head enough that Xannan could see his brother's furrowed brows.

"Not that I can recall."

"Are there gaps in your memories too? I don't remember what happened immediately after meeting Anna and there are various battles where some is a haze of blood and sweat."

"Normal for you in battle, isn't it?"

"No, actually. Many battles I remember each exchange." Xannan tapped his temple with a finger. "I can relive them, remember?"

"And conjure armies of dead," Gailin added dryly, briefly meeting Xannan's gaze. "Don't forget that."

They stood in silence for a moment before resuming their trek to the dungeons. Xannan barely acknowledged the subtle bows given by each of the guards lining the walls leading to the dungeon's entrance.

The stench always lingered. Death and blood and tears. None of which could ever rival the decaying odiousness the droki brought with them. A scent, Xannan realized with muted elation, he should never have to smell again.

Chains rattled, echoing off the stone walls and muddying their father's voice. Xannan stepped forward, stopped by Gailin's grip on his arm. He gritted his teeth, wishing he hadn't waited for Gailin before heading to these dungeons.

Moments later, Seth ventured out of the all-consuming darkness of the hallway lined by cells. Behind him were four guards holding two chained prisoners. The men whom Xannan should have easily recognized were almost indistinguishable from one another. Blood dripped from opened gashes on their faces and arms, clothing frayed. Gaunt, sunken skin covered their bones. Both appeared devoid of life, allowing the guards' grips to support their weakened frames.

"Take the prisoners," Seth said in the simple, expectant tone of a king. "They are to be given a public execution for committing treason against the crown."

"Did they admit to this before or after you had them beaten?" Xannan asked, muscles tensing further with each bruise and gash he noted.

"The when of their admission is of little consequence." Seth cleared his throat and appraised Xannan in a way that made him bristle. His father's tone remained steady. "Since their actions were against you, my sons, you will dole out the punishment. The troops are already being gathered."

Though Xannan tried to exchange a glance with his brother, Gailin didn't move. When Seth snapped his fingers, the guards shoved the prisoners forward. Each sliding step was accompanied by the clink of chains.

Xannan listened, briefly attempting to relive the battle which had claimed his friend's life. But he hadn't convinced his creation to speak. Yet. As of now, he had no way of confirming that Solomon or Ishmael committed treason. Though he disliked how nosy Solomon had been, he'd not wanted the man killed.

"You helped me after I was injured, Solomon," Xannan said, and the loud clanging of the chains dissipated as the prisoners halted. "You knew I was there because you were near when Mikhael was hit." One of the prisoners, whom Xannan barely recognized as Solomon, lifted his head. Xannan bared a portion of his blade and asked, "Did you kill Mikhael?"

"Wounded," Solomon rasped out, coughing and spitting a mouthful of blood. Drops lingered on his lips, and he winced as he tried to straighten further. "We wanted to contr—"

The tip of Xannan's sword rested on the hollow of Solomon's neck, and the younger soldier swallowed, attempting to lift his chin and back away. The guards tightened their grip on the chains. Xannan held the sword steady, scrutinizing the younger soldier's bloodied face and swollen eyes.

"Son—" His father's voice was a veiled warning.

A warning he wouldn't heed. Xannan shoved his sword through Solomon's neck.

"I am not some creature to be controlled," Xannan said, pulling his blade free.

Shock and relief warred with one another on Solomon's features. The bruises became more prominent as the soldier's blood spilled down his front, brighter than the dried patches covering his torn jacket.

Though Xannan could hear the aggravated grumble of his father's voice, he didn't truly listen to the words. The soldier fell to his knees amidst a clamor of chains and wet coughs as his body convulsed. Spurts of blood occurred with decreasing repetition, slowing until only a trickle bubbled through the wound.

"That was not a proper execution, son."

"The traitor's dead." Xannan lifted his sword, and a thin line of blood snaked its way down. The crystal appeared several shades darker than the last time it'd been free of its sheath.

In his periphery, he noted his father's stance. Slow and methodical, the blood continued to drip down his weapon while he held it aloft before him. His father didn't flinch at his glare, but the man's lips thinned as Xannan said, "And I *will* annihilate anyone else who wishes to *control* me."

***

"I'm not meeting with the elves, Father." Xannan grabbed a pack and stuffed several spare shirts into it, mostly his preferred choice of sleeveless brown vests that didn't constrict the movement of his arms. "Both Edmund and Patrick mentioned groups advancing on the northern border, and I'm going with them."

His father's anger permeated the air between them, and he could visualize the lines of disapproval on the aged man's face. But Xannan was old enough now he didn't have to listen to the man. Two more weeks, and he'd be wed. A week after that and he could be crowned in his father's place. So long as his father didn't change that law. Or insist on whatever he meant by taking six months to *prove his worth.*

"The commanders can handle that skirmish, son."

Xannan turned and shook his head; he hated it when the man refused to use his name.

"And I can help them. If it means getting away from you and this ridiculous persistence you have on speaking with those elves, then it's where I'd much prefer to go."

"The elves are here to help you and Gailin."

Xannan snorted. "Unlikely." He retrieved his sword from where it rested against the wall near his dresser full of clothes he rarely wore. Brandishing the sheathed sword, he added, "They just want these weapons back." He lowered his tone, mimicking Eonar's deeper voice. "'Magic must remain balanced between all races. If you use these swords unwisely, we will have to take action.'" Xannan scoffed and hefted the weapon to hold it by its sheathed blade. "I'm surprised they haven't tried to erase our memories and steal them."

Hands in his pockets, Seth pursed his lips into the barest hint of a frown. "Why so callous today?"

"You know why." Xannan buckled the sword belt around his waist and shouldered his pack. "We should return in a week, no? I'll make sure we win." Under his breath, he added, "And no one will harm me this time."

In a condescending tone that felt like nails slicing through Xannan's skin, his father asked, "Because you'll have an army of revived dead to aid you?"

Turning away, Xannan tried to find somewhere on the wall to focus as he asked, "Who told you?"

"Does it matter? I'm not sure—"

"Would you take Gailin's ability to sense the future? If his visions returned, would you try and take those away?" Xannan rounded on his father, almost bumping into the man who had been silently approaching where he stood. "A pathway to the past and a guide for the future, that is what Celena says of Praeteritum and Futurae. And what is it you've always reminded me?" He made a show of tapping his finger on his chin, a facade of contemplation plastered on his face. "The past will always define our future and should not be forgotten."

"I fear—"

"What? Me? Your own flesh and blood?" Xannan let his hand fall to his side, shifting his shoulder so the pack didn't fall off. "Or the magic I'm learning to control?"

"What if—"

"More questions!" Xannan shouted, stepping forward as his father stepped backward. "What if I lose control? Bring more droki?" A hollow laugh, he remembered what they'd not told their father. "Magna trapped them; they're no longer a concern." He took another step forward, grip on the strap of his pack tightening. "What if these revived dead mean I'm *unstable*?"

"Xannan, that's not—"

"That is exactly—"

"Stop interrupting me!" His father roared, straightening to his full height, which was barely taller than Xannan himself. "You refused to let the elves help you understand this newfound ability so of course I fear it. If all of the elves do, then I have reason to as well."

"Gailin doesn't. Nor did Celena seem to." Xannan shrugged. "Leave it alone and let me do what you've trained me to do: fight for this country *you* created." He pressed a finger in the center of his father's chest and shoved as he said the words. "You've taught me all you can, Father. Time for me to find my own way."

Seth sighed and shoved his hands into his pockets, staring at where Xannan's finger pressed against his father's chest. As Xannan lowered his hand, Seth said, "I am still your king, and it is my decision what happens with my crown."

"Meaning?"

Seth stiffened, arms trembling slightly. "Be careful, Xannan. The lure of power is a dangerous road to travel. Blazes protect you." Without another glance, Seth left the room, shaking his head as though disappointed.

Shifting his pack on his shoulder, Xannan mulled over his father's words. He'd never intended to use Blazes as a benediction, but it seemed to fit that way as well.

***

At home atop his dappled stallion, Xannan couldn't shake the thought that someone was watching him constantly. Or perhaps something. It was more than his brother's constant appraisal or Edmund's wary glances. After the last supposed small border skirmish, nerves abounded, making the air feel more charged than the seconds before lightning streaked the sky during a thunderstorm.

Any time Xannan attempted to don the arrogant confidence he'd prided himself on perfecting, he couldn't. The scent of death lingering on the air, the sheer pain as another's blade almost ripped his arm in two. None had voiced it aloud, but he could sense their thoughts. He'd not practiced as often as before. Practicing in the training fields not far from Cantadad's castle dredged up memories. Among other things. He'd not meant to do it the first few times, but he missed sparring with his friend. Many of the soldiers feared sparring against him, both because of his status and how severely he had wounded others' pride in the past.

In the end, he'd taken to practicing in his own space. The castle had many unoccupied rooms, so he used them for his own gain. If needed, he could now command his creations.

A too quick breeze whipped his cloak from his arms, revealing the lack of sleeves beneath, and he shivered despite his attempt not to.

"Idiot," Gailin mumbled at his side. "We're returning north, and you didn't think to put on a shirt with sleeves?"

Xannan shrugged. "Sleeves get in the way."

"But the cloak doesn't?"

"I'll take it off for the fighting."

"Blazing idiot," Gailin grumbled and rubbed a gloved hand along his face. The motion halted and he shifted his gaze back to Xannan. "Gloves?"

Waving both hands, Xannan confirmed he'd at least remembered the benefit of that garment. "How much—"

Shouts sounded down the line, culminating with Edmund's eager glint as he relayed the message to them.

Before Xannan could spur his mount into motion, Gailin gripped his arm. Tightly. After an appraisal of his brother's tension, Xannan pressed his lips together as his brother said, "Be careful, Xannan."

"You as well, Gailin."

"I mean it." Gailin's grip on Xannan's arm tightened, strong enough he could bruise the skin if he didn't let go. "Not because of some sense of the future, but because I know *you.*" He glanced down as he released his hold, cleared his throat, and whispered, "Do not let them define you by your ability as they do me."

Xannan searched his brother's visage for the hint of those emotions Gailin had become so adept at hiding and for the hidden signs of failure or success. Neither appeared.

"We both have more than one ability, Gailin. I will not hide who I am in the shadows."

The remainder of the battalion had bounded ahead, the initial sounds of battle clamoring as horse skidded into horse and sword greeted sword. Several arrows pierced the air between Xannan and his brother and they shared a glance. Alkaanians disliked arrows. But the many clans their father had attempted to annihilate throughout the northern region did.

Despite the raging danger they approached, Xannan grinned, dismounted, and tugged his blade free of its sheath. Almost without thought, the conjured form of Mikhael appeared at his side, sword in hand. Xannan smirked at his brother. "Time to test if his sword still maims, even in death."

Xannan strode forward, dissecting the battlefield as he did. It sprang so quickly. One moment they rode in contemplative silence, and in the next men died before they could spout their last insults to their attackers. His grip on his blade tightened, letting the blood lust and rage consume him.

This time, none would come close to harming him. Nor his brother. Or even his brother's friend whom he found mildly tolerable on the best of days.

The closer his approach, the less margin for error he gave the archers. But he had a companion who couldn't die. A quick shift of thought, and Mikhael's revived form blocked arrow after arrow after arrow. Few spared the figure a glance, likely thinking him a dying companion who wished to do the most damage before his life leaked from him.

Each time Mikhael's form flickered and moved, Xannan felt a slight twinge of pain in the back of his head, near the base of his neck. He pushed it aside. So long as he didn't attempt to control more than the one, he could stave the headache off until the skirmish was won.

He needed to make a statement this time. The last his enemy had seen of him was wounded, bloodied, half-dead.

Xannan wove through the bodies of men tangling weapons against one another, heading for the throng of enemy soldiers whose frames would soon be prime targets for his clouded sword.

The swirls of black quickened as he shifted Mikhael's form again, nearly failing to block an arrow from thudding into his own chest. Grunting, Xannan released the clasp of his cloak, letting it disappear behind him as he ducked and slashed at anything wearing clan markings. Their father believed their destruction would lead to a better world. Perhaps, if Xannan succeeded in completing that task, his father would truly be proud of him. Not the appearance of it, but the reality.

"Xannan!" Gailin shouted from nearby. A warning, not a cry for help.

Xannan crouched, barely avoiding the arrow streaking through the space where his head had just been. Growling, he stood and entered enemy lines. His slashing sword cleaved a path through the men who meant to topple his family's legacy. Perhaps one day stories would be told of the sacrifices he and others had made to create this country.

With one sweep he sliced along three stomachs, wishing he could clasp his hands over his ears as they gritted out their last words. Ignoring their dying voices, he pulled his dagger from its sheath and plunged it into a man's chest while deflecting an arrow with his sword. The revived form of Mikhael flickered at his side, a reminder he needed to maintain focus on the figure for him to remain. Xannan shuffled inside the archer's reach, wrenching his dagger from one chest to plunge it into the one in front of him.

Grinning at the whistle of steel slicing air, he ducked and pivoted on his foot, kicking the other out to knock his opponent to the ground. Satisfied the move had worked, he stood above the soldier, tilting his head as he focused on Mikhael's sword ending the man's life rather than his own. In one fluid motion, Mikhael's conjured form lifted his blade and plunged it into the soldier's chest, piercing the man's heart.

Several more surrounded Xannan, preventing him from being able to savor the moment. The figment of his creation faded as he focused on the weapons pointing at him. Fur coats covered their arms and shoulders but left their midriffs and chests bare.

"Three to one," he muttered under his breath, grimacing as several more approached. The earlier ache he'd pushed aside surged, and he cursed, silently willing his vision not to double.

Six men had surrounded him, each with swords raised. Despite the fear welling inside, he laughed. "So many of your men for one? Thought you all knew how to fight better."

Xannan lunged forward. As the tip of a sword grazed his back, Xannan pierced another's shoulder. The wounded man stumbled backward, grasping at the wound as it leaked a torrent of blood. He spun, swiping up with his sword to create gaping wounds along three of his opponents. The fourth stepped forward into his motion and Xannan's sword sliced along his neck. Gurgling and clawing, the confident six who'd enveloped him became one.

The last of his group, this soldier rested the tip of his well-used sword on the ground and held up a bare bloodied hand. Imprinted on the man's palm was a symbol Xannan had seen only once before. Three birds in flight in a close-knit circle. The crest of the family which once owned his. The clan which had beaten men, women, even children who would have one day become family to him to their death.

"Hold," the elderly soldier said with a poignant glare at Xannan's sword. Clouds of gray and black mingled together within the weapon's crystal facade, twisting and turning like the rivers before they joined and crashed into the ocean.

Xannan stepped back but did not lower his weapon. Quick as he could, Xannan noted their enemy's diminishing numbers. Nearer to him than he expected, Gailin tugged his sword free of a man's side, watching in disgust as his opponent crumpled into a heap. Lowering to wipe his blade clean, Gailin met Xannan's gaze, relief flickering across his visage before being replaced by the ever-present worry.

Returning his attention to the soldier attempting to placate him, Xannan thrust his sword forward, purposely missing any vital organs. He twisted the blade, pushing it in further as he stepped forward. "Let your kin know the LeNoirs got their revenge."

Part Three

"A legacy of scars."

21

Victory cheers and celebrations continued every evening when they stopped to make camp. Jubilant songs rang loud and clear, some men drunk on the high of success, others grinning through the pain of their wounds, grateful to be returning home. Xannan noted the slight grimaces of those who'd lost close companions, frowning at the few bare mounts within their midst. It made him regret not being there for his men when Mikhael passed.

Nevertheless, their return to the city was even more full of cheer than their journey home. Citizens and soldiers alike acted as though Orda'an had won a war. They hadn't. If anything, a war was only just beginning. Skirmishes, small armies like the one they'd destroyed, meant nothing more than an interruption.

Even knowing he would likely spend many more years riding to and from battles such as these, Xannan reveled in the sensation of tossing the severed hand at his father's feet. When Seth's eyes narrowed at him, Xannan grinned and inclined his head. "The owner of that hand is long dead. If any of his family remain, they will meet the same end. As instructed when you first showed me that symbol."

A curt nod was Seth's response, inciting a low boil of Xannan's blood. That small flame ignited when they entered the foyer of the grand castle and were greeted by the elves Xannan would rather never see again. It was a comfort neither their mother nor Anna and Ella were present.

When Edmund and Patrick attempted to follow Xannan and Gailin inside, their father—no, their king—closed the tall, heavy doors in front of their faces. Xannan refused to continue inside, refused to give his father the upper hand more so than he already had, refused to acknowledge what could happen with several of the elves present. He'd seen it done once. One touch, and Eonar could manipulate memories.

Scowling, Xannan scoured the three elves present. Eonar and his son remained as stoic as ever, while the thin, white-haired elf-woman he'd never met wore an inviting and curious smile.

His king faced away from him and spoke in a cool, calculated voice. Devoid of emotion, strategic, almost monotone. "How did you succeed in annihilating this enemy, sons?"

Xannan huffed a laugh beneath his breath. "Same as every other battle we've entered. Our skill and that of our peers."

"The forward scout you sent claimed over a dozen fell to your blade, Xannan." Seth turned around, clasped his hands behind his back, and lifted his chin to peer into Xannan's eyes. "Were they each felled by you?" A hungry pause filled the air, the unspoken question lingering until Seth insisted on giving it voice. "Or by your . . . creations?"

Sighing, Xannan leaned against the closed doors and propped one foot over the other. He couldn't let them think his blood was boiling or that his head had not stopped aching since he'd last created Mikhael's form. Stomach grumbling, throat parched, he wanted to retreat to his rooms and enjoy a small meal before a long bath.

"So you do fear my ability?" Xannan nodded at the elves, focusing on the woman in their midst rather than risk meeting the gaze of either Arjun or Eonar. "My creation killed one; the rest are my own to tally."

Seth's gaze flickered to Gailin, who shrugged. Gailin hadn't witnessed Mikhael's form plunging that blade into the soldier's heart. Xannan wondered if he should have admitted that possibility, but it was too late to take back the words. Here, beneath two imposing staircases and the penetrating gaze of a self-made king, Xannan wanted nothing more than a proper night's rest.

His father's stoicism held firm. "You commanded a being which is already dead?"

Despite the dull throb in the back of his head, Xannan brought Mikhael's form flickering to life before him. He kept his lackadaisical pose and said, "No different than I am now."

A flicker of fear flashed across his father's face, and Xannan let the creation fade. "I have complete control, Father." He motioned with a dismissive hand at the elves and lifted from the door frame, speaking in a more level tone than he believed possible. He channeled that thought, the evenness of his voice, of his countenance, of his posture. "I understand my gift and do not need *their* assistance."

"They are my guests to dismiss, not yours. Son."

The pause, the phrase. Both were intentional and made Xannan work his jaw as he contemplated what to say.

Gailin stepped between them and cleared his throat, the hand gripping his sword hilt pale. "Even victorious, we are weary from travel and need rest. I urge you both to finish this discussion later. Much, much later."

"I will speak with you later, Gailin. For now, leave us."

When his brother paled further, Xannan scrunched his brows together. Something was amiss; something he hadn't been told. Illogical, considering he was the crown heir, not Gailin.

"Secrets will be the death of this country, Father." Xannan crossed his arms and lowered his chin. "Whatever you must say to Gailin, you should say now."

The quiet shuffling of feet—and the subtle clink of bottles that always occupied Arjun's pockets—echoed about the entryway. Decorated with streams of white in preparation for his nuptials, the staircases mocked their stances. Tension coiled down his back and arms, making his arm twinge from the recent exertion. He met his father's fierce, yet tired, gaze. For once, just once, perhaps the man would act more like a father than a king.

"If you wait, it will only be more difficult," Eonar said, and Seth grimaced.

"Your brother is right. That discussion can wait." Seth straightened and tugged at the collar of his solid black coat as Eonar murmured something in his language and ascended one of the staircases toward the hall of rooms the elves always requested. "Enjoy the celebrations of your victorious return. Meat and wine are readily available in the dining hall."

As their father left the entryway of the castle by walking beneath the balcony connected by two grand staircases, Xannan grabbed Gailin's arm and tugged his brother close. "What in the Blazes did you and he last talk about?"

Gailin shoved Xannan's hand off, scowled as he peered around them, and brushed his sleeve. Voice a hushed whisper, Gailin explained, "Father said they plan to bind your memories. Eonar was supposed to do it before we left."

"Bind my memories?" Xannan repeated slowly, cautiously, squinting at his brother as realization dawned. "Thus the warning before the skirmish."

"I really hate calling battles like those skirmishes but, yes, thus the warning."

Xannan snorted a laugh. "They can try, but they're Blazing foolish to think they'll ever succeed."

"Xannan," Gailin said in a veiled warning. "The other elfwoman. . ."

"What about her? Most of the elves require eye contact to be successful in their endeavors." He shrugged. "I'll avoid them and not look in their eyes. Blazing simple."

"And if it's not? If they find some other way—"

"Then I'll have you to fill me in. Right, little brother?" Xannan gave Gailin a playful punch, grin fading when his barely younger than him brother did not return the lighthearted gesture in speech or demeanor.

***

By the time Xannan reached his room after the awkward end to his conversation with Gailin, he'd come no closer to deciphering what else any of his father's or Gailin's words might mean. Other than knowing they wanted to erase who he was, what he could do. Probably try to control him, too.

Whatever it took, none would control him. Eldest of the LeNoir line, heir to a kingdom, destroyer of enemies. His deeds would be remembered, shared with his children and theirs for generations to come, not lost upon the wind as many of the lives he'd claimed several days past had been.

Inside his room, he stripped off the vest, tossing it into a closet off the main room and smiling when he caught a whiff of Anna's perfume. He turned to embrace her, but she stepped back, wrinkled her nose, and wagged a finger at him, pointing to the washroom. Chuckling, he removed the remainder of his clothes. After tossing the soiled garments, he shot Anna a questioning look, but she lifted a book and shook her head while fighting between scowling and smirking at him.

When the water turned tepid, he lifted himself from the bath, grateful the muck of days of sweat, blood, gore, and travel were mostly free of his skin. The blood never truly seemed to wash off. It lingered, as though meant to seep into his skin and make him eager to claim another's life. He shrugged the thought away, grasping the nearby cloth robe as he rolled his head from side to side. Sleeping in his own bed, with proper pillows instead of rocks, would be a dream.

Anna sat curled in a chair, eyes darting as she consumed line after line of text. He smiled and sat on the ledge of the chair behind her back, peering down at the book to determine which she read, but she snapped it shut and tilted her head back to gaze into his eyes. Xannan took the opportunity to kiss her, letting his lips linger and his tongue roam until the book thudded to the floor and they parted. Her eyes twinkled as she took his hand and moved toward the bed, tugging him onto it after she lay down. Xannan rolled to his side, propping his head up with one hand.

Mimicking his pose, Anna trailed her hand up and down his arm first, then his chest. "Another victory," she whispered as she sucked her lower lip between her teeth. "More dead to protect our young country?"

His skin tingled at her touch, and he ached to tug her closer, but she smirked and kept him at arm's reach. Xannan wrapped his hand around hers, halting her movement as his voice turned gravelly. "That is typical to achieve victory."

Anna peered through her lashes at him and lifted to her knees, tugging the shoulder of his robe down to inspect one arm, then the other. The appraisal continued until she whispered, "Not even a scratch on you." She swallowed, gaze growing distant as her finger trailed the thin line down his right arm. "This time."

"I learned my lesson." The thought of breathing life into Mikhael's form at that moment sprouted, stamped down because he wanted to relish this moment with his betrothed, to enjoy her company and erase the cryptic conversation he'd had with his father. "None will ever get that close to cutting me with a weapon again."

Words no more than a faint whisper, Anna resumed her finger's slow glide along his chest. "Because soon these battles will be over. Orda'an will stand on its own." She flattened her palm on his chest, pushing him to his back as she laid her other hand atop him and lowered her chin until the weight of her head was a comforting presence. "We have the elves on our side. And, if your mother and I can find it, we'll have another bargaining chip to convince everyone to get along. A way to help those understand magic better."

That had been part of his father's private conversation with Gailin. Selective words and a clipped tone made Xannan believe there was truth in what he'd been told but not complete honesty. His mother and Anna, escorted by Gailin and a small entourage, planned to search the cave beneath the Cliff of Lycene for the one thing that might prove magic wouldn't corrupt him: a crystal capable of holding the magic instead.

He trailed his fingers through Anna's black hair. "I wonder how Gailin feels about the trip."

Anna sighed, trailing her hand along his chest as she sat beside him. "Either positive or negative, he's always so cautious. Makes him annoying to be around sometimes." She chuckled, as though she'd told herself a joke. "Born the same day, yet you two are less alike than the sun and the moon."

Xannan laughed at the incredibly accurate comparison he'd not heard put to words before. "And am I the sun or the moon?"

Anna smirked, lips crossed between a smile and a frown as she feigned serious contemplation. "The sun." She shifted a lock of his blond hair from his forehead, kissed him, and leaned back with a perfect smile. "Bold, sometimes brazen, but never afraid to let your light shine for all to see."

The restraint he'd managed for several minutes disappeared. Lifting to his knees, he grasped her cheeks with both of his hands, kissing her, longer and deeper until naught but the enjoyment of the moment remained.

22

It wasn't often Gailin wished his room were larger. Fifteen steps from edge to edge. Fifteen steps, a pause, a shake of his head as he grumbled incoherently to himself.

His coat hung loose around him, unbuttoned. His sword lay on the bed, and its hilt mocked him. Those two dragons, the two swords. All of it kept crashing through his mind, and not for the first time, Gailin wished he could relive the past as clearly as his brother. Not that it would change his father's mind.

That day, before Gailin left, his father planned to trick Xannan into having his memories bound.

He walked into the wall and rubbed his nose where it had hit against the stone. Resting his forehead against the wall, he inhaled slowly and exhaled even more slowly.

Flame upon flame upon flame. The stones in his gut sank lower. He'd tried to talk reason into his father, yet the man refused to listen. Shaking his arms, Gailin rounded his shoulders and methodically buttoned his coat. As he clasped the last button, a glint of gold appeared in his mind's eye again, forming a hollow pit in his chest at the implication.

Sighing, Gailin retrieved his sword. In some ways, it was as if his ability no longer mattered. Thankfully, Ella had noted his wariness and agreed to remain in the castle. Even she had tried to convince Anna to remain, but his brother's betrothed wanted to help Xannan. If any still could.

Opening the door to his room, Gailin found his brother leaning against the opposite wall with arms crossed. Clad in his characteristic brown vest, blond hair brushing his shoulders, muscles taut, Xannan halted the tapping of his finger against his bare arm. "Father doesn't want me to go with you, does he?"

Gailin shrugged and shifted his sword belt as the door closed behind him. "You can go ask him yourself."

"I don't understand why he's so fearful of what I can now do and so trusting of you."

"But he doesn't trust me implicitly, Xannan." Gailin soaked in the empty hallway. "Not now, at least."

"Why is Anna going?"

"She requested it." Gailin toyed with his belt again and avoided looking his brother in the eyes. "And you know how stubborn Anna can be."

"Ella's not going?"

"Her sister is visiting."

"Why is Mother going?"

Gailin shifted his hair from his forehead and exhaled through his nose. "Did you think to ask her?"

"What secrets are you all keeping from me, Gailin?" Xannan lifted from the wall, arms remaining crossed as his muscles tensed. "You've seen something, yes? Something you don't want to believe to be true?"

Studying his boots, Gailin said, "A new crystal to store your magic."

Xannan grunted. "The magic is in the sword. All Celena's little stunt showed was that our abilities work better with weapon in hand."

After years of believing that, Gailin didn't know how to respond. The magic was in their swords, but it wasn't. There was something more. Eventually it would make sense. He hoped. While Gailin made a mental note to write his thoughts down later, footsteps approached.

"There you are," came their father's voice, reverberating down the empty hallway.

Gailin met his brother's accusatory glare and winced.

Seth motioned for them to follow. "One last discussion before Gailin leaves. Xannan, I know you would prefer to accompany your brother, but he can handle this task. You have others which require your attention."

Gailin exchanged another wary glance with his brother as the sensation of ice prickling his skin spread outward from his chest and sent chills along his arms and legs.

"We can speak here." Xannan's voice turned to the angry tone Gailin had heard on too many occasions. "Or do you need protection from your own son?"

At the pause in their father's slow walk, Gailin swallowed down several curses. He remained near the doorway to his room, gripping the door handle.

Seth turned on his heel and approached Xannan. "You need protection from yourself, Xannan."

His brother stepped backward as though their father had punched him; Xannan even rubbed his open palm along his chest as though to alleviate the spreading pain.

"I've done nothing wrong, Father." Xannan lowered his hand, gripped his sword hilt, and gritted out. "Year after year, battle after battle, I've protected my family, my people. You. All while *you* hid in this gaudy castle to wait for my return."

"You tread on dangerous words, son."

"I speak truth." Xannan lowered his chin, blond hair falling to cover his face. His tone turned callous. "Sire."

Breaths short, Gailin watched his father and brother's argument.

"Don't you dare question me, son." Seth's arms shook at his sides. "You have no idea—"

"What you went through. What you experienced." Xannan finished for him, stepping closer. "Blazes, you really still believe that?" He tapped his sword hilt and puffed his chest. "I bet I've won more battles than you ever did."

Gailin wished he was anywhere but in this hallway. The rift between his father and brother widened into a chasm. Arms crossed, Xannan glared at their father.

"I know what I've experienced, son." Seth reached out a hand that Xannan skirted away from. Jaw clenched, Seth said, "And I know what you need, Xannan. Trust me."

"Trust you?" Xannan spat the words. "All you've done is lie to us. Blazes know you're probably lying right now. Those tasks I'm needed for here in Cantadad? An excuse to disguise you taking more of my memories."

Seth's gaze narrowed, flickering briefly toward Gailin. He swallowed and stepped away from the door but dared not say a word. Heart hammering inside his chest, his shoulders fell at his father's disapproving shake of the head.

"All I've done, my sons, is to protect you and your futures."

A weight on his shoulder made Gailin turn. He flinched as he recognized Arjun's red-irised eyes. By the time he heard the elf's soft murmur it was too late. Whatever thoughts Gailin had dissipated, as though carried away on a wind, and the pressure building in his chest eased. The elf approached Xannan, who attempted to push Arjun away, to avoid the damning gaze of the elf's red eyes. Xannan called his name, but Gailin's limbs didn't respond.

Frozen in place, he watched Arjun's whisper placate his brother's motions but not the angry glint of Xannan's bright green eyes. Those eyes met Gailin's, littered with one accusation after another, as though their father's choices were Gailin's fault.

When Eonar approached, Gailin's heart sank, and he tried to speak. He couldn't open his mouth to say his brother could learn control. Had been learning to control his newfound ability. Xannan had used Mikhael's conjured form to aid him during the skirmish. Without the creation, Xannan would have died several deaths.

Gailin couldn't even move a finger. Whatever Arjun's command had been, it prevented Gailin from doing anything but watch as the anger etched across his brother's visage descended into confusion at Eonar's prolonged touch.

With a shuddering sigh, Eonar turned to Gailin. Though apologetic, the elf briefly laid a hand on Gailin's forearm. He'd have no way to know what memories Eonar took from him or his brother. Likely something to do with the swords. Or the dragons. Or the elves. It always came back to those three entities. Swords, dragons, elves.

When he could easily recall all three, Gailin frowned. What was missing?

Nothing? Doubtful. Everything? He could remember the cave, Xannan's desire to unite the swords, and his own ability to sense what the future would bring. Right then, the future was an open road. His frown deepened. Not an open road. An empty one.

His father's scarred face appeared before him, forehead creased with the lines of age and worry. "Your mother and Anna await you at the carriage. Find the crystal. Eonar will explain on the way to the stables." More lines crinkled Seth's aging skin as he frowned at Xannan. "Xannan will not accompany you, so be on high alert."

A first clue. The missing memories had something to do with Xannan, not himself. A journey with Anna and without Xannan was an odd request. Never one to disobey his father, Gailin inclined his head to his brother, then to his father.

While Seth led a confused and tense Xannan back toward his rooms, Gailin chewed on his lower lip. Two of his father's personal guards had remained, waiting for whatever he might request of them.

"Leave us." Gailin waited for the two soldiers to leave, rubbing the back of his neck and wishing his forearm didn't itch. Alone with Eonar and Arjun, he asked, "A crystal?"

"An entity which can store magic," Eonar explained, gesturing for them to continue down the hallway as though the elf hadn't just stolen memories from the wielders of the Twin Blades.

Grimacing, Gailin acknowledged that detail remained intact. Both their formal and informal titles could be recalled. The Twin Blades, once the sword Praesidio, now the two halves labeled Praeteritum and Futurae. "Like the swords?"

Eonar nodded and glass clinked behind them as Arjun matched their slow walk. "This crystal is necessary. You will find it near the Cliff of Lycene. Similar to the two halves of Praesidio, the crystals will call to Futurae. Listen to its call so you may find it quickly. Be cautious. Celena believes Eilon may linger near the cliff, possibly in hopes to utilize those crystals for his own gain." They reached the exit to the training yards, and Eonar placed his hand on Gailin's arm. "Be careful, Your Highness."

"The memories you took?" Gailin studied Eonar's hand, so bright against his black jacket. He frowned. Last he knew, most Orda'anians wore brown vests unless traveling to the far north. "I know it wasn't the first time."

"My apologies, Your Highness." Eonar pinched his nose and mumbled something that sounded like an elven curse. "Binding memories takes its toll on me. But it was a necessary action to protect you and your brother. And if you wish to help your brother, and yourself, locate the crystal. As His Majesty explained, Anna believes she is looking for a useful wedding gift. Maintain that guise, but guide her toward a crystal which hums in tune with your blade."

Gailin nodded and rubbed his arm. Perhaps another crystal to harbor magic would finally allow him to be seen as himself and not a tool.

23

Jerk forward, jerk back, slow and steady. A clop of a hoof, followed by another and another. All the while, Gailin ignored the changing scenery. Winter was loosening its hold, giving way to the earliest buds of spring. So much so he had to pinch the bridge of his nose a few times to prevent a sneeze from escaping. As they passed another tree with early blooms, Gailin held his breath, shaking his head when he next exhaled. Even though no enemy appeared to be near, he didn't want to draw any more attention than they already were.

His mother and Anna sat across from one another in the carriage. Small and quaint, its design was meant for no more than transporting someone from one place to another. Anna rested her arms on the open space of a window. It could be covered by cloth if desired, but she smiled at the open land, inhaling with pleasure at each plant that threatened to make him sneeze. It was no wonder he preferred fighting during winter. Cold was annoying, but at least it didn't make his eyes sting and his nose feel like some disgusting fountain.

"No brother of mine should appear so melancholic all the time." Anna weaved her hand through the breeze, grinning as it swung through the carriage and whipped her hair around her face. "Not when all we seek is one small item. The elves insist it will help him."

When she frowned and briefly rubbed at her forearm, Gailin grimaced. Whatever memories Eonar had bound involved her as well. Or something she'd seen. Said? Heard? Gailin ground his teeth. Easier to move a mountain than pry open whatever chest Eonar had locked the memories within. Perhaps if he asked the right questions or said the right words, it could knock their memories loose. But since Eonar had natural magic, his was more powerful. He grunted at the recognition of an additional fact, one he wouldn't be surprised if the elves eventually tried to lock away for him.

"I wonder how long it will take to find the proper crystal." Anna rested her arms on the small windowsill and chewed on her bottom lip. "We probably should have taken this trip sooner, but both you and Xannan insisted on marching off to the last border skirmish in the north."

Gailin remembered fighting, but pockets were absent. Flashes of arrows, of scarred men, of jubilant shouts. Not a single recollection of his brother fighting. He'd made it a habit to keep as close a watch as he could while his brother fought. What could Xannan have done that was worse than annihilating his enemies? Whatever it was, maybe Gailin didn't want to remember. But it felt of vital importance to find what Eonar had trapped. Gailin slouched in the saddle, swaying with the horse's steady clopping movement.

Anna sighed and lowered her chin to her forearm. "How much longer until we see this glorious waterfall?"

"By nightfall if we keep this pace." Gailin shifted in his saddle, mentally recalling each moment of the day before he had left with the caravan to approach the Cliff of Lycene.

Some claimed it was haunted by the ghost of the dragon's past. A foolish story, but one that weighed on him as they approached. None had seen Eilon since Praesidio's breaking. But the droki had been Eilon's creations. The beast of a dragon existed. Perhaps within the cliff?

Gailin surveyed his surroundings. Clumps of budding trees, green grass dotted with bright yellow dandelions, a dissipating dirt path. No dragon. No droki. No enemy.

"Anna." His mother leaned forward and whispered something in Anna's ear.

With a broad smile, Anna tapped on the carriage to indicate a stop. Jumping out, she held her hand up to Gailin, and he almost rolled his eyes but stopped himself as he dismounted and handed her the reins.

Patting the horse's mane, he whispered to his mount, "Be gentle with her. Pretty sure Xannan would skin me alive if she gets hurt."

Anna guffawed, and the dappled gray stallion pranced on all fours. "I doubt Xannan would hurt you, but he wouldn't be pleased." She gathered the reins with both hands, and Gailin boosted her into the saddle. She shifted until she settled into a more comfortable position—if any were possible when her skirts had no slits along each leg. "But he did seem a bit . . . odd before we left, so best not to chance it." She frowned. "You've seemed off as well, Gailin."

He shrugged. If she knew elves could bind memories, she hadn't indicated, and the last thing Gailin needed was for her to want to go racing back home before they had found what they sought.

"Which is why he's coming to sit with me for a moment." His mother held the door of the carriage open and jerked her head as an indication for him to enter. As he climbed into the carriage, she said, "I presume you had a meeting with Eonar and Arjun, same as me and Anna? Xannan too."

Gailin plopped onto the bench opposite his mother, slouching until she tapped his knee and tsked. Straightening, he wiped his palms along his legs and rested them on his knees. "Eonar had to bind your memories as well?"

His mother, the bold and vibrant Queen Dana, grunted and smoothed her skirts. "Apparently." Skin crinkled around her temples. "So thorough, that ability. Made me forget to the point that I have not even an inkling of what it is I was forced to forget."

"I'm sorry, Mother. I should have—"

"Stop taking the blame for your brother's actions, Gailin." Dana grasped his hand, tracing the lines of his palm and smiling softly. "It is my hope and dream that you have a long life ahead. One in which you do not see yourself as some tool to be used by others."

"I know that. I do. It's just—"

"It is how your father often sees you." Dana traced his palm with two of her fingers. "Even some of those soldiers you deem friends."

Thinking back to his last private conversation with his father, Gailin's mouth went dry. Pockets of that conversation were also gone, but his mother was right. Everyone was always right about that. He was a tool. Not a prince, not a skilled soldier. Maybe not even a brother. A means to an end. Something to use for another's gain.

Gailin tugged his hand free of his mother's. "Perhaps that is part of the memories Eonar bound. And without them, I'll be free to live my life as I see fit?"

His hollow laugh cut short when his mother tapped his knee again. Harder this time.

"You've always been free to live your life without the shadow of that ability granted by your sword." She gathered a thin shawl about her shoulders. "Use the tool for yourself, not others."

Gailin squinted at his mother and wet his lips. "You think I should receive the crown, not Xannan? Claim I've seen the damage he could cause?"

Turning her head slowly, Dana lifted a single brow. "That is a bold set of words to claim I thought, Gailin."

He scrubbed his face with both hands. "I'll review these past few weeks with Xannan when we return home. Considering his ability, there are more tunnels which could lead to the truth with his help."

Since the carriage hadn't moved, Gailin didn't need to tap the side to request a halt. He exited slowly, and Anna frowned when he held his hand out for her. Holding her voluminous dress in one hand, Anna dismounted and righted herself, tugging at her bodice and smoothing her skirts. "I wanted to actually ride for a bit, not just sit on him for a few minutes."

"Trust me, Anna, the carriage is more comfortable." Gailin held out a hand to assist her. She flicked her black hair over her shoulders and climbed back inside.

The smirk she flashed down at him made him smile. After a brief check of his supplies, not that they needed it, Gailin mounted and motioned the caravan to continue. This time tomorrow, they'd be looking for this crystal that would supposedly call to his sword.

He tugged each glove tighter onto his hands and pursed his lips. Given his more even temperament, it could be a logical choice for him to receive the crown. Even a smart one. But that was his brother's right. He would be his brother's sword.

A flash of gleaming metal appeared in his mind's eye, and he paused, holding the edge of one glove. Throat parched, he glanced around, wondering if any noticed his sudden jolt at the vision.

None reacted, so he urged his mount into a walk to match the pace of the others. Two soldiers escorted them. Considering the stories of the cliff being haunted, they weren't in danger of an attack from either of their northern neighbors.

Gailin squinted at the horizon. The Jearnian Hills were barely visible, guiding his line of sight to the imposing Cliff of Lycene, a faint image in the distance. He could visualize its rocky facade and cascading waterfall. With another sigh, he peered into the carriage. His mother listened as Anna spoke animatedly. Descriptions of the throne room and castle's entryway floated to him, and he smiled. A wedding. His brother would be a married man within a week's time.

His insides turned cold. The vision of gleaming gold turned to roaring flame. He tugged the reins to halt his mount, chest clenching as he searched their surroundings.

"Gailin?" his mother asked, worry coating her tone.

He shook his head, and the visions faded. "Perhaps we should pause for the evening. Finding this crystal may take time tomorrow."

"But we're almost to the cliff," Anna said, folding her arms on the windowsill and laying her chin atop them. "I'd rather find a room in Lycene than sleep on rocks again."

***

Water crashed against rocks, spraying Gailin's face with droplets as he stood beside Anna on the river's bank and frowned at the waterfall. Like Eonar said, the sword hanging from his hip reacted with a comforting warmth. The crystals called to one another.

At his side, Anna lifted her skirts and frowned at the mud lining the tips of her boots.

"I didn't think to bring a spare set," she murmured. Her dress-skirts swayed with the breeze as she released them. All morning, she'd barely spared Gailin a glance as they ventured away from the town toward this legendary waterfall. "Did Eonar speak true? Do you know where to look?"

Gailin nodded and grimaced as the image of a shining golden crown reappeared in his mind's eye. It made his gut twist. Twice in as many days he'd seen the same vision. Aloud, he said, "Follow me and watch your step. The Guadelaide flows quickly."

"Obviously." Anna sighed and gave him a dashing smile that reminded Gailin of his brother. "But you'll rescue me if I fall in."

Grunting, Gailin stepped carefully from stone to stone, testing his balance and grip before relinquishing his weight to the next space. On occasion, he glanced back. Each time he offered a hand, Anna frowned at him, lifted her skirts, and followed his steps.

Each step closer to the waterfall became more tenuous. Water drummed against the river. In less time than he expected, they stood close enough the waterfall misted their skin. What they needed, Gailin could tell, lay within. But as he considered jumping through the cascading water, an image of flame coated his vision. Every muscle tensed, and he wished he could hear the dragon's thoughts.

"I hope this will help." Anna's words sounded odd as she spoke loudly to be heard over the thunder of water against water.

An ache spread in Gailin's chest. He'd not considered what it might mean for him and his brother to be rid of the magic gifted to them through Futurae and Praeteritum. Though he liked the idea, it felt wrong.

But to live a life without the worry of what thoughts might arise when he least expected, to carry out his days with Ella. He wanted that. When Anna rested her hand on his arm, he turned to her and noted the same desire etched on her face.

"Wait here." He jumped through the cascading waterfall before he could change his mind.

Drenched, Gailin appraised his surroundings with quick glances, blinking to adjust his vision. Thin rocks jutted from the ceiling and the floor, mingled with crystals of all shades and hues. He gripped the sword hilt and cursed at its warmth.

Wet-slicked stone threatened to make him slip with each step closer to the crystals. The cave itself, though damper and smaller than the cave where he'd been bound to his sword, dredged up thoughts he'd long since buried. He understood now why Xannan always saw the ability to relive his past as the opposite of a blessing.

Power radiated around Gailin. Oppressive, suffocating. He almost expected to be flung to his back. Nothing stopped his steps.

A deep rumble echoed through the cave, shaking his bones, and Gailin stilled. Two more steps, and he could reach the closest crystal. Dark and mucky, it reminded him of the tendrils of black coating Xannan's sword.

Gailin reached out, wincing when a second rumble echoed. With each finger he curled around the nearest crystal, flames and gleaming gold coated his mind's eye. He gripped the black-hued crystal tighter and tugged. It didn't budge.

Cursing silently, Gailin studied the crystals jutting from each rock. The one he'd tried to tug free was the darkest of them all. It called to him, to his sword, but they all did. He breathed deeply and allowed the emotions he kept suppressed to well up. A sour taste coated his tongue, reminiscent of the first time he'd experienced magic on the day of the swords' creation.

A second crystal gleamed in his periphery. When he considered taking it, neither flame nor shining gold occupied his vision. So he moved closer, muscles tensing with each deep rumble that rattled the pebbles and his bones. As he edged around the next spindly rock lifting from the floor, Gailin hesitated.

Rocks further in the cave, the ones the sunlight barely touched, moved.

Gailin swallowed, grasped the two closest crystals, and tugged until he stumbled backward once they released.

He peered into the darkness, curious. If he could communicate with Eilon. . . A faint shout sounded amidst the deafening waterfall. Worry coated its tone.

"Anna," he whispered.

Gailin gave the cave's shrouded black depths a final perfunctory appraisal, pocketed the two crystals, and jumped back through the waterfall.

His foot slipped, and he tumbled into the fast-moving stream. Each time his head bobbed above water, he heard Anna's frightened cries. Water sprayed and churned, the quick current sucking him beneath the river's surface time and time again. Gailin reminded himself to remain calm, to move in fluid motions, and to cleave through the water. Uncontrollable submersions transitioned into intentional strokes. He found a rhythm with the current and focused on finding a place to extricate himself from the Guadelaide River's snare.

When Gailin saw several low-hanging branches, he grasped them with a desperate plea the limbs be attached to a solid trunk rather than lying loose on the river's bank. When the branch remained sturdy, he drug hand over hand until his feet met the muddy riverbed. Between the water and the mud, Gailin had lost both of his boots.

He collapsed on the ground and listened to the gushing water. Patting his pockets, he winced. One crystal remained. He closed his eyes and sighed.

"Oh, no," Anna gasped. He shifted his head toward her, too exhausted from his battle with the river to sit up. She lowered the hands clasped over her mouth. "Thank the Blazes you're okay!"

"Thank the Blazes?" Gailin croaked out and grimaced. River water tasted worse than his father's favorite wine. "I thought Xannan meant to use it as a curse, not a benediction."

"Your shoes are gone!"

"Thank you for that assessment." Gailin peered at his feet and wiggled his toes. "I'll get a new pair in town." He tugged the lonesome crystal from his pocket. "Will this work?"

"Are you all right?" Anna crossed her arms and glared down at him. "I thought for sure you'd drowned!" She tugged her hair over her shoulder. "I may be in love with your brother, but I do care about you as well, Gailin. Are you injured? Anywhere? At all?"

The seriousness of her tone convinced Gailin to sit up and appraise her countenance. "Other than my pride for slipping on a rock, not wounded." Gailin moved to straighten his jacket and frowned at the sodden garment. He removed it and asked, "What would you have done if I were injured?"

"Tended to your wounds." She smoothed her skirts and tilted her head. "I think I've done so for you before. I feel like I have, but I can't remember healing you." Anna frowned. "Or Xannan."

"The elves have bound our memories, likely multiple times." Gailin pocketed the crystal and stood on wobbling legs, saved from falling by Anna's outstretched hand. "My guess is both Xannan and I are capable of more than we realize."

The flash of flame against gleaming gold appeared in his mind again, accompanied by a piercing pain that made him gasp and stumble. Anna lowered his hand and pressed two fingers to his temple, face scrunched, until the throb radiating throughout his head and body had eased. A shudder racked her body.

"You have magic, too?" Gailin whispered.

"It was my fault the droki attacked my village." Anna's expression turned distant. "You don't remember that?"

"No. I don't." Gailin squinted at the sun's position in the sky. "Maybe Mother remembers something we don't."

***

After signing to one of the guards to scout ahead, Gailin settled into a quicker pace than they'd used while approaching Lycene. Each thud of the horses' hooves and squeak of the carriage's wheels, each whisper of wind and crack of branches made his muscles tense further.

Dinner, which they'd concluded early a mere hour prior, provided more questions than it did answers. Battles his mother knew he'd fought, Gailin couldn't recall. Several, according to her, had occurred in recent months. Each missing piece sent his insides tumbling further into the depths. Too much of his life was simply void of any thoughts or feelings. Though he had his own memories, he longed for his brother's ability to relive the past.

Gailin swayed with his mount's movement, gaze bouncing across the sprawling landscape of Orda'an without truly seeing anything. Headed west, most was open plains with the occasional cusps of trees. Idly he wondered if binding memories worked on Xannan, given his ability to relive the past.

The prickling sensation of being watched suffused Gailin's body. His spine and neck tingled. If not for the carriage, he'd prefer to gallop away from the small city. But none in Lycene had mounts they could borrow. Lycenian horses were meant for farms, not long treks across the country. So his mother and future sister-in-law sat in that carriage—Anna with the newfound crystal, his mother with lines of worry creasing her forehead.

Gusts of wind whipped through Gailin's hair, tugging at the cloak he'd obtained in the city. A smidgen warmer than the brown vests he once wore, the cloak had to be held tight to trap any warmth inside. Springtime weather would become the norm for the next several months, but the night remained chill. He pressed his lips together and attempted to wriggle his toes in the new boots he'd purchased. Their thin soles allowed him to feel the metal stirrup.

The soldier he'd sent ahead returned, with a perfunctory sign that all was clear. Gailin frowned. Everything felt wrong. The crystal, the journey, even the wind hinted at . . . something.

He motioned for their small caravan to stop and listened. The breeze whipped his cloak until it felt like the garment's clasp was choking him. And then it all changed.

No wind whistled around him. No faint chirps of early springtime birds. No low buzz of nighttime critters. No sounds of normalcy as he searched one dark cloud after another.

Gailin turned his mount in a circle, analytical. Thinking. If they abandoned the carriage, then his mother and Anna could ride behind the two soldiers. The journey would be quicker and allow them to reach the safety of the magically protected castle, but it would exhaust the horses. Or kill them.

The weight of impending danger pressed upon Gailin. Once he felt stones in his gut, the attack was imminent. Grumbling a curse, he made a quick series of signs to explain his plan, dismounted, and approached the carriage.

A moment of otherworldly silence bore down on him. Gailin stood, petrified and unable to lift a hand as a swath of flame descended from the sky and engulfed the carriage.

His heart pounded. His breaths shortened. A second burst of flame surrounded him. He crouched, cowering beneath his hands. Heat licked at his arms, his legs, his hair, his ears, his neck. But no pain.

A brighter swath of flame combated the first. White against black. With the beasts distracted, Gailin raced for the carriage. Fire curled and consumed, licking at the lacquered wood.

He pulled on the glowing orange handle and hissed, shaking his hand. Cloak wrapped around his arm, Gailin covered his nose and mouth, searching inside the carriage with quick, furtive glances.

Ignorant of the heat, he assumed the battle mindset that had, as far as he recalled, kept him alive for the past five years. Grab the one with signs of life. Before the carriage was consumed by heat again. So he did.

Gailin checked her pulse and cataloged her wounds. Hair singed, face oozing black, arms charred. Flecks of her green dress grounded him. His mother lay beside him. His mother was alive. Barely. Which meant Anna. . .

He refused to acknowledge what Anna's death could mean, not when the skin of his mother's chest bubbled from the remnants of heat. Gailin fought his rising gag. Fire had eaten through her bodice and flesh and seemed to have melted portions of her muscles along her chest and arms.

He removed his cloak and debated laying it atop his mother, but doing so could aggravate her wounds. Settling back on his heels, Gailin searched for one of the soldiers and winced. Two charred heaps remained of the men who'd accompanied them.

Hands shaking, Gailin studied his arms. Not a hint of marred flesh to be found, aside from the small burn where he'd grasped the handle. His mother's hand grasped his wrist and weakly pulled him closer.

Dana's dilated pupils darted from the carriage to him and back again. Despair clawed at the hollowness in Gailin's chest as he gave one small shake of his head. "Retrieve your memories." Each word came weaker than the last, and her deformed face blurred in his vision. "Protect—" She swallowed, body shuddering. "Protect each other."

"No, no, no."

Gailin whispered the word over and over. He could see hints of the future, so why couldn't he change it? Desperation, fleeting and useless, encased every thought. He nudged his mother's arm, failing to keep her conscious as her chest rose and fell with shorter movements.

"Help!" Gailin shouted at his vacant surroundings, hoping for anyone's aid. A kinder dragon, a citizen of Lycene, or better yet, an elf with healing potions. "Help us!"

Crackling wood answered him. He tugged at his hair, and the realization hit him like a fist to the chest. The crystal. It housed magic. Gailin's hands shook. He didn't want to see her shriveled form, lifeless and marred. Not after he'd grown accustomed to her kind smiles. But perhaps the crystal had snared her healing magic.

Careful and cautious, he approached the smoldering carriage. Shielding his face with his arm, Gailin climbed inside, and though he tried not to, his vision snagged on what remained of his brother's betrothed. A mangled mess of flesh and cloth and ash, portions melded to the seat. And in her hand, the crystal that, if Gailin had to make a guess, had been the reason their carriage was attacked. Where before it glowed and beckoned to him, it now seemed no more than another object to be carried.

When his fingers grazed Anna's lifeless ones, they disintegrated. He forced down his revulsion and grabbed the crystal. Whatever had been in it was gone. Just as Anna was gone. And his mother would be gone soon if he didn't get help.

For a moment that felt too long yet too short, Gailin let reality settle. Hollow emptiness transformed to shock and anger. Gailin choked on a breath, half-stumbling, half-falling out of the carriage.

Smoke burned his eyes and lungs. He searched the landscape again. Once. Twice. Barren trees. Brown land with patches of green. Those hints of life, of rebirth, mocked him. He scanned the plains again, focusing on each lone tree in the hope it might move. But none of them did. Not a soul to be seen, save himself and his dying mother. Even Gailin's horse had disappeared in the fray or had also been burnt to ash.

Gailin fell to his knees at his mother's side. Skin too pale, breaths too shallow. He took her hand in his and whispered, "I'm here, Mother." Tears welled at the bottom of his vision. Gailin gripped her hand more tightly. "You're not alone."

Each painstaking movement of her chest sent his insides spiraling further. His muscles trembled, and he wished their roles were reversed. Better he, with his apparently useless ability, be the one disintegrating to ash.

His mother squeezed his hand once and went limp.

Night came, the owls hooted, and he knelt beside his mother. Silent tears trickled down his cheeks. Perhaps if he waited long enough, the cold would claim what the heat had not.

24

Relishing in the cool wind, Xannan spun and ducked beneath Edmund's wooden blade. The practice sword sliced through empty air, and Xannan's grin turned wicked as he swiped at the soldier's ankle with his foot and knocked the man to the ground. Lifting to his full height, Xannan pointed his practice sword at Edmund's throat.

"I win. For the fourth time." He shifted the sword away and held out a hand to help Edmund up. "And not a hit from you."

"Thanks for the reminder, sir." Edmund dusted off his jacket and straightened it.

"Usually you get a few hits in. Distracted?"

"Distracted, worried, concerned. My father should arrive today." Edmund lowered into a fighting stance. "Again, sir?"

Wood clacked amid squeaking wheels. One cart after another arrived, burdened with supplies for the wedding. His wedding. Their wedding. A ridiculous grin found its way onto his face. In less than a week, he could call Anna his wife.

Xannan's grin faded as he noted the colors of the arriving carriages. None boasted the shined black lacquer of the royal carriage. His grip on the practice sword tensed. He, too, was worried about his brother's delayed return. Four additional days and they'd received no message?

If anything had happened to Anna. . . He shuddered. But they weren't traversing enemy territory, so the two guards should be sufficient, especially given Gailin's ability.

Xannan motioned for Edmund to put away the blade. "That's enough for today."

He glanced over his shoulder at the entry gates. Open, as they often were during the daylight hours, the gates allowed men and women from the circular city of Cantadad to stream in and out. All carried supplies of some form—food, clothing, drink. The bustling economy supported Orda'an, visible in one long stream of joyous faces.

Interspersed throughout his citizens were the tense faces of visiting emissaries. Those with tanned skin and looser clothes represented the far southern nations; others with straight muscled backs and pale skin were the proud owners of budding plantations beyond the Jearnian Hills.

People walked amongst the carts, flowing in and around the castle whose first stones he'd helped place as a young child. Supposedly. Xannan gritted his teeth. One hour a day to spar, and the rest was a myriad of meetings with those emissaries whose presence was for courtesy. And future leverage. But he itched to use that power thrumming within him. It beckoned and yearned in a way he knew was too dangerous to explore with company. So he focused on the Blazing meetings and prepared to accept his role as king before the year's end.

The ornate castle, gilded with the streaming sunlight, awaited him with the promise of more meetings and polite conversations within those fancy walls. He'd have to be more selective with his words, lest he receive a third lecture about propriety that day.

Sword in hand was much preferred to the uncomfortable chairs of his father's study.

"I'm worried about them too, sir," Edmund whispered at his side.

"I'm not."

Edmund chuckled and tucked his wooden blade back into its place. "Prince Gailin will return in time for the wedding. He has to."

Xannan stored the wooden practice blade in a barrel with others and retrieved Praeteritum. He paused, staring at the sheathed weapon. Vague images surfaced. Silhouettes and shadows. Evidence the elves had bound his memories. Again. Xannan had tried once, on the eve Anna, his mother, and Gailin left, to counter the elves' magic with his own. Pain had ratcheted through his skull, culminating at the nape of his neck and spreading down his spine. Strong enough to make him rethink his next approach. Each attempt had resulted in much the same: pain and darkness.

Someone tapped his arm with the back of their hand. Clumsy and distracted, as though they weren't watching what they were doing. Xannan glared at the hand and grumbled, "Edmund, I said I'm not worried."

"I think it's time to be." Edmund tugged him around to face the gates where a disheveled and pale Gailin entered. Alone. No horse. No carriage. No one else.

The commander was right; time to be worried.

Xannan buckled his sword around him and snapped at Edmund. "Doctor first, then Father. Go."

He didn't wait to see if Edmund obeyed. Each stride lengthened until he was part walking part jogging toward his brother. Dazed, Gailin trudged forward until Xannan gripped both of Gailin's arms.

"Gailin?" Xannan lowered his head to try to peer into his brother's eyes. "Are you injured?"

"No," Gailin whispered, lowering his chin to his chest. "Not physically at least."

Blinking, Gailin slowly lifted his head. Cheeks sunken, lips cracked, Gailin shuddered, and Xannan flinched at the movement. Gailin was calm, collected, and meticulous. His cloak—cloak, not coat—was in shreds, his hands raw from lack of gloves, his blond hair a tangled mess. Gailin's shoulders slumped. His words were choked by sobs. "I'm sorry. So, so sorry. I should have—"

"What happened, Gailin?" Xannan released Gailin's arms and stepped backward. One hand holding the sheath of his blade, the other its hilt, he heard the sinister taint coating his words. "Where are Anna and Mother?"

Gailin rubbed his face with his hand and took a deep shuddering breath. While Xannan waited for the answer to his question, Gailin surveyed the castle's courtyard. Common noises surrounded them. The stomping of a horse's hoof as it was led from the stable. Shouts as others noticed Gailin and as Edmund returned with a physician and their father close at his heels.

When Gailin saw their father, he flinched again.

Xannan's grip on his sword tightened. "Gailin, answer me. Where are they?"

Gailin's gaze flickered from Xannan to their father and back again, skin paling further than it already had. His voice cracked as he whispered, "Gone." Gailin wet his lips. "They're gone."

One step back, and another, until someone's hand rested in the center of Xannan's back, stopping his movement. Xannan clicked his mouth shut. Unable to focus on any one object, his vision blurred as he clenched his jaw. Speak, he tried to command his tongue. No words formulated. His hand was on his sword, so he drew the weapon. A hand reached for it, and he lashed out, his fist connecting with Edmund's nose hard enough to snap bone.

Cursing, Edmund stood between Xannan and Gailin, blood from his nostrils streaming over his lips. "Put the sword down, sir." Edmund reached for it again and Xannan moved backward, stepping on the foot belonging to the same person whose hand still rested on his back.

His father's voice was low, calmer than it should be. "Put the sword down, son."

"Don't tell me what to do." Xannan tensed his arm. He turned back to where Edmund blocked his view of Gailin and looked around the commander to meet his brother's gaze. "Tell me who is responsible."

"Fire fell from the sky," Gailin whispered. "Their carriage, the soldiers, everyone encased in flame." He held out his arms, turning and twisting them, staring at them in bewilderment and awe. "Everyone else succumbed to the heat. I tried—" Gailin's voice cracked. "I tried to help. Too late."

"Too late?" Xannan's arms trembled. He tried to step forward, but his father gripped the back of his shirt. Turning, Xannan jabbed his elbow into his father's forearm. The man grunted and released his hold. Free of another's grasp, Xannan approached Gailin. "You should have protected them!"

His younger brother blinked once. "I know."

Gailin wavered and straightened. "If I could bring them back, return to the moments before we left, think more about whether or not we should go. . ." He frowned and his eyes widened slightly. "No warning. Not a hint. Not even an itch. Not until it was too late to do anything about it."

The sword thrummed in Xannan's hand, begging for him to use it. Power ebbed from the weapon. Xannan lifted his blade, focusing on using his ability to create a pathway to the past and solve this problem. "If we connect the blades, perhaps I could see what you saw."

As he always did when Xannan recommended the swords unite, Gailin shook his head. The motion was slower than normal this time. "You don't want to see them the way I last did, Xannan."

"That's for me to decide." Xannan shifted his stance, and the chilling sensation coating his skin turned to heat. He would find her. Both Anna and his mother. No matter what Gailin said, he could find a way.

Praeteritum flowed with darkening clouds. Pale gray turned to solid black, encompassing more and more of the blade the longer Xannan watched. As he focused on the weapon, he heard a voice. Anna's voice. Whispering at the edge of sound. Too faint to be understood; loud enough to be recognized.

A throbbing pain radiated from the center of his head, through his skull, culminating in a sharp point at the edge of his temple. Xannan faltered a step sideways, frowning at the faint image of Anna glimmering in the sunlight next to Gailin. A second sharp pain followed the first.

***

Xannan inhaled sharply as all sensation came flooding back. The right side of his temple throbbed. He opened his eyes and bolted upright, gaze hunting for Praeteritum and the secrets it could unlock.

Strong hands, Gailin's, pushed him back down.

"You took a nasty fall, son," his father said, voice coming from the opposite side of the bed.

"Liar." Xannan contemplated spitting in his father's face. Settling on glaring at the man, Xannan growled, "You jabbed your elbow into my head. Twice."

Seth grimaced. "You were losing control, son."

"I've a focus like no other." He struggled against the weight of Gailin's hands. "Get. Off. Of. Me."

Seth sighed. "With the number of emissaries here, the last thing I need is you going on a blind rampage through this castle, killing men who could become allies."

"And if one of them is responsible for this attack?" Since he couldn't lift his shoulders, Xannan searched with his eyes. Across the room rested his sword. "Which of these *emissaries* enjoys using fire to attack? Or deems a carriage with few soldiers a threat in the first place?"

"You have to remain calm, Xannan." Seth tugged at the hem of his solid black jacket. "Even in the face of such despair, you must temper your emotions."

"Do you feel so little for Mother now that you can't mourn her loss?" Xannan shoved off Gailin's arms and strode toward his sword. "Or Anna's? Or the other soldiers escorting them?"

"You cannot be the royal and the soldier, Xannan."

With his sword properly buckled, Xannan hunted his father's countenance for a hint of grief, or sadness, or even anger that his mother, their queen, was gone. "And what will you do if I choose to avenge their deaths by killing those I believe responsible?"

"I will name Gailin heir in your stead and punish you according to your unsanctioned crimes."

"Sentence me to death, you mean?" Xannan chuckled. The room swallowed the hollow sound. "Perhaps death would be better. At least I'd leave the world knowing I did what was best for my family."

"Have you?"

Sitting precariously on the bed, Gailin whispered, "I told you it would go this way." He rubbed his palms along his pants, along the clothing still soiled from the ashes of those he'd presumably watched be burnt alive. "Don't make me watch another of my family die."

"No warning?" Xannan wanted to pull his sword again. He wouldn't, not when that action would give them more reason to believe he didn't have control. "Not even an inkling?" He tightened both of his hands into fists when Gailin's demeanor fell further. "Blazes, Gailin, I have trouble believing that."

His brother rocked forward in his perch. Glancing over his shoulder at their father, Gailin spoke in a hoarse whisper. "Eonar bound our memories. Again. The itch on the forearm? The gaps in the last border skirmish?" An audible swallow precipitated a softer whisper. "It must have interfered."

Unspoken words passed between him and his brother, broken when their father proclaimed, "The elves cannot bind memories, they are here—"

"Stop spouting us lies, Father." The pinching pain of Xannan's nails into his palms prevented him from drawing Praeteritum. He needed to focus his fury, his rage, on someone. When he turned to his father, the man stepped back and a hand drifted to the one weapon the king deigned to carry—a jewel-encrusted dagger. Xannan grimaced. "No one else tampers with me or my memories."

25

All in Xannan's path became memories. Rich velvet curtains billowed in the breezeway, no different from Anna's midnight black hair would. Pale stone, bleached by days of endless sunlight, reminded Xannan of Anna's equally light skin. Salt lingered in that breeze, no different from how it would follow Anna after they'd spent hours on that beach.

Laughter echoed in a distant hallway, and he hesitated in his fast-paced walk. It sounded so much like Anna. But his brother claimed she was dead. If only he could relive Gailin's memory to confirm.

Curtains bulged with wind until they flipped upward at the force, and Xannan paused. After blinking several times, he rubbed his eyes. Impossible for her to be standing before him. A curse of the mind, to see that which he desired but could never have again.

Shouts tried to echo against stone walls, difficult to do with the open windows. He had to keep moving, lest they sequester him in some room and feed him one sorry phrase after another. Someone was behind this attack. They would pay. For Anna's death. For his mother's. For the soldiers who thought the trip a simple one. A life for a life.

Deep in the recesses of his mind, emerging with each passing moment, grew the thought that his father could be responsible. The bound memories, the persistence of spending time with the elves, the missing pieces.

Whatever they had taken from him, he needed back.

As Xannan continued down the hallway, he searched through his past memories. Several withered away when he attempted to grasp them. Images floated at the edge of his reach. Fighting alongside Mikhael, his friend who had died... Xannan grimaced and continued exploring his memories as he hunted for where the emissaries were lodged.

He reached the first emissary's door—a young plantation owner who farmed the land just beyond the Cliff of Lycene—and at the same time realized he could not remember how Mikhael had died. Xannan knew of the battle at Falsumbra, knew something had gone wrong and he had been injured.

Barging into the room, he drew his sword and placed the tip between the man's shoulders. Hand frozen with the remaining portion of a half-eaten apple, the emissary bristled. They knew his reputation. Leaving his enemy alive was not in his wartime vocabulary; annihilating them was.

"The voice which commands the act is more dangerous than the hand from whence it came." Xannan spoke in a low growl. "Were you responsible?"

"Apologies, Your Highness." The younger lord's voice quavered. "For your loss. I have no desire to take that which is yours."

The man's words hit Xannan like he'd been stabbed in the side. Like his sword arm had been cut off. He lowered his sword, and the young lord slouched forward, hyperventilating.

Loss. His loss. He'd lost her. The woman he was supposed to protect with his own life. His grip on the sword tightened, and the young lord stilled as Xannan placed the blade on the hollow of the pale-skinned emissary's neck. The man tried to lean back in his seat, but Xannan pressed harder, drawing a bead of blood.

"You could be lying." Xannan's voice sounded strange to his ears. Distant, venomous, calloused.

The young lord's neck bobbed. "I approved of the union—"

"Approved?" Xannan asked, voice cracking. He'd rather suffer a thousand blows to the head then feel the pain crushing in on him from all sides. Approved, not approve.

"And I will support your claim as heir, Your Highness."

Xannan jolted at the statement and lowered his blade. His claim? He had no claim to make. As eldest, he was crown heir. Unless. . .

"What did my father say?"

"He named Prince Gail—"

Xannan knocked the hilt on top of the man's head, grateful for the sudden silence. He refused to hear the end of that sentence.

Sword sheathed, Xannan's fingers tingled as he flexed his hands at his sides. Fist, straighten, fist, straighten. This line of questioning would result in much the same response. Press a sword against their neck and any captive would tell their assailant whatever answer they believed would keep them alive.

Shaking his head, Xannan continued down the mostly empty hallway. Voices gained on him as he moved further into the guest quarters. One turn after another until he stood amid the dark hallway reminiscent of every elven village he'd ever visited.

Xannan cocked his head. How many elven villages had he visited? Just the one? More? His days at Violet Grove had too many gaps to make sense. An injured arm. Question after question from the elf outside whose door he now stood.

He pulled Praeteritum from its sheath, turning it about to follow the path of midnight black clouds. Darker than Anna's hair, they roved in agitation akin to his own. He gritted his teeth and lifted a fist to pound on Arjun's door.

"What will that accomplish, Xannan?"

If his brother was near, their father wouldn't be far behind. If Seth did join them, Xannan planned to return the favor of a bump on the head.

"I could ask Arjun to force you to recount the memory in its entirety."

"Because you think I would lie about Anna and Mother dying?" Gailin reached out, and Xannan turned, sword ready to strike if need be. His brother flinched but stepped closer, hand remaining outstretched. "I would never lie about that. Not knowing what it would do to you." His voice cracked. "To me. Our mother, Xannan. How could you think I—"

"I *have* to do something, Gailin." Xannan's arm trembled, muscles along his upper back and shoulders aching. "I promised I'd keep her safe." His fist struck the wall hard enough the wood paneling splintered. "I need to know how to relive your past memories. I need to see what happened."

Gailin's chest heaved as his lips parted and he shook his head. "I told you—"

"Not because I want to see how they died, but to see who killed them."

"But you can't!"

"Why not?"

"Because—" Gailin's gaze roved up the splintered wood, and he squinted. "Because we were told you can't." He crossed his arms. "I can't remember if you've ever tried."

"And now would be the perfect time. Once we know who is responsible, we annihilate them."

"But Father said—"

"Blazes, Gailin, do you do everything Father says?" Despite the approach of his father's voice, Xannan continued speaking. "*Father* says I can't relive another's past. *Father* says I can't be the royal and the soldier. *Father* says he'll sentence me according to my unsanctioned crimes."

Their father halted behind Gailin, so Xannan stepped around his brother to face the man. "What if I make Arjun persuade you to tell us every memory you've asked Eonar to erase?"

Muscles in his father's temple pulsed with a wild rhythm.

"Follow me." Seth turned, saying over his shoulder, "The elves are not in their rooms. They await us in my study."

"No." Xannan rested his sword's tip on the stone floor. "You can tell the truth without Arjun forcing you to. It's a simple thing, really." Xannan waved a hand about, almost lackadaisical. "A conscious choice. Did you or did you not ask Eonar to erase our memories multiple times?"

Seth paused in his forward movement and turned around. A single nod from his father made Xannan readjust his grip on his sword, a motion which made his father take a step back.

Smirking, Xannan asked, "What are you afraid I will do if I know the truth of the magic embedded in this blade?"

His father's shoulders stiffened. Guards Xannan himself had helped train joined them in the dark hallway. They stood to either side of them, both with hands hovering above their weapons.

Black clouds tumbled and thickened within Xannan's sword, nearly the entirety of the weapon claimed by the black hue. It looked better that way. No bright white, just an all-consuming darkness. The blade's appearance matched how Xannan felt. Without Anna, he had no light left.

Xannan lifted his sword with a silent wish for his father to be honest. To explain why he'd gone from the man who had founded this country out of kindness to a king who'd manipulated his sons.

He could feel Gailin's presence behind him, hovering within reach. If any could prevent Xannan from harming others, it would be his brother. But Gailin would not allow their weapons to meet. No matter how many times Xannan asked. Even then, when Xannan peered over his shoulder, Gailin had a firm grip on his own sword. It was his last option. The only way he could think of to possibly see her one more time.

"Why do you fear the blades combining?" Xannan asked over his shoulder. "They long to reunite. You have to feel it."

Perhaps that was the memory stolen from them, too. But every ounce of anger he added to his boiling blood made him desperate. Reunite the swords, and maybe he could bring her back. Bring Anna and their mother back.

"The thought fills me with a cold dread." Gailin's words were clipped, further betraying his nerves. "And curiosity. What could be done with Eilon's power? Is the lure of such magic worth the consequence?"

A flicker at the corner of his eye. Wide skirts, dark hair. Xannan turned to the form, heart sinking as the image faded into plain wood-paneled walls. "Death comes to us all in the end, Gailin. Why not make the most of what we can access before our end comes?"

Gailin shook his head and stepped closer to Xannan. "Regardless of the power available, we should not take such a risk."

Clouds no longer swirled in his sword; it had turned a solid black. The blade yearned for more, begged to be taken elsewhere. In the darkened recesses of the hallway, Xannan noticed shadows lengthening and stretching. He itched to look but after one step toward it, Gailin grasped his sword arm, his father the other.

He was stronger. But if he tugged too quickly, he could send either his father or brother tumbling over the balcony. Or both. In his periphery, the shadows lengthened, faltered, then reappeared with a vengeance.

His sword yearned for those shadows. And he didn't want to deny it.

"Xannan." Gailin's grip tightened. "Whatever you're about to do, don't."

Faces shimmered in those shadows. Anna. His mother. Mikhael. Hundreds of soldiers whose lives had been the casualties of war. His father's war. Those deaths were on Seth's hands. Not the other countries. Not even the elves. But his father's.

The growing darkness, no longer a shadow, but a black cloud annihilating what little light remained, offered a promise. Xannan focused on controlling his breaths, studying the faces as they surfaced one by one. A promise. A way to revive those whose lives had been cut short.

The guards, ignorant of their king's request for them to remain, backpedaled when Xannan's arms tensed. He tugged his father closer and rammed his shoulder into the man's chest. Seth's grip loosened and he stumbled, driven into the wooden railing by Xannan's foot. The momentum pulled Xannan free of Gailin's hold. Shadows called. Beckoned.

The sword yearned for him to enter. He would reclaim what was his.

Distantly, he heard Gailin's shouting. Cursing? A thud, the roar of falling water. Tendrils of shadows swirled about his feet, encasing his legs, then his hands, culminating around his sword. His heart rate spiked as the shadows pulled him into their abyss.

26

Torn between reaching for his brother or his father, Gailin seized neither. Between the dark clouds consuming his brother and winking out of existence and the crack of wood as his father slammed into the balcony railing, Gailin's words became a series of strangled shouts and curses. At himself. At the situation. At the elves. The dragons. The curse of being a wielder of a magical blade whose power he still didn't truly understand.

The two guards who had backed away from the encroaching shadows halted, staring at him with wide eyes. When his father groaned, Gailin shook himself free of his petrifying thoughts and skidded toward his father, crumpled on the floor. Thankfully, Seth hadn't fallen over the balcony.

Gailin's gratitude dissipated as he realized why his father hadn't fallen to the floor below. The balcony had cracked in several places. One of the wooden spindles meant to prevent such falls had impaled Seth's shoulder.

"Find Eonar." Seth lifted a lethargic hand, attempting to reach the wound.

Gailin moved his father's hand away. "Do as he said. Both of you. He's safe with me."

"With all due respect, sir, your brother—"

"Is gone." Gailin made a sharp gesture toward the empty hallway. No clouds. No faint approaching tendrils. No Xannan.

He should have tried harder to prevent his brother from making such a foolish decision. He could feel his blade yearning for Xannan's and hoped that meant his brother was alive. "And I have no intention of harming my father. Speak to none but Eonar or Arjun. Now go, before his wound is too dire for even the elves to heal."

Both guards saluted and raced off. Gailin searched his father for any additional wounds, ripping his shirt to inspect his chest. A bruise blossomed over Seth's heart, which beat too rapidly.

Gailin tore at his hair and almost screamed. He'd just buried his mother. He couldn't lose his father and brother, too. Not like this. Not this permanently.

"Think, think, think," Gailin whispered to himself while assessing the damage Xannan had caused. Splinters of wood, bruised chest, wet breaths. "Blazes." Gailin removed his coat and pressed it against the bleeding wound as a weak attempt to stop the inordinate amount of blood, hoping his father would remain conscious until Eonar arrived.

"There's no option left now, Gailin." A dribble of blood spilled over Seth's lips as he coughed. "You will be my heir."

"Save the speech, Father." Gailin lifted to see over his father's head, searching the floor below for two guards leading two tawny-haired elves. He even listened for the clinking of glass that grated on his nerves. Never as much as it did Xannan, but the consistent presence was often a source of aggravation.

"No speech, just truth." Seth grabbed Gailin's undershirt and tugged him closer. "You've seen what happens at Praesidio's Linking. And you know how to sever that link. But the memories are bound. Eonar and I are the only other two who know since his magic doesn't work on me."

Gailin settled onto his feet, his application of pressure against his father's wound faltering for a moment. The truth, one Gailin had always suspected. He knew what would happen. The phrase "Praesidio's Linking" made his skin prickle more than his father's paling color.

Blood pulsed from his father's shoulder. Words tumbled in Gailin's mind in time with the beating of his heart. *Memories. Magic. Praesidio. Father. Xannan. Mother. Anna.*

Words halted. He needed to find Ella, needed to make sure she was safe. They, whoever they were, had targeted Anna to get to Xannan, to steal him away. And if they harmed Ella—flashes of a gory forest surfaced, broken when warm liquid trickled between his fingers. Gailin pressed his lips together. His father was losing too much blood.

Eonar tapped Gailin's shoulder and took his place at Seth's side. "Explain while I work." Without preamble, the elf tugged the wood free of Seth's shoulder. The lack of reaction from his father made Gailin's palms sweat. "Xannan?"

"Disappeared." Gailin wet his lips, focusing on not letting himself spiral further into despair. Flame. Blood. Ash. Melted skin. More of his family gone. "Shadows consumed him."

Eonar squinted back at Gailin, hands continuing their work as they placed drops from several different vials into Seth's wound. When the elf's brows creased, Gailin's heart sank, and he fell back into a seated position. All he could do was watch the elf work while his understanding and witnessing of battle wounds made him worry for his father's survival.

"Consumed him or he entered them?" Eonar held a hand out behind him. When another clear vial was set in Eonar's palm, Gailin lifted his head to find Arjun standing above them with a clenched jaw. Seth's incoherent murmurs claimed Gailin's focus until Eonar snapped his fingers in front of Gailin's face and repeated his question.

"Unclear." Gailin swallowed, stood and drew his sword.

"Prince Gai—"

"I'm not going to hurt anyone," Gailin interrupted Arjun as he inspected his blade. Clear with tendrils of white. So similar and yet so different to what had occurred with Xannan's blade. "Xannan's blade turned solid black. As though the night sky itself formed his weapon."

At the glance Arjun and Eonar shared, Gailin considered lashing out with the weapon he'd drawn. But he sheathed it and lowered to his knees on the opposite side of his father. The bleeding had slowed, the wooden rod had been removed, and Seth's chest lifted and lowered in shallow, shaky motions.

Gailin forced himself to meet the red-irised eyes of the Elder Elf. The elf's pitying gaze answered his unspoken question. Not all wounds could be healed. Even with the fancy liquids of the elves' creation.

"How long?" he whispered as he studied his father.

"Depends on several factors. I'll do what I can for him, but I make no promises." Eonar stood and brushed off his tan robes, frowning at the streaks of blood. Motioning at the guards, the Elder Elf instructed them to carry their king to his quarters. Carefully. When Gailin moved to assist, Eonar placed a hand on his arm and shook his head. "You and I must speak. Your father will not be awake for some time, not after the amount of blood he just lost. Arjun will watch over him."

A glance down confirmed Eonar's words. The pool of his father's blood on the balcony had spread, smeared by him and the elf, and limned the balcony's edge.

"Xannan wouldn't want to kill Father," he whispered as the dark blood staining the stone floors consumed his vision. He stunk of ash and sweat and blood. Of death and fear.

"What's happening, Eonar? The attack on the carriage? Xannan's blade? Shadows consuming him? My blade changing?" Too many emotions bombarded his senses. So he shut them out. He didn't want the useless visions. "Father said I know what happens when the blades combine and how to break their connection. But you locked those memories away."

Eonar studied his blood-stained palms and sighed. "What can be locked can be unlocked, even without the key."

"Meaning I can reclaim the memories you've bound?"

A small nod from the elf stirred the roiling emotions in Gailin's gut. Eonar reached for Gailin again, halting and clenching his hand into a loose fist. "You are not ready to receive what I've hidden. Not today. Not now."

"For once, I agree with you." Gailin lifted a hand to scrub his eyes, pausing when he realized his palms were coated in his father's blood. Dried and darkened, permanently stained with his inability to protect those he loved.

His incoherent shouts as he tried to decide what to do reverberated in his mind. Pull his brother from the darkness or make sure his father didn't fall off the balcony. He'd done neither. Petrified, frozen. How could he, someone so indecisive and unsure, ever rule a kingdom?

"You know where my brother is?"

Eonar winced. "I have suspicions, but no confirmation. Eilon can transport between locations using shadows of magic. It is possible that the dragon we thought gone has taken your brother."

Gailin balked. "To what end?"

"To reclaim his magic."

"At the cost of my brother's life?"

"Perhaps."

Despite the blood coating his hands, Gailin buried his face in his palms and chuckled. He didn't know what other response to give. A week ago, everyone in his family was alive and well. Thriving. Preparing for a glorious future.

He swallowed and asked in a meek whisper, "Ella?"

"With her mother, last I saw this morning."

Tension he'd held in his shoulders and neck disappeared at hearing Ella was safe. Exhaustion clawed at his muscles, at the backs of his eyes, and culminated in the throbbing of his head. He sighed and lowered his hands. "Do you have something that can help me sleep?"

27

Darkness consumed Xannan. Time became aloof. It lingered and stretched, shortened and disappeared. Xannan wasn't sure if time passed or paused. Shadows danced along his skin, fingerlike wisps clawing at the sword he still clutched in his hand.

The weapon vibrated. Rhythmically. Slow, steady. Same as his heartbeat. Same as the shadows swirling around him, so thick he couldn't see beyond them. Something roared in his immediate vicinity, and he covered his ears, lowering his hands when the sound ebbed.

A dragon's roar. He'd heard that roar once before, on that fateful day when Praesidio was cleaved in two. Of all the events he'd experienced, that was the one he consistently relived, hunting for explanations as he tried to understand what, exactly, he held in his hand.

Where once that day had held gaps, silhouettes formed. His father speaking with Eonar. A hand on his shoulder and his brother's.

A different roar consumed his senses, steady despite its slightly chaotic beat. Tendril by tendril, the shadows subsided, releasing him from their hold. Xannan flinched at the light streaming into his vision from one side.

He listened and tilted away from the light to acclimate his vision. Slight rustling, like the feathered wings of a bird, to his left. Water crashed against stone to his right, the same direction as the sun's rays penetrating the cascading sheets of water.

Other than the deep rumble and the rustling feathers, Xannan heard no one else. His grip on the sword tightened as he lifted his head. Air caught in Xannan's lungs, then his throat. Eilon. As vast and massive as their first encounter, the dragon watched Xannan with curious beady silver eyes. His body as still as the stone around them; Eilon's tail didn't even twitch. The elves once theorized the beast of a dragon had died, but neither him nor Gailin had ever believed them.

As usual, he and Gailin had been right.

Lifting Praeteritum, Xannan faced the dragon. An orange orb pulsed at the base of Eilon's neck, not far from where Xannan imagined the beast's heart might be. Eilon's color was so similar to the droki that it made blocks of ice slither inside him as cold fear welled. Had Eilon recreated the droki Magna had destroyed? That was a question to ponder later, once he wasn't facing down a dragon whose intentions he didn't know. The beast had brought him there. How Xannan knew that, he wasn't sure, but it sounded right.

When Eilon lowered to his haunches and brought his snout level with Xannan's face, Xannan focused on maintaining his composure. He'd survived droki, he could defeat a dragon if needed. But Eilon wasn't advancing on him, nor did he appear threatening. More curious and quizzical.

Xannan held Praeteritum aloft between him and the dragon, analyzing Eilon's chest so he knew where best to plunge the blade. "You brought me here?"

A single nod lowered Eilon's head enough for Xannan to make out the spikes along the dragon's head, shaped like an imposing crown. The pulsing of Praeteritum almost matched the orb in Eilon's neck, and Xannan furrowed his brows.

Memories approached the surface, memories he wasn't summoning. These had to be Eilon's doing; some were events Xannan had not experienced himself. Gailin's despair. Ella's pity. Him knocking his father toward the balcony. Anna. His mother's death. His father's. . . Xannan grimaced; those thoughts could wait until he knew if this beast would be friend or foe.

"How?"

Faint shadows swirled around Xannan's feet.

"Fascinating," Xannan murmured, lifting an arm as the shadows encased and swirled, feeling like the faintest whisper of wind. Or a woman's finger trailing along his skin. He resumed his focus on the shadows. "That's how you escaped the cave."

Images he'd attempted to repress surfaced, lingering on Anna's face floating amid the shadows. Xannan wet his lips and tensed his muscles. What did Eilon want with Anna? No one could want anything with Anna anymore; there wasn't even a body left to bury. A muscle in his jaw twitched, and a sudden pain sprang through his temple.

Anna's floating face was joined by the rest of her body, completing the mirage. Clad in the wide blue skirts and tight bodice of her own design. Tears gathered as the sob crawled up his throat. Tiny streams streaked down his cheeks. The first tears he'd shed for his dead beloved, witnessed not by his brother, but by a dragon.

"Her death is tormenting enough," Xannan growled. But he held his palm against the facade of her cheek, wishing he could touch her. Hold her again and never let her go. "I don't need the reminder."

Others joined her. All faint representations of who they were in life. Once vibrant, each new person reminded Xannan of all those lost to his father's cause. His mother. Mikhael. Soldier after soldier after soldier.

"Blazes." Xannan hefted his sword, readying for the strike. The hums of the dragon's orange orb and Praeteritum matched. Xannan froze mid-lift.

"Such power inside one," he whispered, gaze flickering from Eilon to the sword and back again. "But you had to have used so much power to bring me here. How?"

Eilon stepped forward, and Xannan resumed his defensive position. A huff came from the dragon, tendrils of smoke streaming through pointed teeth and glazing the dragon's silver eyes.

"Answers first." Xannan met the dragon's gaze. "Take another step and I'll plunge this"—he hefted the solid black blade—"into your chest."

A mocking huff loosened more tendrils of smoke. Sharp pain pierced Xannan's head, and he saw another visual. Himself with Anna at his side. Gailin, Mikhael, and Edmund one step behind them. Crowns rested atop his and Anna's heads.

Another flash of pain, followed by the absolute annihilation of all those who had tried to harm him. The clans to the north and south, Alkaanians whose country wasn't much older than his own. A grand castle, even greater than the one Xannan's father had commissioned, protruded from the infamous bluff. The Cliff of Lycene. Complete with the roaring waterfall protecting the lone entrance to his future abode.

Within the vision and above the castle, Eilon soared with wings spread wide, surrounded by more of his dark-scaled kind. Each seemed a faint color compared to Eilon, as though they weren't real. A mirage. Perhaps a ghost.

Xannan gasped and dropped to a knee, holding his head with one hand as he failed to maintain his grip on his sword with the other. The sword clattered against the damp cave's stone floor. In his periphery, he noticed Eilon's approach.

"Out of my head." He kept Eilon in his sights and felt blindly for the sword.

The visions had to be facades. The dead were gone forever. All he had left of Anna was his own memories, if he could ever bear to recall them with such vividness. The thought made his beloved flicker into being again. Regal. Commanding. Absolutely stunning regardless of what she wore. A ghost of a smirk as he thought of her without clothes on.

Whatever Eilon was doing, Xannan couldn't allow it. Or could he? If he returned home, his father would never allow him the crown. They'd call him unstable, maybe even arrest him for "unsanctioned" crimes. If he'd done more than injure a few soldiers, a cell would definitely be in his future. But the dragon presented a new path. If what the beast showed him was real. . .

Jaw clenching, Xannan surveyed the cavern. Large enough for ten dragons, it had to extend far beyond the bluff. Every wall glistened, damp from the waterfall's spray. The glow of light from the sun turned a deeper gold, causing the walls to shimmer and sparkle.

When his examination of his surroundings landed on Eilon, he muttered, "Now would be an excellent time for Celena to appear." He made a show of looking around, as though saying the elfwoman's name would summon her. It wouldn't be the first time it had felt that way.

Sighing, Xannan sheathed his sword and lowered to the ground, grimacing as the damp sheen soaked through his pants. Hands braced on his knees, he met Eilon's gaze. "You can show me the future?"

Eilon stepped forward and lowered his jaw to be level with Xannan's head. One blink, and the beast's eyes turned solid black.

Xannan refused to scream from the pain, digging his fingers into his legs instead. The grip would leave bruises, but that pain was a small price to pay for answers. Real, unaltered, answers.

Image after image flickered, appearing and fading with increasing speed.

"Blazes, dragon," Xannan gritted out as his stomach churned from the dizzying effect. He'd siphoned through images quickly himself before, but not at that insane pace. "One at a time."

Skin prickling as the cascade of images resumed, Xannan closed his eyes and gritted his teeth. A warm sensation coated his entire body, almost comforting. The images slowed, showing Xannan the future he so desperately desired. Had he known it might hurt this much to lose his inheritance, he would have done more to protect it. Eilon could help him.

All the beast needed was for Xannan to connect the blades to release Eilon's magic. He frowned, eyes remaining closed, urging the vision of him and Gailin reuniting Praesidio to reappear and linger. The darkness of Praeteritum sucked in the bold brightness of Futurae. Two halves of one whole, no different from him and Gailin. But the image was wrong.

Gailin would never agree. Not unless coerced. And of all the things looming in this world, the combining of the blades scared Gailin the most. Did he fear what would happen to them when the blades connected or something beyond themselves? *Blazing idiot, should have asked him.*

More heat surrounded Xannan, and his frown deepened. Hand on his sword, he opened his eyes and all air emptied from his lungs. Black flame surrounded him, spewing from Eilon's mouth.

Before Xannan could draw his weapon, Eilon's long wing slammed into his temple, and all Xannan could do was moan as he lost consciousness.

28

Wind rustled through an open window. Steady drips beat against the castle's stone walls. A spring rainstorm which would give plants life. Gailin's insides went hollow, filling with the tumultuous cascade of emotions attached to that singular word. Life.

Material wrung in someone's hands near Gailin's head. Before he opened his eyes, he laid an arm over his face so he stared at his dark sleeve rather than a bright room. He grimaced. Every source of light reminded him of the flame which had engulfed him yet not harmed him.

Why should he survive while others didn't? Of all in his family, he had to be the least capable. He didn't have the confidence or decision-making skills his brother and father possessed. Nor did he have the calm kindness and understanding his mother displayed. He clenched his jaw. Had displayed.

The wringing of material continued until he lifted his arm enough to arch an eyebrow at Ella. "How long have you been sitting there watching me sleep?"

Her distant hazel eyes darted between him and the floor as she leaned forward to rest her arms on the mattress. "Eonar said you should have woken a day ago," she whispered. "So when you didn't, I made myself comfortable."

Gailin grunted and swung his legs over the bed's edge. After resting his hand on Ella's arm long enough to share a silent understanding, he stood and gathered clothes. He should have changed before downing the vial Eonar had handed him or spoken with Ella before he'd willingly knocked himself unconscious, but he'd needed rest. Unaddled sleep so his body could have a semblance of recovery. Or begin to recover. His legs and back were stiff as he trudged toward the bathing chamber. Ella followed at first, pulled back by a knock at the door. She waved him on, whispering, "you need a bath more than I do."

Bathed and changed, he returned to find Ella pacing. The motion was uncharacteristic, and he grasped his sword from its place by his dresser, buckling it as he asked, "Whatever it is, you could have come and told me rather than beat a path into the stone. News on Xannan?" When Ella froze mid-step at the question and furrowed her brows, Gailin asked breathlessly, "Father?"

Hazel eyes searched his. "His Majesty sent for you." She spoke slowly. Carefully. "Along with Eonar and the High Priest." Ella smoothed her skirts. "No word on this . . . Xannan."

"Logical," Gailin muttered, hoping the movement of fastening his buttons hid his trembling hands. "He did disappear, but he can't stay hidden for long." The last button done, Gailin held Ella's stare. Tears rimmed her eyes, but she straightened and hooked her arm through his.

With a gentle pat of his arm, she said, "Worry about your father first."

He covered her hand with his and focused on planting one foot in front of the other to follow the familiar path to his parents' rooms. Outside the large doors stood several guards, two of whom stiffened at his approach. Their attention went from him to his sword and back again, as though he might try and attack them as Xannan had. Gailin grimaced. They should have known how

Xannan would react to such news. A twinge in the muscles of his forearms brought recollections of a darkening hallway. In Xannan's mind, Gailin was sure, even kicking their father had been a logical and necessary move.

Sighing, he unbuckled his sword and handed it to the guard who hadn't glanced at it warily. "Xannan's the one you should worry about with his sword. Not me." Gailin loosened the collar of his shirt from his neck. "Take me to my father, Captain."

The guard's brows furrowed as his dark eyes flickered toward Ella.

Ella's hand tensed on his arm. Gentle, calming, but worried. For him, for her, for their future? All of it?

"If you prefer I wait—"

"I want you at my side." Gailin breathed deeply, trying to ignore the emotions gnawing at his skin and insides as he inquired, "Arjun and Eonar?"

The guard holding his sword jerked his head toward the large doors granting entrance to his father's chambers. "Inside, Your Highness."

Gailin leaned forward to take a step and rocked back on his heels, grip on Ella's hand tensing as despair swirled in his gut. It tugged at his insides as if something had a grip on his stomach and was pulling it down and out of him. Choking on the words, he whispered, "I don't want to lose anyone else."

"You never truly lose anyone." Ella kept her hand on his arm and turned to place her other hand over his heart. "Not when you can always keep them with you."

His mouth went dry, and he glanced over Ella's blond hair that was too bright compared to how he felt. Staring at the door, Gailin spoke in a measured cadence. "If Father is dying, it would be wrong of me to insist you be there when he does."

The weight lifted from his chest and warmth suffused his cheek. When he tilted his head down, she pinched her lips together and continued appraising him with her piercing intuitive gaze. "Let me be here for you," she whispered as she tugged him a step closer to the ornate wooden doors. "I will always be here for you."

She gulped, and her eyes shimmered with fresh tears. Ella and Anna had become close friends over the past years. *Blazing idiot. Should have noticed she would need me as much as I need her.*

At the internal use of his brother's curse, Gailin idly wondered where Xannan had gone. With his own ability, Gailin was positive he would know if Xannan had died. The swords sensed one another, called to each other, but now he felt a hollowness. Or perhaps the swirling despair masked whatever emotions thoughts of his brother might dredge to the surface.

He'd seen death, witnessed dire wounds and had been the cause of the demise of others himself, and even with all of that past, he struggled to push the door open. Gailin knew what awaited him. More pain and suffering. After a deep steadying breath, he pushed the door open and entered.

Eonar and Arjun stood to one side of the room, conversing in low murmurs. Silence fell after the door's lengthy creak. Gailin's grip on Ella's hand faltered as he recognized the absence of life in his father's frame. Years of abuse and too much sun had wrinkled Seth's skin, riddling it with scars upon scars. Those scars and pain had led to a new life for Gailin and his brother, one that was not supposed to end with such torment and despair.

The small spark of hope flickering within his chest faltered and died, leaving a gaping hole. An emptiness none could ever fill. Less than a week, and those he held most dear were gone. Gone before he could do anything to change the outcome. Though he remained riveted in place, Gailin wanted to scream. Shout, sob, stab something. Was this Xannan's fault? For doing whatever he did that Gailin could no longer remember?

Clammy hands rested on his cheeks as a face swam into his unfocused vision, and he forced his lungs to accept air again. Ella tugged at her lower lip, tears eager to spill from her eyes. He leaned his forehead to hers, forever grateful this grief surrounding him had not scared her away.

"How long ago?" he whispered, curious if there'd been a chance for him to speak to his father one last time. Gailin remained standing with his forehead against Ella's, eyes closed as he breathed in her comforting presence. When neither of the elves replied, Gailin cleared his throat and repeated his question.

Eonar's voice grew louder as he spoke. "Though I attempted all interventions I know, your father's heart was too damaged to aid his body with proper healing. It is possible he would have died soon even without the injuries he sustained." A pause, a gentler voice. "He passed away moments ago, Your Majesty."

Gailin's shoulders stiffened, jaw tensing. "That title is Xannan's. Not mine."

Both elves whipped their heads toward him when he spoke his brother's name. "You are the named heir, Your Majesty." Eonar clasped his hands behind his back, forehead crinkling. "We will speak of this . . . this Xannan when you are ready."

Eonar shared a look with Arjun, but Gailin held a hand for them to stay. He couldn't speak. Not yet. Thoughts coalesced. Tumbling and swirling. An entire country now depended on him. And he couldn't even protect his family.

"One thought at a time, Gailin," Ella whispered, using her thumb to wipe away his escaped tears. She sniffled, rubbing her nose and swiping at her eyes. "Do you want a moment alone with your father?"

"What use is speaking to those who no longer hear?" Gailin shook his head and his shoulders fell. "Are the emissaries still here?"

"Most." Ella stroked his cheek, and Gailin's forming sob of despair almost escaped.

"I'll need—" His voice cracked, and he swallowed.

Raw emotions pounded through him. Not those of a magical gift. No, these were his. Unaltered by the magic he'd grown accustomed to over the years, these feelings *hurt*.

The aching hole in his chest expanded, and he lifted his chin to gaze over Ella's head at his father's lifeless frame. He shouldn't have been so frustrated with his father so often, should have spoken his mind when he thought it necessary, and helped remind his father that he and Xannan needed their father as much as they needed their king.

But any words he said to the man now would mean nothing. With a shuddering inhale and even shakier exhale, Gailin spoke with a modulated tone. "I'll need to speak with the visiting emissaries."

Ella's thumb stopped mid-stroke, and she frowned. "About?"

"Mending the wounds created by my father in the hope to attain a deeper level of peace than he once did." Gailin turned away from his father's deathbed and faced the elves he'd asked to remain in the room, explaining, "I'd like to begin by offering the elves positions within the castle. You've always helped my brother and me, even if Xannan didn't see it that way."

A moment of silence passed between the elves until Eonar said, "Arjun will remain until you are settled. But he need not reside here, especially since I may need him elsewhere over the years."

"Logical." Gailin spared another glance at his father and pressed his lips together as he lowered Ella's hand from his cheek. "I'll need to address the other nobility as well."

"You needn't rush—"

"Father loved this country, the hope he created." Gailin winced at Ella's pained expression. She knew he wasn't allowing himself to feel, that he'd buried his emotions deeper than ever before. "I must show my claim lest Father's legacy die with him."

"A legacy of scars," Ella murmured.

"A legacy of perseverance," Gailin amended. "I'll speak with those my father placed in charge of confirming the heir. After Xannan's—"

"You keep saying that name, but—" Ella peered up at him, forehead crinkled in worry. "Who is this Xannan?"

Gailin frowned and studied their visages. Both elves wore emotionless masks. But for Ella to ask such a question as this? None could ever forget Xannan after meeting him once. His presence commanded a room, making it so Gailin always felt hidden within his brother's shadow.

"My twin brother—" Gailin's words slowed at their furrowed brows. "He . . . he disappeared in a cloud of shadows. But he was the elder and . . . Blazes . . . why don't any of you recognize his name?" He turned to Ella. "Not even you?"

She shook her head, tugging on her bottom lip with her teeth as she rested a hand on his forearm.

"Perhaps we should avoid giving you more of that sleeping potion in the future." Eonar tugged on the collar of his robe, red eyes briefly flashing brighter. "Seems you had quite the dream."

"My brother is real, Eonar. As real as those of us standing in this room. Xannan's gone, but he's not dead. It's like he's been hidden from me. Him and his sword. He wields the other half of Praesidio. The weapon you formed which cleaved in two amidst Magna and Eilon's battle of wills."

At Gailin's explanation, recognition briefly flitted across Eonar's red eyes at the sword's name, replaced by confusion. Gailin rubbed his face with both hands. The swords. Perhaps the past week of torment would never have happened had some other country agreed to receiving a dragon-blessed elven-crafted blade.

Lowering his hands, he almost flinched when the guard holding his sword offered it to him. Given the sudden turmoil inside, Gailin had forgotten the guard had entered the room with them. Hand hovering above the blade's hilt, Gailin hesitated. He let thoughts coalesce, an idle dream of running away to live out his days with Ella at his side. Days in which the guilt of leaving his home and his people behind would gnaw at him until he returned.

Eonar's expression smoothed. "Dreams can feel real to the recipient, King Gailin."

"Praeteritum and Futurae were formed from Praesidio. I the future, he the past." Gailin brandished his sheathed weapon. "Magical abilities intertwined in a way not even you elves ever truly figured out."

Eonar's flash of a frown sparked a hint of anger, but the Elder Elf said nothing. Sighing, Gailin observed his father one last time. Memories of anger and love arose with equal frequency, and Gailin let them.

But these emotions were his, and he would decide what to do with them now.

With the comforting weight of his sword back around his waist, Gailin released a long, slow breath, grasped Ella's hand, and left the room. He paused outside, squeezing her hand as he whispered, "If it is in my power to prevent it, I will never let harm come to you."

"I know." Ella squeezed back, tilting her head up to him. "And I promise to keep you grounded. As I always have, my love."

"Stay at my side today?"

"And for every day to come."

29

Three Months after Gailin's Coronation

"I'm not changing my mind, Ella."

Gailin continued shoving clothes into a bag without turning to meet her gaze. He knew what he'd find. The crossed arms, the judging eyes, the set jaw that was a mixture of aggravation and exhaustion. Once no more items would fit in the bag, he cinched it shut, slung it over his shoulder, and took a deep breath, steeling himself for a repeat of the argument he wouldn't let Ella win. Especially not now. "You need to rest. And stay here where it's safe."

"I didn't realize growing a human inside me made others see me as glass." Ella flipped her head so her hair whipped over her shoulder as she pressed her crossed arms closer against her chest. "I remain capable of riding a horse and walking and sleeping beneath the stars."

"I'm aware of that." He stepped forward and tapped Ella's nose with a finger, grinning at her glare. "This is a journey I must take on my own." At her scoff and raised brow, Gailin amended with a sigh, "Almost on my own. Celena can communicate with the dragons. No one else I know can do that, so she's coming with me. And not a soul more lest another dragon try and—"

"Fine," Ella said through gritted teeth.

He frowned, wondering if it was exhaustion or anger causing the gritted teeth. Or perhaps the constant queasiness he'd heard other women say plagued them in the early months.

"But if you're not back in three weeks, I'm sending the army after you."

"I'm sure sending Edmund would suffice if I haven't returned by then."

"Plus a battalion."

"I can handle myself, Ella." He rested his hands on her arms and kissed her forehead and her nose and then kissed her on the lips. After a long moment, he pulled away and gazed into her soft and kind hazel eyes. An ever-present hint of worry rested there.

The judgment of her visage bothered him more than the fear. Somehow, between the time Xannan had disappeared in a black cloud and when Gailin had entered his father's rooms, it was as if the world had forgotten Xannan ever existed. Each time he'd said his brother's name in the past six months, it had been met with quizzical stares, pinched brows, and worried expressions.

The answer to that phenomenon, among others, was what he sought. If any might know where Xannan now resided, it would be Magna. And if she didn't, Gailin would scour the lands for stories. His brother was not easily hidden.

Outside, his mount awaited. Saddled and ready. An identical one pranced next to his with Celena doing her best to control the dappled gray stallion. Gailin chuckled and grasped the reins, hushing as he rubbed a hand along the stallion's snout.

"Do any horses like you?"

Celena whisked the reins from his hand and nudged her mount forward. At his side, Edmund attempted to cover his chuckle with a cough.

"You know where to send word if I'm needed." Gailin clasped Edmund's hand, grateful he'd not lost his friend alongside his family.

"Yes, Your Majesty." Edmund released his grip of Gailin's arm and offered a proper bow, adding at Gailin's scrunched brows. "It is your role now, and I must honor it. You would do well to expect the same of others."

Pressing his lips together, Gailin mounted and followed the impatient elf outside the castle walls. The soldier was right. But it felt wrong. They all accepted his role so readily, as though there had been no other option than for him to assume the throne upon his father's passing.

And yet, the crown had not been meant for him. He knew that. No one else did. When he'd questioned Eonar about the strength of bound memories, the elf admitted he'd considered erasing a person's existence but had never attempted such, claiming the magic too complicated and the possibility of an error too great. If he forgot one person, all his efforts would be for naught. "From my perspective," Gailin had said, "forgetting just one person seems to have done the job well enough." Unfortunately, or perhaps fortunately, Eonar had had no reply.

Their journey was one of silence and solitude, despite traveling together. Gailin had refused Edmund's idea of an honorary guard. It would bring too much attention, and Celena claimed she would not take him back to the matriarch's home if others traveled with them. He could remember the cave but not how to gain entrance. Another sign his memories had been tampered with time and time again.

One of Eonar's messages to him rattled through his mind as they plodded along grass-covered ground absent of paths. Wherever Celena was taking him, few others had gone. Memories of the previous paths existed, barely acknowledged by the differing colors of grass or the height of the plants which towered over others. According to Eonar, his own memories could be unlocked even without magical aid.

"Continue brooding and you'll march that horse straight into the rocky mountainside," Celena scoffed at his side.

Gailin jolted, snapping his head up and gaping at the mountain towering above them. Last he'd surveyed the horizon, the mountains had to have been a full day's ride away. Or had they ridden for another day?

Sighing, Celena dismounted and grumbled about the aches in her thighs as she attempted to tie the reins to a branch. After sliding off the stallion, Gailin led both mounts to a tree, tying them with enough slack they could graze the nearby grass.

He placed both hands on his hips and frowned at the scraggly rocky mountainside. "We're climbing a mountain?"

The elf-woman almost snorted a laugh. "Climb a mountain? No." She lifted a branch and gestured. "We're going to walk up the mountain, Your Majesty. Unless you're not up for the task and wish to return home?"

Gailin gritted his teeth, ignoring the urge to glance over his shoulder. Tightening the strap of his sword belt and retrieving the saddle bag to sling over his shoulder, Gailin ducked beneath the branch and concentrated on placing one foot in front of the other while not looking too far to his right where, after walking almost two hundred steps, a sheer drop to his death awaited.

It'd been nearly six years since he'd stood near those two dragons and watched their battle of wills result in Praesidio's breaking. A weapon which the elves recalled creating. Celena even remembered the name of Praeteritum, the half which had latched itself to Xannan. Yet not even the elves remembered his brother. They recognized the name and its connection to the blade, but it was as if his brother had become a myth. A ghost who haunted no one's thoughts but his own.

Others called Xannan a figment of his imagination, a creation to help him cope with the loss of his mother and father and his betrothed's closest friend. Anna had been more than just Ella's friend, though. He knew, deep down, what others claimed were lies.

"She knows you're coming," Celena said, pausing at an opening upon a small bluff and gesturing inside. "I'll wait, though I may still hear what occurs."

"I need you to translate what she says."

"Magna's requested to visit with you alone." Celena appraised him and shifted her gaze to the sprawling landscape beyond the mountain path. "If asked, I will join you."

He shifted, turning enough to see the rolling hills barely visible on the opposite side of the valley and smiled. "Enjoy the view," he said and ducked inside the cave.

Damp, yet welcoming, he continued down a narrow opening. He remembered walking this path, nudging his brother in the side and receiving an elbow to his abdomen in retaliation. If Xannan were a figment of his imagination, his brain had done a very thorough job of creating an entire life for the creation.

More memories surfaced. His mother and father had walked ahead, led by Eonar and his son as well as the ever-resolute Celena. Gailin paused and traced a finger along the damp wall. Soon he'd enter the cavern where Praesidio had been split in two. One half rested around his waist; the other had disappeared. He gripped his sword hilt and pressed his hand against the cave's wall, listening.

His thoughts roamed for a time as he tried to make sense of who or what would desire to erase his twin brother from existence. Gailin lowered his hand and continued toward where Magna waited. Not only did he debate what questions to ask but how he should approach the matriarch of a dragon.

Gailin paused at the entrance to the cavern. His heart raced, his breaths quickened, and his grip of his sword faltered. Before him rested the once-bold white matriarch of her race. Scales now mottled with brown and feathers absent from her wings, she lifted to all four feet and spread her wings wide as though to say her strength had not yet been depleted. Magna didn't need to show off; her presence still made Gailin gape in awe.

Gailin cleared his throat and inched forward, hands clenching at his side. "I probably should have asked what to say, or do, but apparently Celena wished to enjoy the view."

A smoky huff came from the dragon, and Gailin's heart thundered inside his chest. Magna lowered her snout and tapped the ground, so Gailin approached the space, unable to decide where to look. At the solid white eyes, at the featherless outstretched wings, at the scales dotted with brown. Everywhere he paused his study of the dragon's features, he felt guilty for studying her.

This time, her huff sounded amused, until she nudged the sword hanging from his waist. Gailin removed it and held the sheathed weapon in both hands before him. "I need to understand what it contains."

He looked up in her eyes, flinching as they closed until he saw an image of a similar sword held by his heirs. Wielded to protect the country his father founded, used to kill those who would threaten the LeNoirs' legacy. Gailin grimaced, wishing for a future of peace that his own ability showed him would not occur for many generations.

The wielding of the blade shifted to an image of Magna herself, of the moment of the sword's creation. The man all around him claimed no longer existed stood next to him. Gailin's arm kept Xannan from approaching, until the sudden force exploded outward from both dragons, landing all sprawled to the ground, unable to sit up. As he watched, Gailin wondered what might have happened had he grasped Praeteritum first.

When Eilon vanished from the cave, the vision dissipated and Gailin's grip on his sheathed sword tightened as though the pain of his grasp could prevent the tears. "Take it back," he whimpered. "Make it stop tormenting me with the unknown."

He dropped the sword at the dragon's feet and fell to his knees while Magna stood and spread her wings once more, nudging the sword back to him with her snout.

"It's useless." His voice echoed. "Everyone, my entire family, dead." Gailin lifted his head and stared into the dragon's solid white eyes, allowing the tears to spill. "Father said this gift you and Eilon gave would help us. But it didn't. It's done nothing more than hurt us time and time again."

Magna rumbled, low and deep, rattling the small rocks strewn about the cave. She touched her snout to the hilt once more, and the solid white blade glowed. The longer it glowed, the harder it became for him to breathe. He clutched at his chest, gasping for air as he collapsed to his side. When Magna huffed another breath along the sword's edge, turning it a simple silver, Gailin shuddered and gulped down air.

He stared at the ceiling, shaking and choking down sobs until he could resume a seated position. "I don't want it anymore. This magic, this ability, whatever it is in this sword which changed us so drastically. Take it back."

In response, he saw a repeat of his heirs holding the silver sword, ending with a young brown-skinned woman holding a solid white blade identical to the one Magna had just changed. The dragon resumed her position prone on the ground, pity in her gaze. Gailin grasped the sword. Visions flashed, more quickly and clearly than any he had seen before. Whatever Magna did had changed how the weapon interacted with him.

He slumped, moisture from the cave's floor seeping through his pants. Running a hand through his blond hair, he hedgingly asked, "Did you attack the caravan?"

Magna's head whipped to him, increasing wisps of smoke escaping both nostrils. One image, of Eilon spewing his treacherous flame. Gailin swallowed. "Why? How did I survive?"

The matriarch lowered, crossing one paw over the other and resting her snout atop both. Eyes closed, her wings flicked. Grimacing, Gailin took that as his sign the conversation was over.

Outside the cave, he found Celena resting against the rock wall next to the entrance. "Told you she has her own ways of communicating." A nod at the sword around his waist, she added, "It communicated with your magic and the magic the LeNoir line possesses."

"My magic? But my magic comes from—"

"You."

"Not the sword?"

"It latched on to you and the other—I know there was another because I saw that vision the same as you did. The both of you already possessed magic you had not yet used; the others of us capable of receiving magic did. Your father, though he never discussed it with you, I presume, gained an ability similar to your own."

"And you know all of this how? Why wait to share this information?"

"I listen to the dragons. What they give is often misunderstood." Celena shrugged. "And no one asked me the right questions."

"No wonder Xannan was always aggravated with you," Gailin muttered while fixing his sword belt. "She didn't explain why Eilon attacked."

Celena canted her head and grimaced. "To recuperate the magic she stole from him. Some of which is"—she tapped the sword's hilt, forcing Gailin to resituate the weapon once more as she added—

"in that sword. That's why his flame could not harm you. Dragons cannot damage their own stores of magic."

"Anything else I don't know but should?"

The elf-woman's red eyes sparkled with the setting sun, coated with amusement. "The sword is now as much a part of you as your own magic already was." Her red eyes deepened, reflecting the glow of the horizon as she smirked. "Don't lose it."

30

Sixteen Years Later

"Calm down, Edmund." Gailin rubbed his temples while keeping a wary eye on his commander and adviser of the past fifteen years.

Before the simple throne Gailin had commissioned to replace his father's, Edmund paced. Back and forth, arms and legs jerking at each step. Though he'd formatted the treaties himself, other leaders had broken them. Thinking of the letters made Gailin resume rubbing his temples in the hope of avoiding the headache of deciding how to retaliate against Alkaan's attack on the Tremaine family's plantation. "Your family will be safe."

The grizzled soldier rounded on him. "Permission to speak freely, sire?"

Gailin raised a brow, grimacing as the throne doors opened and his eldest son slipped through. The boy, Viktor, was barely as old as Gailin's reign of fifteen years. Quiet, observant, Viktor moved through the edges of the room, likely hoping to avoid notice by either Gailin or his aggravated general.

"Too many ears, General," Gailin muttered softly enough that only Edmund should hear.

Edmund took a cursory survey of the room, head tipping back when he noted Viktor's presence. Crossing his arms across his chest, Edmund turned back to Gailin. "I seek permission to assist my family in protecting their lands."

Gailin's elbows dug into the tender skin of his knees, and he massaged each temple. "I need you here, General."

"Oh, drop the show for the boy." Edmund's hands fell to his sides. "Would you sit by if your children were in danger?"

Gailin straightened, and Edmund huffed a breath and said, "You wouldn't, and you know it. Family is everything to you. Otherwise you wouldn't have spent these past fifteen years hunting for a man who does not exist."

"General, now is not the time."

"Do you not wish General Tremaine to speak truthfully to you, Father?" Viktor's voice belied the innocence he sought to hide. Features too youthful to fool anyone, Viktor clasped his hands behind him and tilted his head. "He has made a logical request. Why deny him?"

"Because the Gift shares a sense of overwhelming dread at the thought of letting Edmund leave," Gailin said, threading a hand through his hair before forgetting he wore the crown. He didn't. Not often. But he'd sensed it might be necessary that day.

"The Gift," Edmund scoffed. "I'm so over magic controlling what you choose to do, Your Majesty."

"It has rarely failed him," Viktor said plainly. "Why not send a secondary commander to inspect the Jearnian plantations? Send them with a small troop to be safe."

"Smart," Edmund said. "But I'd prefer to go myself." He paused, fists clenching at his sides. "A new request, Your Majesty. Move me to the base at Vandyl. I can keep watch on the army there and on my family. It was, after all, a castle built to protect those within."

Gailin leaned back on his throne and grunted. Vandyl's newest abode—which many called a castle though it had not been his intent—was meant to house his soldiers since the army had outgrown their barracks at Cantadad. Those numbers were a necessity he despised, but he refused to allow any other country to take back his people. They deserved protection.

"Viktor, thoughts."

Gailin's eldest son tilted his head, lips pursed in thought and displaying more of the boy's youthful innocence. Unlike his youngest brother, Jacob, Viktor kept himself well-maintained. Pristine. Almost pruning. The other two, Simon and Violet, were a mixture of all their personalities. Soon, though, Gailin believed Violet's beauty would rival Ella's. Gailin watched Viktor's stoicism, waiting.

"Let General Tremaine attend the troops in Vandyl. It would allow you to give me the opportunity for leadership here."

Gailin tensed. Viktor was too young to be leading anyone. Gailin gripped the armrests of the throne. He'd been barely three years older than Viktor when his father first sent him to a potential battlefield. And to destroy those deadly droki who'd been gone long enough most believed them a myth, too. Same as Xannan. And Eilon. Too long, Gailin berated himself, he'd waited too long to respond. But even allowing Edmund to relocate to Vandyl filled him with an odd sensation. It wasn't quite dread or despair. But worry.

He surveyed his friend, the only one close to him, aside from his wife, who hadn't died that dreadful week. Agreeing to let Edmund go made Gailin feel like he was once again losing a piece of himself. But the tension coiled in Edmund's stature led to Gailin nodding his assent. The general's posture didn't change when Gailin met Edmund's gaze.

"May the Blaze of our ancestors protect you, my friend."

BOOK ONE
THE LENOIR LEGACY
CRISTEN JENNETTE

Chapter One

An agreement. The words seared into Charles's mind again. He leaned forward in his chair to lay the book he had been trying to read down on his bed. There was no use continuing, not when *those* words were drifting across his mind instead. The mention of the agreement was subtle, but the words were no less poignant than when King Phillippe first created it.

"As if I need a refresher," he muttered to his empty room in the barracks, wondering why else the king had requested his presence that evening.

He ran one hand through his dark brown hair and made a mental note to cut it before the curls appeared again. Princess Rosealyn had not only asked questions about them, she still mocked him for how they looked. Few here had curls. Before he could stop it, a smirk tugged at the corner of his lips—sometimes the way he toed the edge of "proper" was a source of amusement for her, and for him. But the king's words would stomp through his head again, reminding Charles of his role.

His bed sat snug along one wall, sheets disheveled from use with the small book lying face down in its center. The book was fraying at the edges, and a ragged white crack was widening along its spine, reminiscent of the small scar marring his own chin. Given it was his only book from home and written in his mother's flowery hand, he had read it time and time again. Even when pages fell out and had to be stuffed back in, he read it.

He kept glazing over the words that morning though, glancing instead at a thin slip of paper with General Azeiah's crooked hasty handwriting. It stared at him from the small desk a hand's breadth from the door. Between the desk and closed door, hooks held a long-sleeved black coat with white-rimmed cuffs and large white buttons. And his sword.

He moved the chair back and knocked into the small water basin on the opposite wall. He shifted the chair again, angled so he could stretch his legs, though his feet reached beneath his bed. A deep breath in and out, he reread the words the general had sent.

King Phillippe requests your presence tomorrow evening. ~A

He pushed away the swirling anxiety about his meeting with the king. It was almost time to relieve Moss from night-guard duty—and for the princess's next training session. He stood and donned the coat, closing every button despite how the topmost one in the collar's midst threatened to choke him. After a quick tug at each sleeve, he cinched the sword belt around his waist.

Eyes falling on the singular line of the note again, Charles debated what the king wanted to discuss this time. Their agreement was well established after ten years, and Charles had upheld every term so far. As had Phillippe. But still he wondered. *A secret? No, though Orda'anians can be petty. Or maybe she...*

Charles shook the thoughts from his head. Neither Princess Rosealyn nor King Phillippe had reason to distrust him, and her training was going well. After receiving his assignment to train the princess, Charles had insisted she read the books and study the images of the techniques, only to discover she had already read all there was to know. And he was positive she had spied on his training long before her father had given her permission to hold a weapon herself. He smiled. He was proud of her continuous improvement and wondered if she would attempt a new move on him today.

Charles opened his door and walked through the officers' wing of the barracks, noting the glow of sun lighting the castle's walls. Those tall, formidable walls prevented him from appreciating the display of color when the sun crested the horizon. Most mornings he could be found outside the castle walls for a brief run or meandering walk, but sleep had been hard to find after reading General Azeiah's note.

The halls of the castle were quiet in the early morning, and the soft thud of his boots echoed. Dragonstone, as some called it, lined the base of the walls before transitioning into the common gentle gray of regular stone. Wind carrying the smell of morning dew gusted through well-placed windows, making their deep purple curtains billow into the walkway. A winter-like scent lingered on the breeze that shifted his brown hair just into view before he pushed it back.

Charles turned into the main hallway, walking down the center to remain out of the way of servants dashing about with loads of linens or clothing. It was odd to see so many still, given Vandyl's castle housed only the royal family, necessary soldiers, a handful of priests, and enough servants to keep the palace running smoothly. Any excess staff stayed with Duchess Adela at the old castle in Cantadad.

Visits to Vandyl, the capital where Charles currently resided, weren't prohibited, of course, but they had become a rarity as crops dwindled and Orda'an's neighboring countries issued more threats with each passing day. Charles believed the king and his family should have already moved to Cantadad, which was much further south and therefore further from the dangers which continuously approached from the north. Though the eastern country of Jearnia remained silent, he feared what they would try in the future. Instead, the king accompanied the battalions, fighting alongside the soldiers, much to the queen's chagrin.

Servants ignored Charles as he walked, and he grinned inwardly. He spent so much of his time walking beside the princess he had grown accustomed to the honorifics they offered her. A silent chuckle accompanied the invisible grin as he recalled Princess Rosealyn's scowl for each servant who insisted on bowing or curtsying to her.

Lieutenant Flynn Moss stood outside the princess's door, leaning against the wall with one foot propped against the gray stone. His head jolted back up when it touched the wall, and Charles shook his head at the youth. Moss's light hair was short, barely visible above the scalp, and his deep brown eyes were wide, as though only mental effort kept him awake.

"Long night, Moss?" Charles asked.

The younger soldier snapped to attention. "Quiet night, Captain," Moss responded while fighting a yawn.

"I told you, Moss." Charles shifted his weight to one leg and rested his hand on the leather-bound hilt of his sword, fighting a yawn of his own. "Sleep during the day, at least the morning hours. You can't function as the night guard if you don't sleep sometime."

"Yes, sir," Moss mumbled, fist still held to his chest at attention.

"You're relieved, Lieutenant. Of this post, that is. Your orders are to sleep. If I catch you this exhausted at the morning change again, you *will* be reassigned. Understood?"

The younger soldier bristled but nodded. Charles watched Moss's careful, albeit wobbly, steps down the hallway. The gray stone to each side was even lighter in some places, a tinge of white providing evidence of the tapestries which once adorned the walls. Charles turned back to the princess's chamber door and gently rapped his knuckles against it.

"You can come in," came the princess's melodic voice.

Charles opened the door and leaned against the frame. Chairs in their haphazard organization and the colored rugs scattered across the floor greeted him. From her chosen seat in the middle of the room, she looked up from the book she was reading. Rosealyn's brown eyes twinkled as she snapped the book shut and stood.

"Come to relieve Moss, I see?"

Charles nodded, fighting to cool the rising warmth in his cheeks. "Same as every morning this week, Princess."

She wore the beige dress designed for training with the soldiers. And with him. Pale against her skin, the beige looked almost white rather than a lighter shade of brown. After their first few sessions, she had slit the skirts along the sides for ease of movement. The billowing arm-sleeves received similar treatment. It hugged her torso, framing her rather than cinching her like her court dresses. In this dress, she moved with ease—shoulders relaxed, breathing without strain, and no fidgeting.

"Dressed for training already, Princess?"

"Same as every morning, Captain." She flicked a stray strand of auburn hair back over her shoulder and set the book down in the chair behind her.

Charles looked away and studied one of the obnoxiously bright rugs she insisted cover her front rooms. The chaotic mess could make one dizzy, but he'd studied every inch often enough. If danger arose for her here, the designs and strange colors would not distract from his position as her bodyguard. His gaze snagged on her breakfast plate still dotted with food, and he frowned.

"You should finish your morning meal, Princess." He nodded at the plates of wilting fruit and bread. A hint of cooked meat lingered, meaning she had at least eaten *something*.

"No need." She waved a dismissive hand toward the plates. "I told Lori to share the rest with those who need it. That lady-in-waiting of mine would stuff my face every hour if I let her."

Charles studied the princess for a moment, noting the subtle clench of her jaw. King Phillippe had tried to keep her from learning too much, fearful she would act without thinking, but the princess was crafty. She befriended the servants, conversing with them and learning what they overheard. Meaning she knew how the crops continued to grow scarce across the country and had overheard the reports of one burning field after the other.

"You need to eat too, Princess." He approached one of the random chairs.

"I ate several fine pieces of broiled ham," she responded, walking toward her door instead. Charles took two long strides, blocking her path before she could exit first. She gave him a disapproving stare. "I hear the rumors, same as you, Captain. Lori says there is just enough for the castle occupants, much less for the servants. And, for probably the hundredth time now, I'm positive I can enter the hallway without you scanning every inch first."

He nodded but did not move until she waved her arm with a dangerously playful grin. "After you, Captain. Since you'll insist anyway."

Charles glanced to each side of the hallway and waved her through. Two paces behind her, he walked in time with the click of her boots. After a few moments, she slowed to walk beside him rather than in front of him.

"You know it's unlikely an attack will occur here, yes?" She shifted the free-flowing portion of her wavy hair to no avail. Each time she moved one strand, the wind would pick up another and replace it. Two taut braids leading from each side of her forehead held the remainder. Even without the small circlet she wore only in the throne room, those simple braids gave away her station.

"Then why give you personal bodyguards, Princess?"

She sighed. Loudly. At the title, doubtful. He always referred to her that way; it helped remind him of the differences between them. This meant the overexaggerated sigh was in response to his question. "Because Father worries too much."

They continued walking, listening to the increasing bustle of footsteps as the rest of the castle awoke. "The reason probably lies in that Gift of his he never intentionally uses."

The pained yearning in her voice as she spoke sent a small chill down Charles's arms. He could add nothing. Charles was well aware of how the king used the LeNoir Gift and understood the strain with which she spoke of it. The Gift could only be held by one; she would receive the Gift only after King Phillippe's death.

"Father returned last night," she added after a moment.

He glanced at her, a quick break in the monotony of studying the surrounding hallways. With no adornments on the stone walls, it seemed Charles and the princess had been standing still rather than walking several minutes toward the practice yards.

"I'm aware, Princess," Charles acknowledged in barely more than a whisper, grateful the door leading outside the castle proper had come into view.

"He wants to speak with you again, doesn't he?" she asked. The strain of worry had disappeared, replaced with curiosity. He nodded and held the door, watching as she wrinkled her nose at the on-slaught of musky sweat. Had he not been distracted, he would have laughed. The princess practiced outdoors with one of the soldiers every day, and the smell of sweat still bothered her.

"Curious." She walked past him, removing a string from her wrist and wrapping it around her hair to hold it at the nape of her neck. "Swords today, right, Captain?"

"You practiced swords yesterday, Princess. Time to pick a differ-ent weapon."

She shook her head emphatically, steps measured but quick in their approach to the rack of practice weapons. Without hesitation, she grasped two practice swords. They were created of the lightest hue of wood, and could have been mistaken for parchment rather than a blunt force weapon. He chuckled at her mischievous grin which made her brown eyes sparkle while the rising sun brought a glow to her brown-tinged skin. In many ways, she was still the girl he had first met a decade ago, not a woman of marriageable age. At twenty-two, Princess Rosealyn was a few years younger than he and a rarity among nobility. Sole heir to her father's throne as an only child and not yet wed, nor even promised to another.

"Swords today, and then you're stuck with the quarterstaff for all of next week," Charles countered. "But not against me, Princess. Against a well-rested Moss."

She squinted at the suggestion but did not relinquish the swords. "Does that mean you'll be my nighttime guard next week?"

She voiced the question over her shoulder and approached one of several empty practice rings. Others contained sparring soldiers of various ranks. Sword against spear, quarterstaff against sword, spear against quarterstaff. The thwack of wood meeting wood sounded often, while the periodic slap against skin made his arms tingle with memories of the occasional hits the princess managed. Charles paused at the opening between the gates of the ring she had chosen, unbuckling his sword and setting it against the fence, all while watching the princess to see what she would do with the second practice weapon.

He tugged at his sleeves and undid the topmost button. At Princess Rosealyn's smirk, he considered re-buttoning it but decided against it. Given the beads of sweat trickling along his skin beneath the long-sleeved black coat, the entire thing would find its way draped across the fence soon. The wind that continued to swirl the princess's hair around her face brought a dry heat rather than the refreshing coolness of the mountain winds. More than likely, it would be one of the last warm days before the winter winds took hold.

She twisted the second blade, holding the hilt out to him, but he waited. Her shoulders moved first, forecasting where the rest of her body would follow, so he pivoted in the opposite direction.

With one hand, he snatched the second practice sword from her and tapped her in the side with the thin slab of wood. She glared at him and shifted into a proper fighting stance.

"I wasn't ready," she grumbled, gripping the weapon in front of her.

"You should always be ready, Princess," he responded, unbuttoning the rest of his coat and laying it atop the fence. Beneath was a simple, loose shirt, one that wouldn't constrict his movement like the tight sleeves that were not long enough for his arms. "An opponent in battle will not wait for you to be ready. They'll use that hesitation against you."

She scowled at him but nodded her acknowledgment of his instruction, though she didn't take advantage of his own lack of readiness.

Charles's grip tightened on the practice weapon, the natural hue of the wood barely lighter than his own skin, and he tapped her poised weapon, taunting her. She waited, and their gazes met, making that new tension rise up inside again. He looked away first, and she lunged. A slight flick of his wrist knocked her downward strike aside.

Princess Rosealyn grounded her heel and shoved against his block with unexpected strength, but he pivoted away, tapping her back as she almost face-planted into the dirt. He silenced the rising chuckle, leaning left to avoid her wild swing and backpedaling a few quick steps until his back met the fence.

She followed his movement, sword point reaching for his midriff, but he knocked it aside again. Her forward foot dug into the ground, chest rising and falling as beads of sweat made loose hairs cling to her neck.

"Think, breathe, watch my feet and shoulders. Look for the movement before it happens, Princess."

Her gaze darted between his shoulders and feet as he had instructed. She shoved the blade straight at his middle again, her balance growing unsteady when the two weapons met with a loud thud. He grabbed the hilt of her sword and wrenched it away. With both blades firm in his grasp, he shifted his balance to prepare a kick and noticed the king observing from the garden balcony overlooking the training grounds. The simmering adrenaline disappeared, replaced with the common tension that accompanied the king's presence.

Charles put down his barely risen leg and turned so his back faced the princess, lowering both weapons. From this distance, Charles could make out the king's smooth yet hardened features, like the aging man was burdened by an invisible weight. Sunlight made the king's blond hair turn gold, especially since he wore the solid black coat. With a shake of his head, Charles shifted the wooden blades so he held one in each hand and faced the princess again.

"What was that about?" Rosealyn held out her hand for the wooden blade.

"Nothing, Princess," Charles muttered, glancing back up to the balcony again.

The rising sun illuminated the playfulness in her gaze as she followed his eyes to where her father stood watching. A teasing smile softened the sharp features of her face. "Worried what Father will think still? You should be over that by now. Your command is to train me, not coddle me. Again."

"You did well today, Princess." Charles set the two practice blades against the fence and donned the high-buttoned coat. The princess frowned with arms crossed, and he added, "Still need to watch my feet."

Her frown turned into a scowl. His instructions hadn't changed in months, but he was sure he would have to remind her again despite the singular nod she gave. *Especially since she'll be going up against Moss and his quarterstaff again.*

"And *you* need to stop holding back, Captain."

Charles grimaced but tilted his head forward as he clasped each button of the coat. The king's presence above did nothing to assuage the growing apprehension inside. She was right; he was still holding back, but nowhere near as often as before. "As you wish, Princess."

"We *can* continue training. Just because Father is watching doesn't mean we have to stop for the day. We've barely begun!"

"Library, Princess?" He knew they could continue, but the king's steady gaze and his later meeting with the man made Charles hesitate.

"Not until we're done here." She stepped around him and grabbed both practice swords.

Smirking, he allowed her the small victory. It wouldn't take him long to seize both from her hands. Again.

The jitters of his later meeting with the king gave way to adrenaline as he ducked and pivoted away from her twin slashes. Soon he forgot the king watched from above, losing himself in the push and pull of dancing with swords. Rosealyn's youthful demeanor shifted to frustration with each stumble and fall. Smudges covered her skirts, and the streaks of dirt were barely visible along her arms. Each time she fell, she jumped back up, insisting they continue until the sun was well past its midday height.

Lindsey Parks
Photography

Cristen Jennette is a fantasy author, avid reader, and high school English teacher. She's spent many evenings with her nose stuck in a book, and almost as many at the computer. Cristen currently lives in Northwest Missouri.

Find her on Instagram or Facebook with the username @dragonheartbookworm.